HEART BEAT
An Anthology

Sweet Daisy
Diane Benefiel

An Unexpected Rescue
Joan Bird

Marci's Co-Star
Emily Mims

Love in the Time of Hantavirus
J.K. Winn

Heart Murmur
Elle Wright

www.BOROUGHSPUBLISHINGGROUP.com

HEART BEAT
Copyright © 2020 Diane Benefiel, Joan Bird,
Emily Mims, J.K. Winn, Elle Wright

ISBN 978-1-951055-77-6

SWEET DAISY

Diane Benefiel

This book is dedicated to the medical personnel who have put their lives on the line during the 2020 Covid-19 pandemic. You are the heroes of our time. Thank you.

Chapter One

Will parked in the driveway and turned off the car engine. He closed his eyes and breathed deep. For the first time since he'd stepped through the swinging doors of the ER twelve hours ago, he wasn't moving. A bird chirped, and there was the quiet rush of traffic a few blocks away from his San Diego neighborhood. Even his ears were tired. A bus crash on the interstate had brought in multiple patients, some critical. He'd treated a teenage boy with a fractured wrist, a middle-aged woman with facial lacerations, and a pregnant woman with too-early contractions that they'd managed to stop. So far so good on that one. If he didn't get his ass out of the car, he'd fall asleep right there. He pushed open the door and trudged to the porch, the sun setting in the west casting a lavender haze over the sky.

He stopped on the top step. There she was. His nemesis, his personal sparring partner, his too-sweet, perpetually peppy, always chipper neighbor who alternately made him want to throttle her or kiss her.

She sat in one of the padded wicker chairs like a genteel Southern belle, wearing a light summer dress that left her long arms bare. Her wild mass of curly black hair was clipped back, leaving her face unframed. On the little table next to her sat a tray with a plate of cookies and a tall glass of iced tea, condensation dripping down the side. The ceiling fan overhead spun lazily, causing the clutch of pastel-colored flowers stuck in a small mason jar to flutter. He squinted at the cover of the book she was reading. A romance novel. *Figures.*

She placed a bookmark carefully between the pages—no dog ears for her—and closed her book before turning those gorgeous eyes in his direction.

"Hey, buttercup." Her name was Daisy, which suited her perfectly, though he'd slice an artery before admitting to that.

"Teach six-year-olds their colors today? Tie shoelaces? Wipe noses?"

There was that smile. No matter what he said to her, she always bestowed that reward. Even when she wasn't smiling, she was smiling because her mouth naturally bowed up. But when she broke out that grin, it lit her up like a burst of sunshine. Sky-blue eyes, teeth a little crowded, rose-flushed cheeks all combined together to beam out warmth and make a man feel like a precious gift had been bestowed upon him.

The whole package was more than a little annoying.

"First graders are well past learning their colors, I did tie a shoelace, and today was the last day. School is now officially out for the summer." That husky voice twisted his gut into knots. While everything about her was as sweet as a spring meadow, her voice hinted of dark rooms lit by candlelight and bedsheets strewn with rose petals. "Would you like a cookie, Will? You deserve cookies after your very serious and important work saving lives."

He crossed the porch to examine the round cookies dusted with powdered sugar.

"They're Mexican wedding cookies."

He shrugged and shoved a cookie in his mouth.

Then he chewed, swallowed, and licked powdered sugar off his thumb. "Good." He snagged the next cookie, chewing thoughtfully. There was one cookie left on the plate. "You want that one?"

"Nope, it's yours."

He ate the last cookie, then eyed her iced tea.

"Go ahead. I made it for you."

"What's the catch? Did you lace it with arsenic?"

"Fresh out of poison. Drink the tea. You look like you could use it."

No matter what he said to provoke her, she never got mad. She'd parry the zingers, not letting him score points off her, but there was always that glint in her baby blues that made him think she was having fun. He did as ordered and gulped the tea. Cold, refreshing, with a hint of peach. "God, that's good."

"Don't you eat at the hospital?"

"Too busy today." He touched the petals of the flowers. "What kind of flowers are these?"

"Sweet peas."

"Huh. Where do you get them?"

"You should journey into the backyard. There's a whole new world out there that includes sweet peas."

"Your sticky sweetness has gone over the top. You know that, right? You sit on the porch reading a romance novel, you cut sweet peas from your own garden, you offer homemade cookies and tea. And you teach first graders. You're a cliché."

There was that killer smile again, this time with an edge. "I happen to love sweet peas, and romance novels have happy endings. How can that be bad? As you're benefitting from the cookies and tea, you shouldn't complain."

"Not complaining, but everybody's got a dark side. I'm wondering where yours is."

A shadow momentarily dimmed the brightness in her blue eyes, then was gone. "No dark side, Will." She rose to her feet and set her book alongside the empty plate and glass on the tray before picking it up.

He held open the screen door and followed her as she stepped into the small foyer. Her apartment door was open, showing him her tidy living area. "You shouldn't leave your door open."

"Why? I was right outside. Besides Mrs. Gibbs, who is our landlord and is *not* going to steal from me, you're the only other tenant on this floor. Are you planning to rob me blind?"

"The upstairs tenants can come down here if they want, and you don't know me all that well. You shouldn't trust me not to steal from you, and you should always lock your door when you leave your apartment."

"You're too suspicious."

"You're too trusting."

"Why don't you go play a violent video game? That should help you feel better." Her smile showed a dimple in her left cheek. One more item to add to the too-sweet list.

***

Daisy shut the door to her apartment, throwing the deadbolt with what she hoped was a click audible to Will. She took the tray to the small kitchen area and began running the hot water to wash the dishes. Sticky sweet, that's what he thought of her. She preferred to think of herself as having a positive attitude, and if she liked to surround herself with pretty things that brightened her day, why should that bother him?

Doctor Will Sloane's opinion shouldn't matter, but it did, too much. It wasn't only his looks that pulled at her, though god knew they pulled hard. She loved his longish, curly hair that spanned colors from burnished gold to dark brown. People paid good money to get streaks like his, but she knew for a fact his were earned compliments of the sun. Then there was that surfer's body—long arms and legs, narrow hips, and wide shoulders. He'd laugh his head off if he knew she thought of him as anything other than her irritating neighbor.

She squirted dish soap into the basin, throwing a scrubber into the suds.

Looks alone wouldn't have held her interest. No, what had her thinking about him more than she wanted was that he was a fundamentally decent human. He didn't show that side often, but she'd seen small things he'd done, like patching up the little boy from down the street who'd scraped his knee.

Then there was the time he'd charmed Mrs. Gibbs into letting him give her a checkup and had diagnosed an ear infection. But the capper had come from Mrs. Gibbs, who had told Daisy that before— eight months ago—he'd moved into the house they all shared, he'd worked at a refugee hospital in Syria. One that had been bombed by government forces. He'd saved the lives of the most vulnerable people in the most war-torn country on the globe. Daisy would never be brave enough to do something like that, which made her admire those who did even more. No wonder he saw teaching first graders as nowhere near the same stratosphere of importance.

She rinsed soap off the glass Will had used and set it on the drainer. Her apartment was one of the nice things that made her happy. Her childhood had been rough, no other way to describe it, and from a young age she'd made it her goal to create happiness, and she'd succeeded.

The house she lived in was a gorgeous Victorian that had been divided into apartments in a beautiful neighborhood of San Diego. The darling Mrs. Gibbs encouraged Daisy's desire to grow things by letting her do what she liked in the yard and garden area. All this on top of loving her job. Six-year-olds were so fun and eager to learn.

She wasn't naïve, and the circumstances some of her kids endured broke her heart, but she was a good teacher and her little charges loved her. The result? She'd created her own happiness.

She sighed, looking out the window to her tidy side yard. Bees circled the purple spears of the lavender she'd planted, and finches took turns at the bird feeder she'd hung from the pergola. Those were exactly the type of things that gave her mood a boost, and if Will Sloane would unbend a little, he'd find comfort in the small things, too.

Daisy scrubbed the baking tray with a little more force than necessary. There'd been too much ugliness in her life to take being in a good place for granted.

After setting the tray on the drainer, she dumped the dish water and opened her refrigerator, a finger to her chin as she examined the contents. She'd make it her mission in life to make Doctor Sloane lighten up, to get him to enjoy the simple things, like the iced tea and cookies.

Going with the idea, she began pulling items from the fridge.

Chapter Two

Already running late, Will opened his apartment door to leave and nearly stepped on the bag sitting on the floor of the foyer, squarely in his way. The party bag was covered with curling, multicolored ribbons, one ribbon tied to a bright yellow balloon. The attached note read "Take me to work, Will!" in loopy script. He picked up the bright green bag and noticed it was covered with tiny white flowers with fuzzy yellow centers. Daisies. He didn't have time for this. When he got to his car, he tossed the bag onto the passenger seat and fought to keep the balloon from obscuring his view as he drove through the early morning drizzle to the hospital.

He parked in the underground garage and started getting out of the car when the balloon bounced in front of his face. The dismal gray parking garage, the dismal cloudy gray day, and a yellow balloon that wouldn't be ignored. Muttering under his breath, he grabbed the bag and strode through the staff entrance, the balloon trailing behind him like a puppy.

In the staff locker room, Will tugged his navy scrubs over the base layer he always wore. It got damn cold in the hospital.

"Hey, Will, whose birthday is it?" Hari Patel put on the white coat stitched with his name and shut his locker.

Will eyed the anesthesiologist with a raised brow. "How should I know?"

"Because you brought a present?"

Will glanced at the bag with its balloon he'd set on the bench. "I'm not giving that to anyone. My neighbor gave it to *me.*"

"Oh, so it's your birthday. Happy birthday, man," Hari clapped a hand on Will's shoulder as he walked out.

Rolling his eyes, Will put the bag in his locker, and since the balloon wouldn't fit, shut the door leaving the balloon floating above.

He entered the ER as a paramedic wheeled in a man on a gurney, another man in uniform riding on the side as he performed chest compressions.

"Tell me about him," Will demanded.

"John Polanski, sixty-six years old, history of heart disease and diabetes," the paramedic replied, reading from an electronic tablet. "Suspected heart attack. Went asystole on the way in."

The hospital staff took over, and for the next forty minutes Will and the nurses put everything they had into bringing back John Polanski's heart rhythm.

"Come on, John, hang in there," Will muttered as he checked the monitors. "Okay, we've got a pulse. Damn, ventricular tachycardia. Paddles."

He thought it was going to work. He shocked the heart, they got a few beats of normal rhythm, then a flatline. They fought to bring the heartbeat back, then the patient's blood pressure crashed, and in the end, he'd had to call it.

Pulling the mask off his face, Will made his way to the small room where the family had been asked to wait, and did the part of his job that never got any easier.

When he stepped out again, one of the nurses patted him on the shoulder. "Hard to lose a patient, and on your birthday, too."

"It's not my birthday," he called after her as she walked down the hall.

Some days just sucked. Four hours after losing John Polanski to a heart attack, he headed back to the locker room to change out of scrubs soiled by a woman who had puked on him.

That about a dozen people had wished him happy birthday for some reason made his day even worse. He turned down the row, and there it was, the balloon floating above his locker like a sunbeam.

He stripped down, grabbed a towel, and made his way to the showers. Ten minutes later, feeling a lot cleaner, he pulled on knit briefs and a t-shirt, then sat on the bench facing his open locker. The bag looked so damn cheerful with the little flowers that reminded him of Daisy. He opened it. There was a small folded note. *Hi Will, I made you lunch so you don't get grumpy. Enjoy. Your friend, Daisy.* She'd drawn a cute flower with a bumblebee next to her name. He stuck the note to the inside of the locker door with a magnet.

The first thing he pulled from the bag was a peanut butter sandwich, cut into neat triangles, and wrapped in wax paper. He lifted the crust to find strawberry jelly, his favorite. Suddenly ravenous, he stuffed a triangle in his mouth and chewed as he pulled out the rest of the food. A glossy red apple, carrot sticks, four cookies of the same kind she'd offered him the evening before, a small bag of Fritos, and, of all things, a juice box. He couldn't remember the last time he'd had a juice box, or if someone had packed him a lunch in the last fifteen years. He sat in his underwear and ate his lunch, thinking about Daisy, and felt better than he had all day.

***

Daisy let herself into the house, carefully closing the door so as not to wake her neighbors. She leaned against the door, raising a shaky hand to her forehead. She couldn't believe what had happened. She'd gone out with a guy, a friend of a friend, but he'd made her uneasy. He'd seemed a little...off. So, when he asked her out for a second date, she'd turned him down. And then he'd body checked her right into a wall. He'd apologized profusely, claimed it was an accident, then suggested it wouldn't have happened if she hadn't made him so mad. Jerk.

She crossed the foyer and entered her apartment. In the bathroom, she leaned toward the mirror to examine the lump that was sure to leave a bruise above her right eyebrow. In the morning she'd wear her hair a little looser, hoping nobody would notice.

She started her bedtime routine, letting the ritual soothe her. Cleanser, toner, eye cream, night cream, her favorite pajamas, then snuggling under the light quilt with her bedtime book. Sometimes life threw ugly things in your path, but the nice things, sweet peas, a romance novel, the bees in lavender, far outweighed them.

Next morning, dressed in baggy cropped pants and a t-shirt, and armed with gardening gloves, she stepped out her door. She took a detour out the front to Will's car, a Subaru that had seen better days. For as much grief as he gave her about leaving her apartment door unlocked, he *always* left his car unlocked. He said it kept thieves from breaking a window if they wanted the change in his cup holder.

She put a CD on the dash in front of the steering wheel so he'd see it.

She opened the gate to the back, walking under the pergola with its blooming wisteria. Today was a perfect San Diego day. A few puffy clouds floated in a gorgeous sky of deep blue, the bright yellow blooms of the sunflowers along the fence turned their faces to the sun, and a mockingbird sang from a tree. Working in the garden would help root out the nagging distress from the nasty end to her date the night before.

The green beans she'd planted were unfurling their glossy leaves, and climbing tendrils were starting to search for something to grab onto. Her job today was to make a trellis for them to climb. Mrs. Gibbs had told Daisy to use whatever materials she could find in the garage, so that's where she'd start.

She rummaged through an amazing assortment of garden tools, some likely dating back fifty years. She collected what she thought would work—long wooden stakes, a section of chicken wire, and, bonus, a staple gun.

Thwack. She used the staple gun to attach the wire to the stakes. *Thwack, thwack.* The backdoor slammed and she glanced up to see Will coming down the steps. No one had the right to look that good. The sun brought out the golden highlights in his tawny hair, and his jaw was shadowed with dark whiskers, the giveaway that he didn't have to work today.

Her fingers itched to rub and see if they felt as good as they looked. He wore a faded San Diego Padres t-shirt and cargo shorts frayed at the hem.

He strolled over to where she knelt by her project.

"Hey there, petunia."

She rolled her eyes. Calling her the name of some random flower was a thing with him. "Hey back, Doctor Sloane. Funny how I'm able to remember your name."

"I remember your name, but Daisy is such a syrupy sweet name it makes my teeth ache. I might get a cavity."

"You're a funny guy."

He stood over her, watching as she stapled another section of chicken wire to a stake. "Right now, I'm an appreciative guy, having had an excellent and nostalgic lunch yesterday. Thank you for that. Kind of made my day."

"Really?" She rose to stand.

"Yeah. Bright spot after a really crappy morning."

"I'm glad."

"What are you mak—" He broke off, brows slamming down and all humor leaving his face as he lifted the hair from her forehead. "What the hell's that?"

"What?" Memory returned. "Oh. Nothing."

"Fuck that."

She'd never seen him angry before, never seen those tawny eyes spark golden fire or his jaw go rigid. She took an instinctive step back.

"How'd you get that bruise?"

"It's nothing." When she would have turned back to her project, he gripped her shoulders.

"You went out last night. Did someone lay a hand on you?"

"It doesn't concern you, Will."

"You concern me." His hands gripped tighter and he pulled her closer. "Tell me what the fuck happened. Did your date do this?"

"Dammit, Will. I was having a perfectly nice morning until you came out here. Yes, my date *accidentally,*" she gave the word extra emphasis, "bumped into me. As this was after I'd turned him down for a second date, I'm not buying the accident part."

"Did you report him to the police?"

She gave a disbelieving laugh. "What would they do?" At his stubborn look, she gripped his wrists to tug his hands from her shoulders. "He apologized, said it was an accident."

"That's bullshit."

"Yes, it is. But I took care of it, Will. There will be no second date with him, and he knows it. I can take care of myself."

"You take care of everyone, from me to the neighbors to the mail carrier who you greet with cold drinks. But no one can look after you?" He slid a finger along her temple as he lifted her hair again, and she forced back a shiver.

With his hand cupping the side of her face, he leaned forward and pressed his lips to her forehead next to the bruise. She couldn't remember the last time someone had kissed her to make her feel better.

"It kills me to see you hurt."

Her gaze locked on his and her heart took a slow, languid tumble in her chest. Oh no. She couldn't fall for Will Sloane. Falling in love with someone put your heart in their hands, and experience told her that was a dangerous thing. She moved back, but had a sinking feeling she might be too late to protect herself.

Will let his hands drop, but his gaze remained riveted on hers. "Who was it? Who'd you go out with last night?"

"I'm not telling you that. I don't need a white knight to ride to my rescue."

"I'm not a white knight. Do you have family or anyone who looks out for you?"

"I have me to look after me, as I've always had. Leave it alone, Will."

He looked unconvinced, and she had the uneasy feeling that the thoughtful frown meant letting the subject drop was only temporary.

He motioned to her project. "Want help?"

Chapter Three

Will's day off had been spent taking care of the basics—grocery shopping, paying bills, FaceTime with his parents. They didn't live far away, but if he couldn't visit them, FaceTime did the trick.

The smartest thing he'd done since returning to the States was hiring a college student to clean his apartment, so he hadn't had to deal with that. Coming home from work to find not only that the house sparkled, but also his laundry was done, was worth every penny.

On the way to the grocery store he'd listened to the CD Daisy had left on his dash. The Post-it had read, "Play me, and sing along. It'll make you smile. Your friend, Daisy." He'd tucked the note in his pocket and put in the CD. The playlist included ELO's "Mr. Blue Sky," "I Can See Clearly Now"—he didn't know the artist—"Don't Stop Believin'" by Journey, and other upbeat classics. He'd blasted the tunes, and yeah, he'd sung along. And damn if that hadn't given his mood a boost and made him think of his neighbor.

His week had been busy and every one of his shifts had gone into overtime. Upshot? He'd missed seeing Daisy.

Stepping out onto the porch, he looked around. Ah, there she was. Early evening was lengthening the shadows, and Daisy sat on the wide porch swing with a book. As he watched, she pushed with her toe and set the swing moving. She glanced at him, gave a hesitant smile, then returned her attention to her book.

He wasn't sure what to make of her new wariness around him. Or the fact that any time he was with her was the best part of his day. Something about Daisy smoothed out any rough edges he was feeling.

"Let's go for a walk."

That brought the baby blue gaze back to his. "Around here?"

"No. Let's go to the beach."

Momentary indecision crossed her face, and he found himself insanely grateful when her sunny smile bloomed and the dimple winked. "Give me five minutes and I'll be ready."

She was good as her word. In five minutes she was back, wearing canvas shoes, shorts, and carrying a sweatshirt. He liked her in the flowery summer dresses she often wore, but he couldn't complain about the long, toned legs bared by little white shorts.

Daisy rolled down her window and the breeze sent her hair flying as he drove west. He wound through a residential neighborhood until the street came to a dead end at a small parking area occupied by a couple cars and an ancient VW bus.

They climbed out of the car. "Have you been here before?"

She shook her head. "No. This must be a locals-only place. I bet it's not marked on a map."

"Got that right." It seemed natural to take her hand and lead her down a narrow walkway. Flowering plants on each side grew so tall overhead they formed a tunnel exploding with color.

"This is beautiful." She tilted back her head. "I love the variety of colors of bougainvillea. Oh, and look at the hummingbirds."

There had to be a dozen of the tiny birds zipping through the foliage. "These flowers are bougainvillea?"

"Sure are. You're seriously deficient in the flower identification department."

He tugged her hand and they started walking again. "I know what daisies look like."

"Which is?"

"Black hair and beautiful blue eyes."

"Are you flirting with me, Doctor Sloane?"

"Maybe." He smiled. "Okay, daisies are white with a yellow center."

"That's one variety. Daisies happen to come in all colors. Pink, yellow, red, variegated. There's even a blue daisy." They came to the end of the walkway and she put her hand to her chest and sighed. "The flowers are a perfect frame."

He got what she meant. The deep blue of the ocean was visible at the end of the tunnel, the view bordered by burgundy, orange, and cream flowers that he now knew were bougainvillea. They stepped out of the tunnel and onto the wooden landing of the stairs that led to the beach.

The wide expanse of the Pacific glimmered under the lowering sun, swells undulating to form waves that broke near the shore. Surfers sat on their boards beyond the breakers, waiting for the perfect wave.

"This is so nice. Why don't I come to the beach more often?"

"We're correcting that. Let's go down."

They descended the steps zigzagging down the bluff. At the bottom, Daisy pulled on her sweatshirt and shed her shoes to carry them as they crossed the sand. "This is wonderful. Look, there are tide pools. Let's go see."

She ran ahead to a rocky outcropping, long legs eating up the distance. He caught up with her and they crouched at the edge of a clear pool.

"There's a whole world in there. I love the anemones."

He dipped in a finger and lightly touched the tentacles of a purple anemone to feel it contract. He could remember doing the same thing when he was a kid. "Do you see the starfish?" He pointed to the underside of the rock.

"It's gorgeous. And there's a hermit crab."

A wave hit the rocks with a crash, spraying foam. "The tide's coming in." He took her hand again. He was becoming seriously addicted to touching her.

They walked along the wet sand as the sun dipped to the horizon. The last ripples of waves frothed around their feet. An evening breeze had come up and Daisy pulled a band from her wrist and caught her hair in a ponytail. She smiled as she took his hand again. "Your hand is cold."

"I should have brought a sweatshirt. Usually I'm wearing a wetsuit."

"Do you come here to surf?"

"Yeah. It's a good spot. It's hardly ever crowded, and the waves are reliable. Do you surf?"

"I've never tried it. It looks fun."

"Can you swim?"

"Varsity swim team in high school."

"That'll do. Come out with me. I'll teach you."

"To surf? I'd love that."

He stopped and pointed to where the sun was sinking below the horizon. "We have to watch for the green flash."

"Green flash, what's that?"

"You've never heard of it? When the sun sinks below the horizon and you can see only the very top edge, there's sometimes a flash of green."

"You're making that up."

"Are you always so suspicious? I am not making it up. The legend is that if you see it, you'll never again go wrong in matters of the heart."

"Aw, that's romantic."

"I can be romantic. Let's watch."

She turned to face the water and he drew her back against his chest, folding his arms around her. It took a minute until she relaxed against him. They watched in silence as the sun looked like it was setting into a molten pool. The ocean turned dark as the sun slipped below the horizon. It hung for a moment, flashed brilliant green, then disappeared.

"I saw it! Did you see it?"

"Yeah, I saw it."

She turned in his arms, eyes bright in the fading light. He didn't think he could have done anything but kiss her. She froze, but then her lips were moving under his. He angled his mouth, dove deeper, and felt himself drowning in the sweetness. He let out a low groan as her tongue slid along his, and he had to battle back the urge to gobble her up in one hungry bite.

He held her hand where it pressed over his heart, and moved his lips along her jaw to her neck, breathing deep the flowery fragrance of her.

She drew in a shuddering breath, then pushed back. "This is too much, Will."

"It's not too much. What I feel for you is growing, Daisy. You feel something, too. I know you do."

Her nod was hesitant.

"Will you go out with me?"

For once he couldn't see the light in her eyes. "I can't."

"Why not?" He stepped back to better see her face in the waning light. "What I'm feeling for you is different than anything I've experienced before. Are you telling me you don't feel it?"

"I do, and that's why I can't. I like you, Will, a lot. But even if it's more than like, this can't go anywhere, so it's better not to start."

"You went out with the asshole who gave you that bruise on your head, so it's not that you don't date." Irritation gave his voice an edge.

"It's because I like you. I *really* like you."

He stared at her hard, gave it another few seconds, then shook his head. It still didn't compute. "You're not making sense. Really liking me is a good thing. I want to know you better. I want you to know me. We should build on the really like. We could go out to dinner, make out on the couch, maybe partake in other adult activities."

He was encouraged when she shivered and closed her eyes.

Then she was shaking her head, her gaze firm on his. "I didn't care about the other guy, and I only went out with him to be nice." She held up her hand when he opened his mouth to speak. "I know that's lame, and I didn't know he was going to accidentally on purpose hurt me. But he didn't mean anything."

"You didn't care about that guy, and you went out with him. But you care about me, so you won't."

"Exactly." She said it like she was giving his homework a gold star. "If I care about you, I'd want it to be more, and I don't do serious relationships. I don't want a boyfriend, Will, and I'm never getting married."

Chapter Four

Daisy elbowed open her door. If Will hadn't made a big deal of her locking it, she wouldn't have to juggle the Dutch oven full of soup she was holding with hot pads while dealing with the door. It had been three days since their walk on the beach. Will had acted like he'd been sucker punched when she'd told him she basically didn't do relationships, and she hadn't seen him since.

She kicked the door shut, turned around, and nearly walked into the man standing in the foyer. Her stomach gave an unpleasant roll. "Oh, Raul. What are you doing here?"

"I wanted to see you."

There was that look in his eyes that made her uncomfortable. "You shouldn't have come. I told you I wouldn't go out with you again. You pushed me into that wall, remember? I'm taking this soup to my neighbor, if you'll excuse me."

She stifled a groan when the door across the foyer opened and Will stepped out, looking like a surfer dude in boardshorts and a t-shirt. She hadn't seen him for three days and, granted, he'd been working every day, but he had to choose this moment to show up? His tawny hair was in its usual curly disarray, dark brows furrowed as his golden gaze gave her a once-over before locking on Raul.

"Hey there, Daisy. Who's your friend?"

She opened her mouth to reply, but Raul turned on Will with a snarl.

"Fuck off, man. I'm talking to my girlfriend."

Daisy drew a sharp breath. "Ah, listen. This is hot, and I don't want to stand around. You should go, Raul."

Will strode across the foyer. He took the pot and set it on a little side table. "Is this the guy who hurt you?" His gaze drilled into hers and she found herself nodding.

"You make food for this asshole, Daisy?" Raul sneered, his gaze traveling over Will with derision.

Will turned on Raul. "You're leaving. Now."

"Who's going to make me? You, pretty boy?"

"Yeah. Leave."

Raul hung his arms loosely at his sides, body squared to Will's. "Not leaving, asshole."

In a blur of motion, Will grabbed Raul's arm, twisting it behind him and, with a hand behind his neck, forced him to the floor. Raul's arm was wrenched up toward his shoulders and Will leaned forward with his knee pressed in Raul's back. Daisy blinked while Raul gaped like a landed fish.

"When I let you up," Will hissed, "you're leaving. Don't come back, and don't bother Daisy again."

"Fuck, that hurts. You're breaking my arm."

"If I'd wanted your arm broken, it would be broken." Will crouched closer to growl, "Only assholes hurt women, you fucker. And you hurt Daisy."

"That was an accident." Raul let out a muffled scream when Will twisted tighter.

"It was no accident. Deal with your anger issues. You are never to contact Daisy again. Agree or we'll call the cops right now."

"Fuck you."

"Wrong answer. Daisy, call nine-one-one."

Daisy didn't have a chance to move before Raul babbled, "Okay, okay, I'll leave."

"And you won't come back."

"Shit, no, I won't come back." Raul was sweating profusely, his voice strained.

Will eased his hold on Raul's arm, not letting go until the other man gained his feet and Will pushed him to the door.

Daisy had never seen someone move that fast. She certainly never expected that Will could handle himself so well.

He pulled open the door and shoved Raul through. Raul waited until he got to the sidewalk to turn back and yell, "It's not over between us, Daisy. You're mine."

Will surged toward the door and Daisy caught his arm, holding tight when he pulled her with him. "Will, it's okay. Let him go." Raul hopped in his truck and peeled out from the curb, tires squealing.

Will shut the door with a snap, and Daisy blew out a shuddering breath. "Wow."

He shoved a hand through his hair. "Look, I'm sorry that happened."

She realized her hand holding his arm was shaking.

"Hey, you okay?"

"Of course, I am." She released him and stepped back. "I want to take this soup to Mrs. Gibbs. She's sick."

"Wait a minute." He tipped her face up, and whatever he saw had him frowning. "Come here." He drew her into his embrace, tucking her head under his chin as he wrapped his arms around her shoulders. He felt so good, so strong and solid. She breathed in deeply and felt steadier. He smelled of the sunscreen she'd used as a child, the one that brought back memories of her grandmother taking her to the beach.

She stayed in the hug probably longer than she should have before stepping back. "I'm fine, Will. I guess I never expected that you'd take Raul down that way. Where'd you learn to move like that?"

His hands stayed on her shoulders, rubbing lightly. "I studied various martial arts through my teens and twenties." He shrugged. "I've only had to use what I learned a few times."

She raised up to her tiptoes to lay her lips on his. She kept the kiss brief. Given that she could feel the zing of it all the way to the tips of her toes, she thought the idea was wise. "Raul is a bully, and you dealt with him for me. Thank you, Will."

She retrieved her pot of soup, and Will walked with her down the short hall to Mrs. Gibbs's door. "What the hell was that asshole doing here, and why did he call you his girlfriend?"

"Both good questions, for which I don't have an answer."

He raised his hand to knock. She shook her head. "Open it, it's unlocked."

He gave a frustrated sigh and turned the knob. "Of course it is."

Daisy called through the open door. "Mrs. Gibbs, it's me and Will. I brought you chicken noodle soup. Can we come in?"

A faint voice answered from inside.

She crossed the living room to the small kitchen and placed the pot on the cooktop.

"What's wrong with Mrs. Gibbs?"

"She's been sick for a couple days with an upper respiratory bug." Daisy opened a cupboard and found a sturdy, wide-mouthed mug.

From the fridge she retrieved a bottle of ginger ale. She poked around until she found what she wanted, a reusable water bottle with a straw and screw-on lid. She added ice and poured ginger ale over it. All the while, a frowning Will paced the small kitchen, arms crossed over his chest.

Placing the mug and drink on a tray, Daisy tilted her head to study the man who appeared ready to run out the front door and chase down Raul. "Are you okay?"

He gave an abrupt nod. "Yeah. You? This is the longest I've seen you go without smiling."

"A guy I don't like or trust showed up at my door and said I was his girlfriend, my hot neighbor went all Jackie Chan and took him down, and my eighty-eight-year-old landlady is sick, so smiles are scarce at the moment." She shook her head. "Go away. I need to get this to Mrs. Gibbs."

"Hot neighbor, huh?"

"That's what you got from all that?" She pointed to the door. "Go. I need to take care of Mrs. Gibbs."

He pointed a thumb at his chest. "Doctor, remember? I'll check her over, make sure it's not something serious."

Oh. Well. "Let me go in first. She won't like it if a male visitor is suddenly sprung on her, even if he is my hot doctor neighbor."

"I'll be back in a couple minutes."

She crossed the hall to the bedroom door. Mrs. Gibbs pushed herself upright and gave a phlegmy cough. Tiny to begin with, she was dwarfed by the fluffy comforter. A coughing spasm shook her entire body.

"How are you feeling, Mrs. Gibbs?" Daisy set the tray on the crowded nightstand, pushing aside the pretty vase with pastel-colored sweet peas she'd brought in that morning. She helped Mrs. Gibbs sit up and arranged the pillows behind her.

"I'd feel better if I could get rid of this cough." The old woman's gnarled fingers covered Daisy's as she held the ginger ale for Mrs. Gibbs to drink.

"Will is going to be here in a minute to check on you."

"Oh, that's fine." She sipped more ginger ale before pushing it away.

Daisy set the bottle back on the tray. "Did you call your daughter and tell her you're sick?"

"I did." Mrs. Gibbs leaned back against the pillows. "She'll come by this evenin'. My Ruthie watches her grandbabies during the day while my granddaughter is at work." Despite having lived in San Diego since her husband had been stationed at the Navy base during World War II, Daisy could hear the South in her neighbor's long vowels and relaxed elocution.

Mrs. Gibbs lifted the mug and sipped broth as Daisy helped steady it. "You're a good girl, Daisy Medrano." Mrs. Gibbs covered her mouth with a lace-edged handkerchief and coughed so hard Daisy was worried she'd crack a rib.

With her skin normally a polished mahogany, Mrs. Gibbs's pallor alarmed Daisy. But being ill didn't prevent Mrs. Gibbs from calling out when there was a rapping sound on the doorframe. "Come in, Doctor Will."

Ah, the power of a handsome man with a stethoscope hanging around his neck. Mrs. Gibbs had been thrilled to have a doctor as one of her tenants and had been dropping hints to Daisy that Doctor Will was a fine catch indeed. It made Daisy think she should run out and buy a fishing pole.

Mrs. Gibbs sat up against her pillows and Daisy straightened her nightgown. "How'd you like that pie, Doctor Will?"

"You got pie?" Daisy asked.

Will shot her a smug look as he crossed the room carrying a black case. "Best peach pie I ever had."

Mrs. Gibbs gave a wheezy laugh, black eyes shining. "Doctor Will paid a house call on my Ruthie," she told Daisy. "Gave her a prescription for those headaches of hers, and that medicine's helping. Wouldn't take money so Doctor Will got a pie. Give me another sip of that broth, Daisy."

Daisy held the mug, let her sip, then got the spoon. "How about some noodles?"

Mrs. Gibbs accepted a small bite. "Thank you, dear."

Will set his case on the end of the bed and unzipped it. "Do you mind if I give you a checkup, Mrs. Gibbs?"

"You anglin' for another pie?"

"Yes, ma'am, if you're making it."

"Okay then." She held out a thin arm that Will wrapped with the blood pressure cuff.

He pumped the bulb and listened with his stethoscope. "Are you normally on the low side?"

Mrs. Gibbs nodded. "Low blood pressure keeps my heart ticking."

He listened to her heart, then had her breathe deep, an action that brought on a coughing spasm. After a series of questions, he hung his stethoscope around his neck again and pronounced, "You have bronchitis, Mrs. Gibbs. Do you have a humidifier?"

"In that closet over there." She pointed. "Daisy, will you get it?"

Daisy busied herself setting up the humidifier. Will got on the phone to the pharmacy to order meds. When he disconnected, he told Mrs. Gibbs, "You need rest. No pie baking until you're over this. Eat the soup Daisy made for you, and drink lots of fluids. Daisy and I will pick up the meds, and anything else you need. We'll be back in an hour or so."

Chapter Five

Carrying the list Mrs. Gibbs had insisted Daisy write down, she and Will descended the steps from the porch. "Why do we both need to go to the pharmacy?"

Will jiggled his keys. "Maybe I want to spend time with you."

"Give me a break."

"God's truth. I like spending time with you."

"Right. That's why you've been avoiding me."

She caught his frown. "I was working something out."

"Fair enough."

They got in Will's car and Daisy buckled her seatbelt. He backed out of the driveway and drove through the residential neighborhood. "We're making another stop."

"Where?"

"There's someone I want you to meet. I called a guy I know when you were in with Mrs. Gibbs." He caught her narrowed gaze and shrugged. "Mike's with San Diego PD. I want you to tell him about Raul."

"A cop? I don't want to talk to a cop."

He raised a brow. "And I don't like how that fucker Raul looked at you."

"I can't go to the police because a guy looked at me wrong. Besides, you sent Raul on his way. I doubt he'll be back."

"We'll tell Mike what's going on and let him decide if he wants to do anything."

Daisy remembered Raul's threat that it "wasn't over" between them. "I don't know. I'll admit that he scared me. But I don't like cops. What can they do, anyway?"

"That's what we'll find out."

Will took the turn into the parking lot of Sunshine Coffee, the small, independently owned coffee shop that locals loved. He parked next to a San Diego PD SUV. Just seeing the black-and-white made Daisy uneasy. They parked and the officer exited his vehicle.

"Mike, thanks for meeting us." Will shook hands with the officer who looked like he could moonlight as a linebacker. "How's the rookie?"

"Back at work and complaining about the physical therapy." Mike nodded at Daisy. "The doc treated my partner after he dove out a glass window and fell about fifteen feet."

"He's lucky he landed in bushes. Mike, this is Daisy Medrano, my neighbor. Daisy, Sergeant Mike Pacheco."

They shook hands and Daisy hoped he didn't notice her sweaty palms. Will gestured to the coffee shop. "Let's go in. I'm buying."

When they had their hot beverages and were seated, Mike nodded to Daisy. "Will says you have something to tell me."

Daisy sipped her latte, then set down her drink and, giving her anxiety a mental push to the side, squared her shoulders. Sergeant Pacheco had kind eyes. She'd focus on that. She spoke, relating what she knew about Raul, which admittedly wasn't a lot.

Mike made notes in a small notebook. "You went out with him once but turned him down when he asked for another date. Why is that?"

She glanced at Will, then back to the officer. She was hardly going to admit that one reason was that she had the hots for her neighbor. "I wasn't attracted to him. I only went out with him the one time because he's the friend of a friend. I thought maybe I'd like him more if I gave him a chance."

"But he didn't improve over time?"

"No. He talked about himself the entire evening, about how he's the manager at the tire shop where he works, how he likes ordering employees around. He bragged about taking advantage of his customers, padding the bill, faking problems and charging to fix them, that kind of thing. He acted like taking advantage of people was a positive character trait."

"Sounds like a prince. How'd he take it when you turned him down for a second date?"

Daisy caught Will's look and sighed. Why should she be embarrassed because Raul had hurt her? "He got angry, made rude comments. He shoved me into a wall. I banged my head, then he gave a lame apology."

"I saw the bruise the next day," Will interjected. "Classic hematoma on the forehead."

Mike scribbled in his little notebook, then looked up.

"Anything more, Daisy?"

"He, ah, texted me the next day and sent inappropriate photos of himself." She shifted uncomfortably. "I blocked his number, and since I hadn't heard from him, I thought he'd given up."

"Do you still have the photos? Sending them could constitute harassment."

She shook her head. "I deleted them."

"We may be able to recover them." More jotting in the notebook, then Mike put his pen down. "Tell me what happened today." Daisy appreciated Mike's unruffled demeanor. It went a long way toward calming her nervousness over his uniform.

She told him what had happened, from Raul's unexpected arrival to Will flattening him on the floor. "Will got Raul to say he was leaving and wouldn't come back. But Raul waited until he was out of reach to yell that we weren't done."

"Do you know where his tire shop is?"

Daisy gave him the location, and Mike said, "I'll stop by and have a word. Most of the time with cases like this, that's all that's needed. In case it's not, I want you to report anything that happens. If you think you're being followed, if he shows up at work, or home, if you see him at the grocery store. Anything, understood?"

Daisy nodded. They left the coffee shop, watching as Mike drove away in his patrol vehicle. She slid into the passenger seat of Will's Subaru and leaned back in the seat, eyes closed.

Chapter Six

Will gave a quick glance at the woman sitting in the car beside him before returning his attention to the road. "What's the issue with you and cops?"

"Who said there's an issue?"

He gave a short bark of laughter. "I'm pretty good at reading people, Daisy. I thought you were going to take off running."

She stared out the window. "Not everyone's interactions with the police are positive."

"Usually that's because they've done something illegal." He shook his head. "Can't see that with you."

"You don't know me."

"What, you're telling me your sweetness is a façade? Are you faking me out with PB and Js and juice boxes?"

She flattened Mrs. Gibbs's list on her knee. "The life I've built now is different from what I came from. Bad things happened when I was a kid. Sometimes the police were involved and that involvement wasn't always good. So cops make me nervous."

They pulled into the drugstore parking lot, but instead of getting out of the car when he shut off the engine, Will turned in his seat to face her. The shadows in her eyes made him want to wrap her in a hug and hold tight. The thing he was developing for Daisy was getting to be more than a thing.

She fiddled with the list, folding and refolding the paper. He caught her hand in his. "What happened when you were a kid?"

"I don't like talking about it."

"Sometimes talking helps."

She brought up her gaze. "Do you ever talk about when you were in Syria?"

He raised a brow. "You know I was in Syria?"

She nodded, face solemn. "You must have seen some traumatic things. Do you talk about it?"

"Yeah, I do. I have a therapist to help deal with the PTSD. I'll tell you about Syria sometime, but right now, I want to know about you."

She was quiet for so long he thought she wasn't going to say anything, then she gave a little sigh and spoke. "I've worked hard to limit the influence my past has on my present. I can't control my past, but I can control how much it affects me now. I don't mind you knowing, but don't think it defines me."

She squared her shoulders like he'd seen her do when talking to Mike. "My parents didn't have what you'd call good parenting skills. They didn't get along, argued a lot. One or the other of them would storm out of the house and be gone for days. But there were other problems. The first time I remember seeing the police was when they showed up at our apartment with a warrant. I was five. I remember being scared and crying. They took my dad away in handcuffs. He was arrested for dealing drugs."

"You were just a baby."

"Yeah, I was. Then when I was seven my mom was arrested for child neglect. I'd been found sleeping in the car in the parking lot of a casino."

"Alone?"

She nodded.

"Was your mom working there?"

"No, she was gambling there. She liked slot machines."

He pinched the bridge of his nose. "Do you remember her leaving you in the car?"

She nodded "Mom had made a bed for me in the backseat. She'd done it several times before she got caught. A cop broke the window to open the door. It took a while to find my mom, then they wouldn't let me go with her. They took me to a foster home."

"Jesus." He could imagine a tiny Daisy, black hair and big eyes, being taken from everything that was familiar. "How long were you in foster care?"

"A while. Then my grandmother, my dad's mom, got wind of what was happening. Turns out Mom regularly gambled away her paycheck. When child services came to check out my living situation, they found there was hardly any food in the house. Upshot was that my grandmother got custody, so I moved to San Diego to live with her."

"Where are your parents now?"

"My dad lives here in San Diego. He's managed to stay out of prison for the past ten years. We see each other occasionally. Mom lives in Phoenix with her boyfriend."

"Is she part of your life?"

"Not much. She's not a bad person, but she doesn't always make the best choices."

"Were things better with your grandmother?"

"Yeah. Much better."

"But you were left with a lifelong distrust of the police."

"Seeing a cop brings back the memories. The guy in uniform breaking the car window, the cop holding my hysterical mother back when they were putting me in the police car to take me away. It's hard to get past that association."

He brushed his thumb over the back of her hand. She had long fingers and neatly trimmed nails and a small birthmark on her wrist. "Is your grandmother still around?"

"She lives in a senior care facility in what they call the memory unit. I visit as often as I can." Her voice had roughened when speaking of her grandmother.

"She has dementia." It wasn't a question.

"She does. I visit her but she doesn't remember me. We grew sweet peas every year, and sometimes she remembers that when I bring her a bouquet."

Will thought Daisy's sunny personality was a testament to her resilience. He brought her knuckles to his lips and brushed them with a kiss. "You're amazing, Daisy."

"I'm not amazing. I do what comes next."

He shook his head. "I've seen too many people who've gone through less trauma than you who coped by dedicating their lives to the bottle or the needle. Sometimes both."

"Yeah, well, my way comes at a price. I can't enjoy adult beverages because I'm afraid I have an addiction gene and I'll turn into an alcoholic, which also explains why I refuse to go to Las Vegas." She looked down at their joined hands, then into his eyes. "I'm glad we're having this conversation, Will. I want you to understand why I won't have a relationship with you."

"The most important people in your early life let you down in the worst way. I get it. But you're too late on the no-relationship deal, because we're already there. And remember, we saw the green flash."

"So we can't go wrong in matters of the heart?"

"Exactly. I want to be with you, Daisy. You can trust me."

He could read the indecision on her face. "Let's start with something easy. Come with me on Sunday. I'd like you to meet my parents."

"That's something easy? Even if I was tempted—"

"You're tempted."

"Humble, aren't you? Skipping ahead to the 'meet the parents' portion of the program? I don't know about that."

"I want you to meet them. If it helps, I can tell them that we're just friends."

"How many female 'just friends' have you brought to meet your parents?"

"They've met some of my friends."

She gave him a look that had him breaking out a grin.

"Okay, none to meet them like you mean. But they'll be cool. Trust me."

"I think we've established that I have trust issues."

"Maybe, but this is me we're talking about." He ran a finger along her arm. "When you come home with me, you'll also get to see my mom's awesome garden. She has dedicated her spare time to growing flowers."

She narrowed her eyes. "Your mom has an awesome flower garden and you don't recognize bougainvillea, one of the most common flowers in California?"

"The flower interest has been since she's retired so I'm off the hook for that." He paused. "Come with me Sunday afternoon."

"I don't get it. Why meet your parents?"

He shrugged. "A couple of reasons. One, we *are* in a relationship, which, full disclosure, I'd like to develop. And two, I want you to meet them. They're good people."

"I'll think about it."

"How can I convince you?"

She fluttered her eyelashes. "Be romantic."

She'd meant it as a joke, but he nodded, expression serious.

"Game on."

***

The knock on the door had Daisy rising from her desk where she'd been working on lessons for the next school year. Sliding her feet into flip-flops, she went to the door, opening it to find a delivery man clutching a plant bursting with flowers.

"Delivery for Miss Daisy. You Miss Daisy?"

"That's me."

He thrust the pot at her. "Have a good day."

Daisy stared at the flowers. She recognized the variety, Cape Town Blue Daisy. They had soft blue petals with fuzzy yellow centers and were absolutely gorgeous. She shut the door and found the envelope addressed to "Miss Daisy."

She opened the folded card. *Blue daisies to match your eyes. Say yes. Will*

Her heart melted. Why was she such a sucker for sappy gestures? The flowers certainly hit the top of the romantic scale. Plus, Will was cagey. If he'd given her cut flowers, she would have thrown them out in a few days when they wilted. But a potted plant could live for years, reminding her of him every time she looked at them.

She put the plant on the shelf next to the wide abalone shell she'd found on the little table in the foyer the day before. The bottom was covered with beach sand and edged with a small pink spiral shell and three perfect tiny sand dollars. In the sand had been drawn "WS + DM," encircled by a heart. Who'd have known Will could be so sweet?

Chapter Seven

She worked until late in the evening pulling together resources for a lesson she could use in the fall that combined early map skills with learning about community. She couldn't help that her gaze kept drifting to the flowers. Or that she'd moved the abalone shell to her desk.

Chin in hand, she stared at those letters in the sand. What if she let herself have the relationship with him that he wanted? That, deep down, she wanted. How bad could it be? Love was an ephemeral thing. They'd both move past it at some point. She stopped that train of thought in its tracks. The pain of losing someone you loved was the cut-you-off-at-the-knees kind of pain. It was the kind that made you search for numbness, like dulling that pain with the thrill of pulling the lever on the slot machine, the money-sucking, mother-stealing, one-armed bandit.

But Will was different. Besides the smokin' hotness, he was steady, reliable, and essentially *good*. Added to that, she wasn't her mother. Her grandmother had taught her that you dealt with problems as they came along. Maybe Will was a work-out-the-problems kind of guy in relationships, rather than the kind who yelled and argued and scared the kids. Perhaps with Will, they'd face hard times together. Be a team.

Interesting concept.

When she finally shut off her computer and stacked papers and notebooks on her desk, she noticed with a start that it was nearly midnight. A noise from the front of the house had her frowning until she identified it as the faint creaking of the porch swing. She looked out her window and, sure enough, a dark shape showed someone lounging in the swing.

Without giving herself the chance to talk herself out of it, she slipped outside, closing the door softly behind her. She crossed the porch to Will, who sat in the gently swaying swing.

"What are you doing out here?"

"Thinking too much. Came out for some fresh air."

She leaned against the rail. "Want to tell me about those thoughts?'

Light from the streetlamp filtered through the trees and she saw him leaning back in the swing, eyes glinting gold while everything else was in shadows.

"Nothing happy or sweet in my thoughts right now. You won't want to hear it."

She moved to sit on the cushion beside him, drawing up her knees and curling her bare feet under her as she turned to face him. "Try me."

He picked up her hand to hold in his. He was quiet so long she thought he wouldn't say anything, then he started speaking, voice quiet in the darkness. "Last week we got a woman in from that bus crash. She was nearly twenty-two weeks pregnant and contractions had started. Odds for the baby surviving at that point in gestation aren't good. We got the labor stopped and I thought we'd done it, but this afternoon, she was back to the ER. This time her labor was too far along to stop. We didn't even have time to get her to the labor and delivery ward." He cleared his throat. "Her baby girl didn't survive."

"Oh, Will." Daisy swallowed against the tightness in her throat. "That's got to be the hardest."

He shrugged. "It seemed to have opened the floodgates, because ever since, I've got this endless loop of the worst of what I saw in Syria playing in my head. Couldn't sleep, so I came out here."

"Why did you go to Syria?"

"I was with a program that sends doctors to places in need around the world, and in return helps pay student loan debt. I was there for eighteen months. If I were ever asked to describe hell, that's where I'd draw inspiration from."

"What was it like?"

"They say Syria was a beautiful country before the civil war started, but there wasn't much evidence left of that. What I did see were incredibly resilient people desperately trying to keep their children alive and fed, and still educate them, and a government using the most brutal means at their disposal to crush the people's will to resist tyranny. War like that strips life down to the bare bones. We delivered a baby in a field hospital there. The mom didn't know how far along she was. I'd guess about thirty or thirty-one weeks. If he'd been born in a developed country, that baby would have been in NICU for a few weeks, but would have been fine. In Syria, all we could do for that little guy was let his mom hold him until he died."

She blinked against the tears. "I heard how bad it was there, about the bombing of hospitals and schools. It boggles my mind that anyone would ever consider hospitals legitimate targets."

"Tells you something about the depravity of the people making and carrying out those orders. Our hospital was bombed. Twenty-three people were killed, including a friend of mine, Abdul. He worked as a translator. He was a decent, kind man, the father of six. They didn't have much, but he invited me to his home and his wife made the most amazing meal. They shared their food with me and acted like it was an honor to do so."

"Were you hurt in the bombing?"

He shook his head, the streetlamp illuminating the flash of his teeth as he gave a humorless smile. "No. I'd put in a thirty-hour shift and gone back to the barracks. The bombing woke me, and by the time I got outside, the hospital was in ruins. Fucking bastards."

They sat quietly. Will used his foot to start the swing swaying, the quiet creaking sound overlaying the crickets chirping.

He had begun brushing his thumb back and forth over her palm while he'd been speaking. He stopped and stared at her hand, seemingly just realizing what he was doing. Then he raised her hand to his mouth and pressed a kiss to the center of her palm, the glint of his eyes visible as he watched her.

She leaned forward and offered her lips to his. The kiss started softly as a comfort to the warrior, then evolved as it drew heat. Everything Will had told her only confirmed that he was a man of great passion and integrity. No one went to help the people of Syria during a civil war simply to pay student loans.

He had a drive to care for people, and he'd gone to where they were the most vulnerable and the need was greatest. Emotions she'd been trying to tamp back were spiraling out of control. She'd promised herself she wouldn't risk love, and now she knew the joke was on her, because she could no more stop the feelings she had for Will than stop the tide.

He shifted and pulled her onto his lap, spearing his fingers into her hair as he kissed her with a thoroughness that left her breathless.

"God, when I'm with you I feel like the world is a little more bearable, that no matter what's thrown my way, I can handle it." He kissed her shoulder, nudging aside the strap of the tank she was wearing. His lips moved to the swell of her breast as she rocked against him.

He lifted his head. "Do you want this?"

She nodded, then rose to her feet and held out her hand. "Come to bed with me, Will."

He laced his fingers with hers and followed her into the house.

Chapter Eight

Daisy let herself into the foyer of the house. Waking in Will's arms had been wonderful, especially when they'd taken the opportunity to make love once again, this time slowly and sweetly, with none of the desperate yearning they'd built between them during the night.

She jiggled her keys to find the one to her apartment. After the endorphin rush of early-morning sex, the visit to her grandmother had dropped her mood and left her feeling plain sad. The woman who had saved Daisy's life, who had given her security after so many years of uncertainty, no longer knew her.

She stepped into her apartment and discovered a folded paper had been slipped under her door while she'd been out. *We have a date tonight. Be ready at half past seven. Will*

Now she understood why he'd casually asked her earlier if she had plans for the evening.

She'd suggested he be romantic, and he was hitting all the marks. He'd asked her to meet his parents and this evening she'd tell him that she would. Meeting Will's parents didn't mean she was committing her life to him. They were having dinner. Nothing more.

After spending the rest of the day running errands, as evening fell, she took her time getting ready. She left her hair loose to curl over her shoulders and chose a white halter dress that left her upper back and shoulders bare. She rarely wore makeup, but she applied eye shadow and mascara, and coated her lips in red.

A knock sounded at her door. She opened it expecting it to be Will, and had to look down to see the little boy from down the street, the one whose knee Doctor Will had bandaged. He wore a dark suit jacket and a bow tie.

He smiled, showing a gap where his top two teeth should be. "Miss Daisy, I'm Eddie. Your presence is 'quested in the pugula." He frowned up at her. "I don't know what that is, but it's outside. I'm supposed to escort you." He held up a bent arm.

"Oh my." She took the arm of her adorable escort, and he walked her out the front door and around the side of the house. Dusk had fallen and fairy lights glimmered around the pergola. A wrought-iron table with a mosaic top had been moved to the center of the brick floor, and red candles flickered seductively beside a sweating bottle of wine. She peeked at the bottle. Not wine, non-alcoholic apple cider. He'd remembered. Sweet peas sat in a vase next to two wine glasses.

Eddie pointed to a chair. "You're supposed to sit there, so Will can bring out stuff."

Will stepped out the backdoor carrying two plates covered with inverted pie tins. He had dressed in khaki chinos and a wine-colored, button-up shirt. He set the plates on the table.

"Thank you, my man," he said to Eddie. "You're off duty."

With a high five, Eddie trotted back toward the street.

Will bent forward and kissed her cheek. He whispered, "You look beautiful. Back in a minute."

Will followed Eddie, returning a couple minutes later. "He made it home. I'll bring out the food."

"Do you want help? I worked as a server in college so I'm qualified."

Will shook his head. "No, you sit and relax. I'll be right back." He disappeared back into the house. A slight breeze stirred the leaves in the trees, causing the candles to flicker. He must have hidden a speaker somewhere because the bluesy wail of a saxophone added to the ambience. Will returned with a breadbasket that he sat in the middle of the table.

"This is really nice, Will."

"How am I doing on the romance?" His gold eyes glittered in the candlelight.

She grinned at him. "Ten out of ten. But, full disclosure, I've already decided to go with you to your parents' home. I'm looking forward to it."

"Good." He lifted the pie tins off the dishes. "Had to improvise here."

"Oh wow. This looks amazing." He'd prepared shrimp Florentine pasta, with red peppers, wilted spinach, and lemon wedges. The side was a caprese salad with yellow and red tomatoes.

The meal was served on white plates with a beautiful flowered pattern and gold rim. "Mrs. Gibbs let you use her china?"

"Yes, she did. She told me that since she only has daughters, she's considering adopting me." He smiled smugly. "The pie tins were her idea to keep the food warm. And she felt well enough today to make our dessert, which is strawberry rhubarb pie."

"Yum, that's a favorite of mine." Daisy swirled pasta around her fork and took a bite. "So good. Did you make all this?"

"Yeah." He put a piece of garlic bread on her plate. "I don't cook often, but I enjoy it."

"Who taught you to cook? Your mom?"

"Ha. My mom's brilliant, but the kitchen is not where her skills lie. No, my dad was the cook when my sisters and I were growing up, and he made sure we all knew how to cook."

"Cooking is tops for me in the romance list."

"I'll have to remember that." His brows lowered over his eyes. "Look, I want to get this out of the way so we can enjoy our evening. Mike stopped by earlier when you were out."

She set down her fork. "And?"

"And Raul's been arrested on a variety of charges around customer fraud at the tire shop. They're even gathering evidence for possible money laundering. Mike says detectives may be in contact with you about harassment charges."

"Wow. I should have listened to my instincts about him."

"Yes, you should have. At least you won't have to worry about him bothering you again since he's going to be occupied elsewhere."

"I guess he is. Thank you for doing what you did. None of this would have happened if you hadn't contacted Mike."

"I protect those I care about."

"God, Will, when you say things like that you make my heart literally stumble."

"Now you know how I feel whenever you walk in the room."

Daisy fanned her hand over her face. "You are so getting lucky tonight."

His grin flashed, fast and wicked. "I look forward to it."

If they were going to get through the meal, she'd have to steer the conversation in a less provocative direction.

They talked about a variety of topics including how much she loved teaching. Will was intelligent and charming and there was an undercurrent of attraction that added an extra sparkle to the evening. Daisy closed her eyes as she savored a bite of strawberry rhubarb pie with the flakiest of crusts.

"Tell me, why aren't you married, Will Sloane?"

"I was once."

Her eyes popped open. He couldn't have surprised her more if he'd said he'd joined the priesthood. "What happened, if that's not too personal?"

His gaze caught hers. "It's not too personal. I meant it when I said I want you to know me." He set down his fork and pushed back his empty plate. "Short version, we were young and dumb. I was a sophomore in college, Brandy had been my high school girlfriend. We hooked up during Christmas break, condom broke, and she got pregnant. We got married, then our baby, a little girl, was stillborn at five months. There were problems with the placenta." Heaviness seemed to settle on his shoulders. "I guess that's why cases with babies always hit me so hard."

"It broke your heart."

"Yes, it did. It took me some time to get over that."

"How was Brandy?"

"Devastated. It didn't matter what I said, she felt it was somehow her fault. After that our marriage fell apart. We were too young, and in a lot of ways we weren't compatible." He lifted his shoulders. "Neither one of us worked very hard to stay together. She married a good guy a few years later. They have three daughters."

"I'm glad. Did that experience have anything to do with your decision to go to medical school?"

"That's the direction I'd been leaning, but yeah, it tipped me over the edge. It made me grow up." His gaze lingered on her. "But enough about me. You're too far away."

"I am?"

"Yeah." He rose to his feet and held out his hand, palm up. "Care to dance?"

When Daisy finally lay replete, curled into Will's body, his fingers playing lazily with the ends of her hair, she was floating. No one had ever gone to such effort to make her feel special, to woo her. Hands down, swaying in Will's arms with the music playing softly and fairy lights twinkling above them was the most romantic moment of her life.

If she was tumbling into love with Will Sloane, she wasn't looking too hard for something to break her fall.

Chapter Nine

Will's parents' Spanish-style home sat on a wide lot in an old, established neighborhood only blocks from the beach. Instead of going to the front door, Will led Daisy around the side of the house and through a gate. A walkway made of stone pavers was lined with potted plants along the house and bougainvillea in a profusion of color on the other side, bordering the fence. Daisy nudged Will with her elbow. "Quiz time, can you name those flowers?"

"Daisies? The most beautiful of all flowers?"

"Oh geez, Will. Now you're getting corny."

"I don't know what you're talking about. I've developed a taste for daisies."

Daisy could feel heat warming her cheeks as they rounded the corner to the backyard. The view helped distract her from thoughts of the times she'd spent in Will's arms.

"Oh, how beautiful." The stone pavers had been used for a deck bordered by a short, white stucco wall inlaid with colorful tiles that maintained the Spanish theme. The backyard stretched up a hillside and showcased a beautiful garden in full bloom.

"There's Mom."

A woman with long gray hair wearing loose clamdigger pants and a breezy linen blouse came down the slope toward them, brushing her hands together. "I see a weed and I can't help pulling it, and one leads to another and before I know it, I've forgotten that I came out to fill the birdbath." She held out a hand to shake Daisy's. "Daisy, it's so nice to meet you. I'm Nancy."

"You have a beautiful garden, Nancy."

"Thank you, we enjoy it."

She turned to her son, who wrapped her in an eyes-closed, all-in hug.

"Hi, Mom," he murmured before releasing her.

"Hi back, my boy." She turned back to Daisy. "I'm so glad Will brought you. Let's go inside where Keith's prepping dinner. He got himself a new barbecue that I swear does everything but cut your food for you, so all the cooking today is being done outside."

They passed the impressive chrome barbecue before going up steps to the spacious kitchen with granite countertops. A center island skirted by barstools held a bowl full of fresh fruit.

Keith Sloane had a wide smile and hair much like Will's, though streaked with gray. His lined face told her he spent many hours in the sun. He was busy skewering strips of meat for what she guessed would be kabobs, while peppers, mushrooms, and onions sat on a cutting board.

After introductions, Daisy asked, "Can I help? I can cut the vegetables."

"Of course." Keith got a knife from a drawer and set it beside the vegetables. "Nan grows flowers, and I grow vegetables. The peppers are from my garden."

Daisy washed her hands and began chopping. Conversation flowed, the family including her as they talked about an upcoming trip the elder Sloanes were planning.

"We haven't been to Europe since we took Will and his sisters when they were teenagers," Nancy told her. "Keith and I have decided to join a tour group for a trip to Italy."

"That's the old folks way to go," Will said as he snagged an orange pepper from the pile Daisy had chopped.

"Since there's no way in hell I'm going around with a backpack like you did," Keith pointed a skewer at his son, "a tour will suit us just fine."

Will chewed on the pepper. "There's a lot of room between backpacking around Europe and having a trip planned down to the last minute."

"We'll see how this trip goes," Nancy chimed in. "Then maybe next time we'll do something different."

By the time they sat down to dinner at an outside table in the shade of a mimosa tree, Daisy had a pretty good idea why Will had wanted her to meet his parents. They were a *couple* in a way she had never experienced with her parents. Casual touches, finishing each other's sentences, the warm affection when their gazes caught all served to show Daisy what could be if two people worked together to build a life.

They said their good-byes, but instead of opening the car door, Will led her to the end of the driveway. He pointed to where the ocean gleamed blue between houses. "Want to walk down to the beach? It's only a few blocks. Sun's going down. Maybe we'll see another green flash."

"That's a hard invitation to resist."

Will took her hand and they strolled leisurely down the gently sloping sidewalk. When they got to the sand, he insisted on carrying her sandals. At the shoreline, tiny shells and smooth stones gleamed in the wet sand like pirate's treasure.

"I like your parents. They seem so...real, I guess. Down to earth."

"They've been married nearly forty years, and still enjoy spending time together."

"It's obvious they love each other deeply." She hadn't intended for her voice to sound wistful.

"The only thing they like better than being together is when they're together with their kids." He stopped her with a hand to her arm. "I wanted you to meet them because that's what I want," his gaze burned brighter, "with you."

Daisy waited for the clutch of panic. It didn't come, but she still felt wary. "This is coming from the guy who up until a couple weeks ago never called me by my name, but whatever flower you could think of. And you made fun of me."

His quick grin was hard to resist. "Consider that foreplay. It got you to pay attention to me, didn't it?"

"I was paying attention, anyway, whether I wanted to or not. There's something about you, Will."

"Yeah? Is that something enough to get you to reconsider the ban on boyfriends?" His face turned serious. "You said you weren't letting your past dictate your future, but I think that's exactly what you've been doing. The pain you endured as a child is keeping you from trusting my feelings for you."

Her gaze remained locked on his. "I've been thinking about that a lot lately. You have a way of making me question myself."

"I know I'm moving fast, Daisy, but you're what I want, and I'm willing to wait as long as it takes for you to love me, too."

This time her heart did clutch, but not with panic. She couldn't look anywhere but into those brown eyes flecked with gold as the feelings inside her swelled like a bud preparing to open.

"That sounds perfect, but I'm scared."

"I love you, Daisy. I have from the first moment we met. I've only been waiting for you to catch up."

The swell of love opened like an entire bouquet of daisies coming into bloom. She launched herself into his arms, burying her face in his neck. "I love you, Will. I love you. I love you."

He boosted her up and she wrapped her legs around his hips. She leaned back, and his full-wattage smile had her catching her breath.

"That's good, sweet Daisy, because we've got our life to build. Together. Let's get started."

Epilogue

Sixteen months later

Daisy gripped Will's hand so tightly he was sure the bones would be permanently fused.

"You did this to me." She panted the words. "We are never having sex again. Ever."

A nurse coughed to cover a laugh.

"Whatever you say, honey."

Daisy puffed, then ground the bones in his fingers again as another contraction tightened her belly. She held her breath and bore down, panting when the contraction eased. "Even if you look at me with that sexy look of yours, no sex. You're moving into a separate bedroom."

"Okay." He kissed the back of her hand. "You got this, sweet Daisy." He glanced at the monitor. "Another contraction's coming. Hold on to me and breathe."

"You hold on and breathe." Her words ended in a howl as the contraction hit.

The fear that something would go wrong had plagued him from the moment Daisy had peed on a stick and the little cross marks had appeared. Since his wife had ignored his order of bedrest for nine months, he'd watched her like a hawk and done everything in his power to keep her and the baby safe. And Daisy being Daisy, she'd followed the advice that worked for her and ignored the rest.

He looked in the mirror. "There's her head. Daisy, look, there's the top of her head."

The next contractions came quickly, and with a last mighty push, Lilah Rose made her entrance into the world with a wailing cry.

Feeling shaky, Will pressed his forehead to Daisy's. "God, you're amazing. You did it. We have a daughter."

She turned her face to his and whispered, "You're a daddy, Will. We have a little girl."

The nurse laid Lilah on Daisy's chest, draping a light blanket over the baby.

Tears streamed down Daisy's cheeks. "Oh, look at her." She cupped the precious bundle between her breasts.

"She's beautiful." Will stared at the scrunched newborn face, lightly trailing his fingers over his daughter's head. "Her hair is black like yours."

"She has such tiny fingers."

The tiny fingers of one hand wrapped around Will's much larger one, and he had to swallow a lump in his throat.

Daisy raised her gaze to his. "She's perfect, Will. We made the perfect baby."

"Too bad she's going to be an only child."

"What are you talking about? She won't be an only child. We're having at least two, maybe three."

Will smiled and kissed his daughter for the first time.

Life was perfect.

AN UNEXPECTED RESCUE

Joan Bird

The term "first responders" took on a whole new meaning for many of us on a sunny New York morning 18+ years ago. Perhaps we even took their presence for granted until countless heroic actions became global news. Yet, as time healed our collective pain, it may also have muted our respect for those who serve, at least until we are forced from complacency by another catastrophic event. With gratitude, I dedicate this story to all who first rush to save, and to those then tasked with repairing damage to tissue, bone, hearts, and minds borne of human calamities.

#

I cannot write without acknowledging Boroughs Publishing...Where Story Matters. Thank you for the opportunity to join with exceptional writers in the creation of stories with roots in a cause. For the encouragement, the subtle but clever editorial suggestions/corrections, and the continued faith in my ability to craft a beginning, an end, and the-often-a-struggle, middle, I shout (because I dare not use the outlawed exclamation point), THANK YOU.

Chapter One

"Dammit, Monkey, where are you?" Cat Morgan blew a dust bunny away from her face. She hated having to look under the furniture. "Oh well." Squinting, Cat stared into the shadowed area beneath the sofa, hoping to spy the errant rescue.

Good thing she lived alone because nobody would tolerate the menagerie of creatures that paraded through her cozy cabin twenty-four/seven. Cat never considered luck as a regular part of her life until she landed the caretaker's job six months ago. There wasn't much to the post, house-sitting really. An absentee landlord and 200-plus acres of woods fifty yards from the cottage's back door preserved her sanity and nurtured her tendency to quirkiness. With no one to judge her lifestyle, she could write. And she had done so, diligently, feverishly, and with commitment until the block.

Of course, every writer had these, but the worst case Cat had ever experienced smacked her upside the head three weeks ago. Nothing she did unleashed any clarity in her writer's head. Not yoga, meditation, running, baking, or eating warm sugar cookies. She'd even ridden the beat-up bike with questionable tires that sat against the fence like a piece of artwork into town. The exercise hadn't produced a single paragraph. Maybe the underlying cause was her not feeling well. Fever, achy—that kind of crap put a body off creativity.

Cat pulled her face out from under the sofa and was greeted by a nubby tongue across her nose. Heathcliff, a kitten, saved from starvation, stared into her eyes. "Sweetie, have you seen Monkey?" First appearing to consider an answer, the wary kitten instead jumped onto her shoulder. Wicked little claws grabbed on for a ride, poking through the thin cotton fabric of her favorite shirt. "Shit, Cliffy. That hurts."

Sometimes, not often, but sometimes, Cat had to ask herself why she hadn't let the hawk snatch up the obnoxious calico kitten to feed its babies. But screeching from high up in the nearby grove of trees convinced her that the furry terrorist now drawing blood by clinging to her skin did not deserve to be a snack.

Odd, Cat didn't much care for the four-legged variety of the genus feline, and that she had rescued one was the sort of irony she wished she could write.

Twisting to unlatch the kitten, she nearly fell. "Dammit." She tugged at the kitten while trying to keep her balance. Multitasking sucked and, at this moment, failed. Cat crash-landed over a footstool, Heathcliff still entrenched in the cloth of her shirt, its needle-like claws had made matters worse. And Monkey remained on the lam.

"Hello?"

She hadn't heard a car door slam, she wasn't expecting anyone, and Cat could have sworn she'd closed and locked the front door to the cottage despite the sunshine, a welcome break from days of clouds and rain. If there was a downside to paying zero rent for the place, it was the occasional fear that rankled at being isolated and alone.

The cabin was almost at the end of SR 211, and although the main thoroughfare out of town, it dead-ended about half a mile from Cat's driveway. California's transportation gurus had long abandoned the idea of a road along the Lost Coast. Consequently, folks had little interest in traveling much farther than the stop sign at Dairy Lane. Without traffic, the highway simply settled in as if part of the countryside, and not a single car passed for days. Sometimes, like now, the isolation forced Cat to accept her complete vulnerability.

Standing, Heathcliff swung from her shirt, which now stretched below one shoulder, and she decided to face her fears and the stranger head-on.

"Damn you, Heathcliff."

"My name is Case."

Well, bully for him. Drop-dead handsome some-kind-of-the-law-gun-toting-uniform-wearing-dude-with-a-name-like-that…well,

maybe she'd have to shoot him. Except she didn't have a permit for the gun tucked under her ugliest underwear in the dresser. Damn, but her uninvited visitor was good-looking. All chiseled and blue-eyed and six-foot something, hot—sizzling hot.

She expected the officer would announce his last name and purpose at some point. Still, Cat tried to make out his identity. She squinted her eyes, but neither the nameplate pinned above a pocket nor the shield clipped to his belt were readable from where she stood.

She needed to get a grip on her brain because for a second or two, she had tried picturing the officer with his shirt off and his belt buckle undone. Geeze, fantasizing with an illegal monkey loose somewhere in the room while a hunk of male with a badge stood blocking her exit, and in a manner that seemed to hold her hostage, was idiotic. And what if her gorgeous visitor was an ax murderer? She swallowed the lump in her throat and vowed to stop watching *True Crime* on TV.

If he was here to wring her neck, she could only hope he'd ravage her instead.

***

Case Gallagher wasn't much fond of beautiful women, though the ones he'd met in his life refused to believe it of him. He wanted character, class, stamina, a woman in hiking boots with fire in her gut, a spark behind a gaze that spoke of intelligence and a sense of humor.

Truth was, Case had failed to connect with too many of the female species to count, and wouldn't tolerate bimbos. At the moment, it appeared he was in the presence of just such a creature.

He stared at the woman dressed in a flimsy sweater-like thing, a baby cat pinned like a broach to one sleeve, and his first thought was a judgment. He studied the gatekeeper's current resident while trying to decide if he should dismiss her as a typical blonde, and never fill in the blanks.

She *was* a towhead, and the color had to be real because freckles were splashed all over her skin as if Jackson Pollock had dropped by to clean his brushes by flicking brown paint on the girl's otherwise fair skin. For one moment, his brain tried to plant an image of where else those freckles might be on a sort-of sexy body.

So the rumors were true. Case had heard this new tenant brought a menagerie when she moved in two months back. Checking up on her sooner would have been appropriate, especially since his primary duties fell under the title of game warden. But, between torrential rains and a nasty version of Type A flu, the community was reeling. Case had no chance to meet the new no-rent-hippie who had moved into Zack Brennan's dilapidated cabin. Zack was in a rest home down in Healdsburg and let the cottage be cared for by anyone willing to keep it clean and in reasonable repair.

The woman wearing a kitten sneezed, and Case swore under his breath. Despite his job—one part of which involved close contact with people—he'd managed to avoid the flu since the first reported cases in Humboldt County over six weeks ago. Still, under the current circumstance, he got a crazy notion to dig a moat around his A-frame. He'd be fine burrowing in until spring officially arrived.

But here he was, and orders were to be carried out without question. For now, he could only deliver the recommended voluntary evacuation order, even though by tomorrow the storm would upgrade evacuations to the mandatory variety. Case guessed she wouldn't want to leave. It didn't take a genius to figure that out. He refocused his attention on the woman occupying the cabin.

The kitten dangling from the fabric of her shirt had likely dug in enough to puncture the skin. Dammit, but that exposed freckled shoulder kept rushing him like a linebacker. Toss in a long neck, strong clavicle bones, narrow hips, and some kind of plaid leggings that fit her thighs and legs like cling-wrap on cheese, and he had to reevaluate his thinking.

The woman wasn't just *sort-of- sexy*. Nope, rescue-animal-lady was hot. Pick-up-in-a-bar-take-her-home-and... He shook his head, chasing the image out of his mind. Every alarm hardwired to his brain about females, and the hazards of getting involved with them, clanged in his head like a 90s grunge band. Still, skin dusted with some sort of glittery substance begged a nibble. He reminded himself that although she didn't appear to be a living contagion, it was best to avoid contact.

Maybe.

The bigger problem was the weather and evacuating areas subject to flooding. Somehow, Case had to convince her to take a hotel room in town before the next storm exploded over the area. Meteorologists were warning it could be the last straw for the Eel River, and the gatekeeper's cabin sat on a marshy flat known to flood.

"Ma'am?"

"Cliffy. Let go." She snapped her head away from the kitten and stared at Case. "Do I really, truly, and actually look like a 'ma'am' to you?"

"I need a favor." Something about nature-girl compelled him to move closer. He stepped around the sofa.

She didn't pull back, "Okay, but I've no clue who you are, and I'm kind of busy." A grin broke into a broad smile as the woman gently disconnected tiny claws from fabric. She held the wannabe tiger by its scruffy neck. The cabin's apparent sole human occupant seemed to be considering a criticism of the bad behavior, but instead kissed the cat's pink nose.

"Ma'am, Case Gallagher. I'm a game warden for two counties. Also, when needed, I'm a deputy sheriff around these parts."

"Spoken like a cowboy. Isn't it supposed to be *these here parts*?" Her smile widened, marshaling freckles into lines like shadows within the dimples on either side of her grin. For unknown reasons, Case wanted to kiss her. And that twist in his thoughts was plain nuts.

"I'd appreciate a little respect for the law, ma'am."

She broke into a laugh that burned his ears and pissed Case off. Seriously. "And I'd appreciate not being called ma'am for another thirty years or so."

Case shifted his weight, knowing full well the move compromised her personal space. It also made his leather gun belt squeak. The ordinance was one of two parts of being a lawman that he tolerated. The other was the badge on his belt. Otherwise, he usually managed his duties with green khaki shirts and Levi's. Case knew his height and the breadth of his shoulders brooked little resistance. At least for the kind of crime that occurred on occasion in a small tourist community off the northern coast of California.

He stared at the girl. *Another day, another dollar.* Trite thinking got him nowhere, but the wood nymph, bless her heart, was working some unwanted magic on a particular part of his anatomy. The reaction surprised him because it was difficult to imagine even a remote attraction to a woman covered in animal hair.

Good thing he didn't have any allergies.

As for other animals, so far he'd noted a worn-out-looking gelding in the dilapidated corral and an equally antique cow aimlessly munching on long grass in one corner of the fenced area when he first came through the gate.

Observations aside, he needed to focus on the serious matter of her safety. Between

epidemic flu and the miserable weather, the town was gasping for the benefits of its tourist trade. Hotels, restaurants, cafes, and even the boutiques and pottery shops that marched up and down the town's main street, were cutting rates and "sale" signs filled every storefront window. His duties included the safety of all citizens, and that meant convincing the nutty female scolding an obnoxious kitten that she needed to leave the cabin.

Case refocused on the tree-hugger, an unfair thought but one that stuck. "Ma'am, I need your full attention here." Animal hair, fur, and what appeared to be a solo spaghetti noodle attached to her sweater. Her leggings looked as if a vacuum bag exploded. The idea of all that dander landing onto his truck seat should have sent him running, but duty called.

She tossed her thick mane of sunshine hair, licked her lips, smiled again. "You'd like my full attention, right, officer? It is officer, I mean, is that how one addresses a game warden? I can try, sir. Will sir do, or do you hate it? I, for one, detest being called ma'am, so…"

"Tough." She didn't flinch, so he continued, "I don't know your name, I'm not even sure when you moved in here—or if you even have a *right* to be here—but I have a job to do. And it's urgent. For now, you'll have to settle for ma'am."

"Cat."

"You're holding one, so what?"

"Cat."

"Ma'am, this is not funny. I don't know what your game is, but I'm here on official business." Case shifted in his boots, which further lessened the distance between him and the woman. He rested his hand on the butt of his revolver, thinking to get the message of his authority across to the crazy person playing games.

No such luck. Her laughter filled the small room, and the sound struck him as one that any other time or circumstance would have filled him with joy. But not now. "This isn't funny, ma'am."

"But of course it is. It's hysterical. My name *is* Cat. And despite appearances, I don't have two thousand of the four-legged mouse catchers hiding in the wings. Also, for the record, no children are being plumped for cooking in the basement, and I don't try to communicate with Martians when the moon is full."

"Your name is Cat?"

"Catherine Morgan. I go by Cat. And that last little speech was funny, which means you should be laughing. I always make people laugh, and in truth? I'm devastated that you don't find me humorous." She frowned, but Case could see it was a fake expression.

"Somehow, I think you'll get over it." He forced himself to take a step back. Catherine, Cat, whatever her name might be, was on the verge of ruining his day. On top of which, she could be exposing him to the flu or some ungodly virus borne on vermin prone to wildlife.

He knew the cabin had been without a tenant for over two years. Glancing around the place, it appeared as if she'd given it a thorough cleaning, but with a damned ark in her living room, viruses could still be problematic.

Case returned to studying Cat. Instinct confirmed that doing this job spelled disaster.

Duty engrained after almost eight years in the Marines meant he would get her out of the cabin and off the marsh even if he had to arrest the fur-covered blonde, who now seemed to consider whether he'd make a good pet.

He needn't worry about any attraction anyway. His heart was protected from emotional pain because he'd locked it down. On his return to the states at the end of his final tour of duty, over five years ago now, Molly Reynolds hadn't been there to greet, hug, or kiss him. Instead, his mom had delivered the news. Molly had married some real estate mogul named Brad-something two months prior to Case's return. No *Dear John* letter, no gentle letdown, but another IED, only it killed emotions rather than leaving jagged scars like the one across his belly. Helmand province, Afghanistan was no picnic, but the broken heart bit was worse.

He shoved the past out of his head. Case had no choice but to save the animal-hair-covered woman grinning at him as if she had his personality all figured out. Whatever draw she had would not alter his rules about relationships with women since Molly. Those dictates included zero relationships with women he met while working. In effect, the total of these conditions resulted in no females. Period.

Still, the fact of closing his heart to emotional involvement didn't foreclose on the occasional dalliance to satisfy physical needs. Especially as now, when Cat ignored him and returned to peering under the couch, her shapely rear end his only view.

***

The primate landed on the lawman's head as if planned. Maybe the beast had been in the rafters, which mattered little since now tiny human-like hands dug into his hair.

"Shit."

Cat pushed up from the sofa as if popped from a toaster. "Monkey." She shouldn't laugh. However, that inherent knowledge couldn't curtail a fit of giggles. She should have known what would happen next.

Ordinarily, she anticipated the warning signs. Excitement, then shortness of breath, an attack no doubt to follow. It never helped that she surrounded herself with pet dander. But watching the game warden, deputy, or *whatever*, trying to extract the rescued chimp from his head was too much fun to ignore.

"Dammit, Monkey. Let him go." Cat ignored the tightness in her chest and reached the lawman's side. Reaching up, she wrestled the baby monkey's fisted hands, freeing the animal's grip on her visitor. "Shush now." Calming the wild pet as best she could, Cat quickly deposited the confused animal in a cage on top of the beat-up coffee table.

"I'm so sorry. The little monster is super-protective of me." She dared a step toward the deputy, studying his face for scratches, blood, any damage caused by Monkey. Case, that's what he said his name was, right? Yes, and he was impossibly close.

Embarrassed, she ducked her gaze, afraid of her reaction if she looked him straight on. In an earlier glance, she had thought his eyes might be blue, but she'd been wrong. They were green, but not ocean green. The color seemed more akin to the shallows under trees in a lake. Making a decision was dizzying. She looked again and noted the fury building in his expression. Gray, there were flecks of gray, he was gorgeous, even totally pissed off.

Cat might have dared an apology to the man who had rattled her since he first barged in, but it was too late. She reached in her pocket. The inhaler wasn't there. Her lungs had tried to warn her, and she spun, lunging for her backpack, but then everything went black.

Chapter Two

"Sip, this."

A steady hand cradled Cat's neck from behind as a glass rested against her lips. "Huh?"

"Sip, not too fast."

"Margarita?"

"Okay, funny, at least that means you're not dead."

"That or my version of heaven is a beach in Puerta Vallarta."

"Passé. And, from what I hear, it's no longer the hot spot south of the border."

"You don't seem the type to have insight into so-called hot spots for touristas." Cat's stranger again tipped the glass to her mouth. She tried to ignore the heat resulting from his touch, the nearness of his body to hers. He hadn't stopped being gorgeous because she'd passed out.

"I'd take insult by that remark if I gave a damn about being bored while melting under a sizzling sun. Now, drink."

"It doesn't matter. I'm too old to enjoy lying on a beach even dipped in SPF two hundred."

"How old?"

A cough stopped Cat's retort, and water dribbled down her neck. "Damn, that's cold."

"Rhymes with old. I need your age, ma'am."

"No, you don't."

"Yes, I do." The ranger rescuer hunk whipped a clipboard with official-looking papers rammed under a metal brad from behind his back. "Health questionnaire."

"Over my dead body."

"Well, it might have been if I hadn't been here when you had that asthma attack."

"I've had them before."

"The way you dove for your backpack, I figured you had some kind of medical condition. You might try keeping more than one inhaler." He held the red and gray canister, then set it back on the coffee table. "Be even better if the one I found had been in say, the side pouch, instead of wrapped between wet socks."

"There's an explanation."

"No doubt."

"Geeze, smug, arrogant, and a know-it-all. I hit the jackpot, folks." Cat tugged on the

blanket. As she leaned forward to get up, her progress was halted when a coughing fit slammed her back against the pillow. The cup, jarred by her movement, flew from the deputy's hands, and icy water splashed her again.

Whatever Cat expected, it wasn't jumping up to find her sweater and shirt gone. "Poop, squared." In an ordinary world, a girl might jog, garden, and walk children clad in only a flowered exercise bra such as the one she had on now. But standing in the small living area in front of a drop-dead-gorgeous stranger was anything *but* ordinary.

"Ma'am, you're cute, but you need to settle back down."

"And you're an asshole."

"Well, I appreciate you might feel that way, but saving your life didn't warrant my asking your permission."

"You didn't save my life."

"Argue that point all you want. Fact is, I made a judgment call about removing those vermin-infested items of clothing on your body." Cat's visitor pointed at the heap lying at the end of the sofa. "What," he pointed in the direction of the piled clothing, "is that anyway?"

"Evidence of a rape." Cat accepted she was overreacting, but his overt familiarity when she was vulnerable justified outrage. She knew how bad her asthma attack must have been, and she hadn't been feeling well for the last few days. Still, she refused to let the flu warnings get to her, and she wouldn't ever accept that she had allergies to her animals. "I'm not sure how your credentials as a game warden or whatever the heck you are extend to removing my clothes."

"In most circumstances, you'd have a point."

"And now you're going to insist a dumb old asthma attack justifies the ends? "

"Correct." His grin and the pinpointed study of her body forced Cat's temperature up another few degrees. At least it felt that way. A surge of weakness struck, so she sank back onto the couch.

Sir Badge-Wearing Lancelot plopped down next to her as if he belonged there "That was not any old asthma attack. Did you know that as many as three people die each day from asthma?"

"Mr. Case, whatever…"

"Gallagher. Case Gallagher. But you can call me officer, or sir, or even Mr. Saved-My-Bacon, if you'd like."

"Your ego is a little too big for this cottage, buster."

The rumbling laugh that followed Cat's comment took her by surprise. She'd thought he couldn't have a sense of humor given the size of his ego.

"Buster? Listen, Cat-Woman, I'm good at what I do, and in a past life, my job duties extended to EMT. I was better at that than policing, so you're lucky I'm here."

This time Cat laughed. "I only have one cat, the kitten. So you can't officially stick me with the Cat-Woman title."

Instead of a retort, the deputy leaned in and seemed to be taking stock of her features. For a crazy moment, she hoped he'd kiss her, but then her airways pulled their short-sheeting game on her lungs again.

Kissing would have to wait.

Chapter Three

Case figured he might have to come back to the cabin later, all that mattered now was to get the sick woman in the rear seat of his truck to the hospital. It meant barreling through the tiny tourist attraction that was now his home. For the town of Ferndale, the closest hospital was Fortuna up on the 101. The last thing the woman's lungs needed would be the addition of anxiety. A panic attack, coupled with her aggravated asthma condition, could kill her.

"Ow."

He glanced at the lump under the blanket via the rearview mirror. "Sorry." Case tried to avoid another pothole, but Cat's condition spurred the lack of caution. And why was he calling her Cat in his head? He needed to stick to the *woman* or *girl*. Or what was her last name, Morgan? That would work. She wasn't a girl, but he figured if his brain perceived Cat that way, he'd be more likely to avoid further involvement. She mumbled something else, but a second glance over his shoulder confirmed she remained snuggled back under the blanket.

The road was slated for summer repairs because of potholes, and the recent rains made the condition of the asphalt that much worse. The bounces were inevitable and better than a delay in getting his charge admitted into the ER. He narrowed his eyes to focus on the road. He didn't like the look of the incoming weather. The sky was angry, and the clouds that formed had dark underbellies. "Dammit." From his perspective, the next predicted storm had no intention of following the timeline plotted out by diploma-ed meteorologists or the science of Doppler radar.

Case turned on the truck's siren and lights when he hit Main Street. He was vaguely aware of the Victorian houses and the storefronts, a blur as he focused on getting to Fortuna.

***

Cat wasn't at home. Noises. The same sounds, over and over, filled her brain. Her arm itched. And it hurt. *An IV?* Why would she have an IV? Plastic prongs poked into her nose. Oxygen.

And then she remembered the asthma attack, not one, but two. At least she believed she had a second one, which seemed the most likely cause for her being in a hospital. But how? There wasn't one in Ferndale. She also had no recollection of flashing red lights or being wheeled out on a gurney. A memory emerged—she'd been carried to a vehicle.

An EMT or a game warden who wore different hats. A lawman who looked phenomenal in a khaki shirt and Levi's. The details filled her brain with help from the oxygen: the memories returning like staccato beats in music. A handsome man who made Cat stupid had ministered to her after the asthma attacks. A truck that bounced along the road as if hauling bales of hay instead of a person.

Case Gallagher. That was his name. She'd sue him or something. What about the animals? There was supposed to be a bigger-than-ever storm, and she'd been preparing for it. She had. But now she couldn't get back to the cottage.

Dammit. Cat was here against her will, at least as far as she was concerned, and if anything happened to her animals, well, Case Gallagher would feel her wrath.

Geeze, Cat, can you be less dramatic?

She closed her eyes to force recollection, knowing full well that when she had a bad asthma attack remembering the moments leading up to the event often disappeared. It pissed her off—the asthma thing. Cat had researched her disease over the last two years, and knew about eosinophils, all the reasons not to live in a wet climate, not to have animals, not to inhabit a drafty old cottage surrounded by reedy grass, marshland, water, water, and more water. But the dry climate from which she'd run, the near-desert environment of Temecula, a *new wine country*, held nothing for her now. She'd never go back.

And why did she fall for guys with weird names? Not, mind you, that she was so-called falling for that Officer Neanderthal. Not a chance. Her romantic history was more connected to fit men who didn't feel a need to reveal their physique and instead wore expensive suits, had their nails manicured, and God bless them, they knew their wines. Men like Ryder Benton.

And shouldn't it be that way? Her folks had retired to the unknown land that was dryer than a popcorn fart until irrigation. A small boutique winery, self-sufficient, good Cabs, a living. Her father had designed and helped build the rock-and-log home that reminded Cat of her childhood vacations to the mountains. The cellars were five times cooler than the air, with oaks and willows stalking the small creek that ran full in a good winter and did little during a drought. Eventually, the five-star cottages added money for the operating expenses of the fledgling winery.

The Oak & Willow Vineyard was in its eighteenth year when Ryder stole it from her widowed mother. Its eighteenth year when she'd relocated her mom to assisted living in San Diego. Year eighteen, when the wedding planned for months disintegrated into lawsuits, and Cat conceded her parents' vineyard, their home, and life's work to a greedy, manipulative shit-heel. She'd lost too much, so the diagnosis of adult-onset asthma, like some freaking icing on the proverbial cake, had been the last straw.

"Shit, shit, shit." She pounded her fists against the hospital bed. Alarms sounded, bells started ringing. "Quadruple shit."

A nurse came through the door as if she expected to find the bed on fire. Cat stole a quick look at the dry-erase board on the wall. Kelly. Her nurse was Kelly. "Hi," coughing, "Kelly."

"Hi yourself. You know whatever you did set off bells at the nurse's station like a stock market crash. You okay?"

Cat would have responded, but she was coughing up a storm.

"Dr. Miller is down the hall. He was planning on stopping in to see you anyway. How long did you say you'd been using inhalers?" Cat rolled her eyes. "Well, it's in your chart somewhere." The nurse fiddled with the oxygen feeds in Cat's nose so that tears formed in the corners of her eyes. "Oh hon, don't cry. You won't be in here but another day tops. Maybe the doctor will change your medication. Did you say you'd been on steroids at one point? You know adult-onset asthma can be more challenging to manage. Maybe you know that, but the doctor can explain the details. I don't see that anyone brought you fresh clothes. Can I call someone for you?"

With a nurse babbling as if she'd mainlined three shots of espresso, Cat thought bliss might come in the form of an immediate embolism to her brain. Except she had to get out and see to her animals. And, to be fair, Nurse Bubbly was trying to help.

Whoa. None other than her intrepid deputy/EMT etc. stood in the doorway, one hand poised to knock. Cat took a shallow breath as a test of her lungs. No cough. She inhaled more deeply. He was gorgeous, and she felt immediate embarrassment again. It couldn't be coincidental that she blushed anytime he was near.

A hospital gown, IVs in her arm, tubes up her nose. Lord, if she'd only had the forethought to slip into a little black dress before that last asthma attack in the cabin, the man holding a brown bag and smiling goofy behind chatty-nurse-Kelly would have a memory of Cat looking hot.

And wait a minute. Why did she care? It must be the drugs or something because she was pretty sure she remained ticked off at Deputy Do-Good-Gallagher.

"Hi. You here to spring me?"

"Ms. Morgan."

Chilly reception. Well, she was mad at him anyway. If he didn't want to be civil, she could be equally frosty. "Do you need something in particular, because the doctor's on rounds and…"

"No, nothing much. I stopped into the Western shop, picked up a shirt and jeans. Carol Whittaker said she knew your size. She mentioned you'd shopped there when you first got into town."

"Did you put the items on my account?"

"Nope, Carol didn't mention you having one."

Cat didn't, but at least by making the statement, he'd know she wasn't going to renege on his expenditures. She thought about telling him buying her clothes was too personal, but Nurse Kelly took that moment to emerge from the bathroom, drying her hands with a paper towel.

"Hey, Deputy. How you doing?"

"Fine, Kelly. Heard you had a bad bout of Type A. Glad to see you're back to work."

"It was awful. Had a flu shot, we all did here at the hospital, but it didn't do much to curtail the symptoms. I was down for ten days. Fever, chills, that tight feeling in my lungs…you had your shot, right?"

"Yes. But still at risk, I haven't had it—the flu, or least ways no symptoms."

"Well, try to stay that way." Kelly looked at Cat as if she were Typhoid Mary incarnate. "I'll leave you to chat with the patient, but

I'm going to change that IV in a few minutes. Don't get too close. You of all people know that coughs, sneezes, touching, equals exposure."

"Thanks, Kelly. I won't be long."

For whatever reason, Cat felt an unexplainable ache at the prospect of Deputy Gallagher leaving. Worse, she felt a pang of jealousy and wondered how her deputy came to be on a first-name basis with the helpful and cute Nurse Kelly.

"Kelly worked at the River Grill when she was in college."

News flash. Officer Gallagher reads minds. He dropped the bag of clothes unceremoniously in her lap. A sense of being angry replaced any embarrassment by his unannounced visit. "Gee, thanks." Cat looked in the bag. Jeans, check. Shirt, double-check. Whoa, long sleeves? Plaid? Were those snap buttons on the cuffs?

"You bought me a cowboy shirt?" Glancing up, she glimpsed a spark in his eyes. Case Gallagher might be trying to curb a grin, but he was lousy at it. "And you're laughing at me? What an ass."

"Badass, in fact."

The bag caught him off guard and straight on the chin. A small dabble of blood appeared—paper cut.

"Oops."

"Oops?" He stepped around to the uncluttered side of the bed. She had no place to go, and he was quick. IV or not, he had her free hand in a killer grip, twisting her elbow enough to be menacing but not to hurt. "Do you always bite the hand that feeds you?"

"Kind of trite, don't you think?"

"You've already decided what kind of man I am. Brute, a Neanderthal? What other adjectives float around in that free-thinking brain of yours, sweetheart?"

"I'm not your sweetheart." Cat turned her face away, and for the first moment that day she wished that chatty Nurse Kelly would materialize through the door.

"Yeah, you kind of are. I saved your life."

"That some old Indian lore? Take a girl out of her home on a horrible bumpy truck ride with half her clothes missing and plop her down in a hospital? Oh, and then bring her a checkered cowboy shirt?"

"Cowgirl shirt."

She spun back, and the IV needle pulled. Pain shot up her arm. "Damn, this hurts."

Case sat on her bed, released the captive arm, and reached across to her right hand. "Let me see."

"No." Cat tried to retrieve her appendage.

"Stop being a baby."

"I'm not."

"And don't whine."

"Screw you, officer. Because of you, I'm stuck in this hospital bed. My arm hurts, and," Cat dared a peek at the outside window even though it meant risking being pinned by his impossibly green/gray eyes, "it's raining." *I will not cry.* But she did. "Heathcliff, Monkey, Old Bess, and Topsy, not to mention Clyde and the others, they need water, to be fed, access to shelter, or the ability to get outside—"

"Hold on, Cat. I met the kitten, um, and that monster of a primate." He took her free hand and placed it on the ridge between his hairline and forehead. "But what's a Clyde?"

Cat felt it, did he? Her blood raced, heat rushed from the tip of her finger up her arm, and a swooshing filled her ears. There was a scab forming where her hand rested against his head. "A rabbit. And I'm sorry, deputy."

"Case."

"Deputy Gallagher."

"You are a stubborn woman, Catherine."

"Cat."

"You see how you are? You call me Case, I'll call you Cat. I had to get a tetanus shot, and," he reached and pulled her chin up so that she had no choice but to stare into his eyes, "Monkey's in quarantine."

"No." She tried to tug away, but despite the reach, her damned rescuer managed to grip both of her shoulders. Cat already knew the consequences for Monkey. "They'll take him away from me."

"No doubt. It's illegal to have any primate as a pet in most states. California is the strictest in all fifty states."

"I know."

"So you deliberately broke the law?"

Was he sympathetic or ready to slap cuffs on her already miserable self? God, she wanted to trust him. No, she wanted to kiss him, but she loved Monkey. Still, she couldn't keep the creature anyway. She'd known that from the beginning.

And what about the deputy? His eyes seemed to express disbelief in Cat's sincerity. She didn't want him to doubt her, nor could she stand it if he stayed angry. *I just met you, you arrogant, controlling, beautiful man.* He relaxed his grip, dropping his arms. Cat studied his hands, which now gently held each of her wrists. She wasn't sure if he stayed in contact because he wanted to, or because it allowed him to reassert his hold on her if she tried something stupid. Cat dared a glance at his face. She'd been right about his eyes. Intent. His gaze unwavering. The sensation of his fingers loosely holding her wrists? Delicious.

"Ms. Morgan, the law?"

Shit, they were back to Ms. Morgan. That sucked. "I took Monkey from a house in Gardena. Do you even know *where* that is? The dad worked on fishing boats. He had a jillion kids and traveled as far as Central America with a private enterprise. No fish, no money. Don't ask me why I spent any time in the area. Okay, ask. I was driving a school bus." Cat tried to gauge his reaction to her gibbering. She inhaled, avoiding his gaze, and continued. "The yard was off the PCH in Lomita. And, *if* you know where Lomita is, I owe you a steak dinner."

For whatever reason, Case had begun a slow circular rub of one wrist with his thumb.

"I knew the family couldn't care for him. Monkey, that is. Carlos had brought him home thinking it would entertain his children, and perhaps he could sell the imp on the black market. It didn't take long for Monkey to exhibit his natural craziness, so I took him, promising to find a sanctuary."

"And?" Case held Cat in some kind of tractor beam. She could not keep staring into his eyes. She dropped her focus to his thumb, mesmerized by the continued circular motion; the contact of his skin against hers.

"And I got the gatekeeper's cabin, free of charge, no questions asked, at the same time my publisher accepted a new book idea. Monkey ended up in a small carpetbag, with dried bananas, and tossed in the back of my car for the six-hundred-plus-mile drive to Ferndale. I couldn't place him with a sanctuary before I left, then deadlines, isolation, horrible cell service. You know about the cell service out there on the marsh, right? Enter macho deputy/EMT guy, an asthma attack and," Cat raised her head, stared Case straight on, adding, "tada!"

Chapter Four

It was all Case could do not to burst out laughing. He wanted to turn her in. God knew he wanted to, but it would only be for the moment of her reaction and then another chance to rescue Ms. Catherine Morgan.

Instead, he sneezed.

"You're sick."

"No, I'm not."

There was no time for dispute as ever-diligent Nurse Kelly, burst into the room. "Hi, all. Did Dr. Miller get here?"

They answered no simultaneously, and Case got off the bed. He didn't want to. He'd been ready to slip in under the covers and surround Cat Morgan with all parts of him that would fit on the narrow hospital bed.

Kelly prattled on as if she hadn't busted in on an intimate moment. Case recognized the past few minutes with his law-breaking charge had been precisely that, but bit his tongue on further comment. He suspected the nurse's enthusiasm was about to violate patient privilege.

"Well, it's up to Ms. Morgan, but I can give you the test results for several things. Dr. Miller got called away, so I guess he couldn't finish rounds. The rain is causing havoc just south of the one-oh-one junction. There was a big wreck, and he's down in the ER."

Case glanced down at Cat in the bed. She looked small, weak, and vulnerable. Still, she responded, "Tell me. I want to get out of here."

"To be sure, it's okay if I release this information to you with Deputy Gallagher in the room?"

"Sh— I'm sorry. Yes."

"Okay, you do not *currently* have Type A or B Flu." The nurse looked down at the chart in her hand, studying maybe. Case gave the nurse the benefit of the doubt. One thing was clear. His fugitive appeared somewhat relieved, but not the least bit satisfied.

"So, what does that mean?"

He was glad to see that Cat wasn't a "yes, ma'am" patient. She had more questions. Case pulled up the visitor's chair and sat down.

The nurse thumbed through the chart and moved closer to the bed. "Well, that's the good part. You had A, maybe within the last twelve to fourteen days, but you have no symptoms now. So, it may have been a mild case, and now you likely have antibodies to at least that strain of flu. No guarantee, but Dr. Miller seems confident that the prior exposure will help stave off reinfection, or lessen the chance of getting another flu. But there's also not such great news."

Not such great news? Case bit his tongue to avoid offering the nurse some advice on grammar.

The whir of the bed rising filled the air as Cat pushed a button on the handheld device to raise herself to a seating position, "What's that? I mean, 'not such great news' sounds ominous."

"Gosh, I wish Dr. Miller were available. It's your eosinophils. The numbers mean your asthma could respond better to a different medication, but if not, you are going to have to exercise caution. Asthma kills, you know, and I'm not saying that to scare you, and I'm overstepping my bounds, but we're so shorthanded and are out of the medication, but it's been ordered. We have a visiting resident, but I'm not sure she can sign you out without the supervising physician to back it up."

"Okay, I can wait a bit longer, but I'd really like to get out of here. Can you track down the resident? I've got pets at home."

Case caught the look of concern on Kelly's face and thought they might be in for another lecture, this one on the probable hazards of animal allergens for someone with asthma.

Case sneezed into his sleeve. He hadn't planned on it, but there it was. Instead of leaving, Kelly spun on squeaky rubber shoes. "Deputy, are you okay? You know Ms. Morgan was likely contagious, the last *few* days." Case ignored the insinuation that he and Cat had rendezvoused for a few days. He kind of liked the idea, though.

Kelly moved her hand to check his forehead. "You feel hot."

He was. But not from fever. Nope. The heat Case felt was for the pitiful-looking Cat Morgan, who should be in jail for the damned captive monkey thing, but also should remain in bed. Case's bed. *Damn, that thought came out of left field.* But Case didn't scuttle it. He'd felt genuine amusement at waging dialogue with Ms. Catherine Morgan. And he couldn't ignore the physical attraction. Brushing the RN's attention away, he nudged Kelly back to the chart and Cat's status.

"Uh, well, as I noted, asthma can kill. You'll need to follow up with Dr. Miller or your personal physician within a week. And with all hell breaking loose tonight, I'm not sure if I can get anyone up here to release you until tomorrow."

"Like hell." Cat sat up straighter, and Case noted the pained expression. Her fingers rubbed at the IV.

Case sat back down in the bouncy visitor chair and was studying his boots when she coughed, drawing his attention once again.

She raised an eyebrow at him, and then leveled her gaze on the nurse. "You can't keep me here."

"Well, if you leave, you'll have to sign out as against doctor's orders."

"Kelly, you've been a great nurse, and I appreciate all you're doing. It's a difficult job, and a bossy patient doesn't make it any easier, but it's not my idea to leave."

"Huh?"

Case let his half-shuttered eyes come to attention.

"You see, Deputy Gallagher here," she waved an arm and hand in his direction," is about to arrest me."

Chapter Five

They were in the truck. Cat refused to bounce around in the backseat this time and sat huddled against the passenger door bundled in a blanket. Beneath that, Case had draped her in his jacket. It smelled of male and gun oil. Add in her new jeans and the cowboy shirt, and she was ready to take up line dancing. She'd never worn any so-called *cowgirl* shirts before.

"Thanks for the underwear."

Case didn't drive off the road, a good thing, and Cat knew she shouldn't have mentioned it, but it was commendable that he picked out a pair of undies when he bought the shirt and jeans.

Rain pelleted the windshield, and he needed to concentrate. Cat knew it. Still, something about him compelled her to push further. "Most guys wouldn't have thought about it. Clean underwear, I mean."

"Ms. Morgan, we're driving through a massive storm, there are places where this road has likely washed away, and we wouldn't know it until we were floating towards the Eel River. The fact that you are wearing clean underthings is not a big deal right now." He had shouted his response out of necessity; the noise of the storm, the old truck, the road, made normal conversation impossible.

Cat yelled a retort. "Well, you never know. Might be important later."

Adjusting her seatbelt, she turned to study him as best as possible, given the minimal light. All she could go on were shadows cast by the headlights reflecting against the torrent falling from above. Strong jaw, fierce concentration, shoulders rigid against the seat...battling with the wheel had to be tiring. Four-wheel drive or not, slick mud rolled over the road, and sheets of water swept away with each slap of the wipers that returned in an instant. Cat figured he'd need a massage before the night was through.

For whatever reason, the image of her kneading his naked shoulders filled her head. She flexed the fingers on both hands—opening, closing—into her palms.

Cat was lousy at feminine wiles, and she needed to get to the cottage and check on the animals. So, giving him the idea arresting her was appropriate seemed brilliant at the time, if not unwelcome in the execution.

That she seemed drawn to him remained a puzzle, but she couldn't deny it. Add in the unbearable prospect of staying in the hospital another night, and the ruse of being his prisoner stuck.

Lightning flashed, further illuminating the inside of the truck. It startled Cat out of her rumination. The flash revealed beads of sweat on Case's brow, and she didn't think the mere mention of delicate woman's garments was the cause.

He's sick. I got him sick. My pets attacked him, he saved my life, and now I've manipulated him into taking me home under house arrest, in a stupid big storm, no less. And he's sick.

Cat would have insisted they turn around and check him into ER, but the hard right into her driveway brought them to a skidding halt at the cottage. The next strike lighted the corral. Topsy stood drenched in the ramshackle paddock, Old Bess looked weary and scared in the opposite corner.

It didn't matter that the storm was at a peak. Cat leapt from the truck and ran toward the two animals stuck outside.

***

Case couldn't be angrier, but Cat was already hiking her sweet ass over the fencing and plopping herself into the mud of the corral. She didn't even give him a chance to undo his seatbelt and turn off the ignition before unclipping hers and lunging into the storm.

And he didn't feel right. All his training confirmed a self-diagnosis. The vixen writer/ animal activist/monkey-harboring fugitive was out of her mind, *and* she'd given him the flu. Okay, it could have come from exposure on another call. That's what he and others like him risked as first responders. Except he'd been relegated to game warden work for a full week before he stopped in at the gatekeeper's cabin.

Seven days and nights of camping under the stars, or crashing in the back of his truck because of fog and rain. He'd tagged deer and foxes. Counted coyotes, and confirmed several brown bears were still inhabiting the general geographical area—all of this he'd done without human contact.

None until, minding his own business—well, doing his job— he'd arrived at Cat Morgan's front door.

The storm couldn't care less about Case's condition, so he shoved the door open and jumped from the truck. Damn, it was coming down, enough that it was challenging to see, but there she was, tugging the milk-less old cow under a narrow lean-to that ran along one end of the corral. Case couldn't believe the rickety thing was holding up, but it would at least give the poor bovine some shelter.

If he felt better, if they weren't functioning under the onslaught of a near typhoon, if the girl in tight button-downs and his jacket hadn't been in the hospital for a severe asthma attack, and if none of those things were in play, Case still would've been at her side.

He moved toward the fenced pen where Cat had at last secured the cow. The stubborn woman sloshed through mud and muck toward the horse. What had she called the swaybacked animal? Topsy. In Case's head, Topsy should have been the rabbit she mentioned. She also said the old thoroughbred had been a racehorse. Looking at the worn-out gelding now, you sure wouldn't know it. The lightning had moved on, and the rumble of thunder sounded in the distance. Case refocused his attention on Cat. Hair plastered against her head, soaked, mud splattered everywhere, she could star in an animal rescue commercial.

Damn if he wasn't falling for her.

"Catherine," he yelled into the wind. "Give it up. The horse will be fine." She motioned with one arm as if asking him to complete some chore. "What?"

Before he could figure out what she needed, the wide gate swung open and slammed against the corral fencing. With the horse lead held tight in her other hand, she trudged by. "Close and secure the gate, okay?"

Case knew then that his next purchase for Catherine Morgan would be a Stetson. Nothing like a good hat brim to keep the rain off one's face. He watched for a moment as she marched Topsy toward the cabin, and for one second, it seemed perfectly rational that they would bring the old horse inside. She coaxed the animal up the porch steps and gently nudged its haunches around so the horse could head forward going back down.

When Case latched the gate, he double-checked the strength of the carabiner. Figuring Cat would kill him if anything happened to the aging cow, he spied a rope on a hook next to the lean-to. An unexpected smile as he recognized the knot at one end. The girl now securing a knock-kneed, but proud racehorse between pillar and post of the cabin's overhang had been practicing with a lasso. That meant his tree-hugging animal rescuer was a wanna-be cowgirl.

Turning, Case did a quick recheck on the gate for resistance. Satisfied, he headed toward the house. He couldn't wait to tease Cat about it. Maybe even while he tugged on that shirt she hated, pulling her close enough to unsnap a button.

Or two.

***

Cat couldn't keep her eyes off Case. In the truck, it had been all she could do not to thank him for everything by resting one hand on his thigh. Or faking exhaustion and accidentally, sort of, falling over and snoozing on his shoulder. That way, she could inhale the scents that clung to him. Some remnant of a subtle aftershave. Sunscreen. Sweat tenured by soap and time. Nothing that would turn a girl off, and everything that turned her on.

A flash of lightning with the simultaneous crack of thunder meant the storm's fury had returned. Case made the third step and stood, drenched, but out of the rain on her porch.

It was dark, yet she could feel his intensity.

"We went to a lot of trouble to tie up two animals that might have to fare on their own."

"No." Cat bit her lip.

For the second time that day, Case tipped her chin up with his thumb. His touch seemed to have a hotline to her heart. "Cat, these flatlands flood. It's why I came out here to issue voluntary evacuation orders yesterday."

"I have a trailer, do you have a hitch?"

"Well, yes, but in this storm, unless it lets up, I'm not sure we can do anything but get the small animals and go."

She needed him to be safe, but she couldn't bear the idea of leaving Old Bess and Topsy. Cat could plead her case, but then he sneezed so hard his hat flew off. She fumbled for the key under the mat while he retrieved his worn Stetson.

They'd be safe inside. For a while anyway, leaving Cat to wonder what kind of mess she'd made of everything.

Chapter Six

After getting the lights on, Cat had escorted Case to the bath. He'd protested, but his sneezing fit had turned into coughing. "You know, I don't *have* the flu, remember? I'm over it. The steam will loosen that cough. While you're in there, I'll find some aspirin and cough medicine."

"Cat, I'm fine."

You sure are. Mighty fine. She banished the prurient thoughts that filled her brain and pushed back. "You're not fine, but either way, you can shower, and I'll gather up all my pets that can transport if we have to leave."

"I'll shower to get warm. You said you had a dryer? Good, because I know we have to leave, even if you refuse to face facts. You're right, though. Exposure won't cause the flu, but it can make it worse."

Cat watched the wheels turn in his head, realizing she was falling for a rational man. Well, that would be a first.

"My whole point in coming out here was to get you out of harm's way."

"Well, things change."

"Not that much." Case's chin could have rested on the top of her head, and for a brief moment, she thought he'd kiss her. Instead, he tucked her hair back behind one ear. "I'm going to check in with dispatch."

"You have to go back outside for that, right?"

"Unless your cable's working."

"Take a hot shower. I'll check the cable and pack some things, including pets and cages." In the time she'd looked away, he'd removed his shirt and jeans. He grinned and handed her the clothes. Cat pushed his chest with the palm of one hand, holding his soaked jeans, socks, and khaki shirt with the other. Admittedly, it was all she could do not to suggest they save water and shower together, but she turned and slammed the door on the image of his boxer-short-clad body.

After she'd tossed his wet clothes into the dryer, Cat started to gather animals. Once the rabbit was fed and secured in its travel hutch, she found Heathcliff on the bed. The little kitten stretched and purred as she lifted him for a greeting. She put Cliffy in his carrier with a small bowl of Kitty Whiskers Salmon.

The ducks lived outside, eating bugs, snails, and worms. Besides, they'd be okay under the porch or at home in the marsh. Well, except for Winston. A young mallard who'd taken to following Cat around the garden and catching snails mid-air when tossed. As a consequence, sometimes he tried to get inside the little house. A quick search assured her the sort-of-domesticated duck would not swoop from the rafters or wiggle out from under the sofa and snap at Case.

The steps to avert a crisis seemed easy enough until she thought about getting an arthritic old cow and a cranky thoroughbred into the same trailer in the rain. Cat would deal with that scenario in the event they had to leave because of the storm. Except she had developed an understanding of the man in her shower, and if duty was in the picture, they would go. And on his terms.

She stopped in her tracks at the sound. Case—singing in the shower. Cat smiled, at least until she heard him coughing. Wiping palms along her thighs, she was reminded that the pants she wore remained caked with dried mud. She dashed into the bedroom and donned clean jeans. Catching a glimpse in the dresser mirror, she was surprised at how shapely the snap-down Western shirt made her look. It hugged her form, and since the cotton fabric had dried, she opted to keep it on. Grabbing two pairs of clean underwear—she fingered a black nightie in her drawer, ignored it, grabbed another shirt, and slammed the drawer closed. The wardrobe items were shoved into her backpack on a hook behind the door. Cat realized she might be gone a few days and added a T-shirt and sweater. *Dammit. Jeans*. The clean pair she'd donned would be a mess after she went back outside, so she crammed a pair of so-called skinny pants into the pack. It would have to do.

"Cat?"

"Yes?" She stepped out and closed the bedroom door.

"The shower helped." He sneezed.

"Not enough. I have aspirin and cough syrup on the coffee table."

"Wine?"

"Really?"

"Yeah. To take with us. Never keep it at my place."

Okay, he was suggesting they drink? If he didn't keep alcohol, then maybe Case wasn't a crazy womanizer. There was no doubt he had the body for it. Perhaps he was gay. No, there was something intense going on between them, and the realization excited and scared her. She loved wine and thought, they had some things in common after all. She ducked into the laundry room and grabbed his things, tossing him the items. "Not dry, but close enough."

At least the action stopped the self-babbling in her brain. She turned to face him straight on. Reading the look on his face was easy enough. "So, we're definitely leaving?"

"Got to, Cat." She nearly drooled as he punched one foot into a jean leg. "It's my job. And I've been here when the river floods. Not a good thing. I promise."

"Strange promise, but okay."

"So maybe that's the wrong way to put it. Will you trust me?" Case took three steps in, close enough that if either of them breathed deeply, the physical connection would be complete. He had the jeans on but not the shirt. The contact, like stones skipping across water. "Has anyone ever told you that despite being a tad quirky, you're adorable?"

"Only a tad?"

"Okay, maybe a lot quirky."

"Anyone ever accuse you of being inflexible and authoritarian, Case?"

"That's nice."

"What is? A woman describing you as controlling?"

"No. You saying my name, even if a bit derisively."

Cat surrendered and rested her head against his chest. The moment might have lasted forever, except the air outside split with a clap of thunder, and the old cottage rattled under its force.

"Shit."

"You know, you say you're a writer, but if you have any articulate moments, I've yet to experience them."

"Damn. My computer." She extricated herself from his hold and dashed to the desk by the fireplace. "You say we have to go? Okay, my backpack, the pet carriers next to the washer/dryer...and get dressed. Uh, more dressed. Grab those and gather everything at the front door."

***

Case might have laughed at her bossiness, but for the reality of their circumstances. Then he got a little dizzy, and sitting on the sofa, he took advantage of the aspirin Cat left. He vowed to close his eyes for just two minutes, but he'd dozed. What? Twenty minutes. Cat wasn't in the cabin.

First, he grabbed the items she'd mentioned. The kitten seemed content licking one paw next to the half-empty can of cat food. The rabbit, docile enough, seemed content with some kind of pellet mix. Both cages easy to carry. What he saw when he opened the front door to the cottage, however, initiated minor panic.

Cat, getting drenched again, was at least wearing some kind of poncho. He didn't know how, but she'd set the trailer on the hitch of his truck. He saw the old cow's head inside the rickety-looking trailer. Cat waved. She stood partway up the ramp, urging Topsy forward.

Unbelievable. He was going to transport two long-lived animals in a trailer that appeared unstable, if not unsafe. He also considered that the road might be gone, washed out, that they had to tackle the Oak Creek Bridge, and if making town proved impossible, then make higher ground.

Saving Cat seemed a package deal. The animals were included, even if they didn't survive the trip. Case hoped the aspirin, which had diminished the feverish feeling, would keep more symptoms at bay. So, to quote the woman he was pretty sure he'd fallen for, he looked out at pouring rain and muttered one of her catchphrases, "Double shit."

Tugging his hat tight against his scalp, Case headed toward her while she coaxed a retired racehorse with a ridiculous name up a ramp, wishing he'd grabbed and kissed her silly in the shower while he had the chance.

Chapter Seven

Cat watched Case as he concentrated on the road, the rain, the mud. Despite four-wheel drive, the slipping and tugging from the stupid trailer took her breath away. The ordeal of getting Topsy into the damn transport had been bad enough, but seeing Case get soaked again, sneezing, made her feel guilty. Still, when he double-checked the hook-up she got annoyed. Of course, she could be pissed off about his lack of trust in her trailer-hitching skills, but she figured to let that go.

"I'm sorry. I should have left Topsy and Bess at the cottage."

"No. I get it. They are no longer able to care for themselves. A younger horse, we'd open the corral, and the animal would be okay. Not your Topsy. Old coot probably would have stood in raging water up to his shoulders while trying to eat the grass beneath."

"You know, you've got a soft heart under that rough exterior."

"No, I don't. I'm mean, bitter, and a Neanderthal, right?" Case slowed, letting the truck and trailer come to a stop under some thick pines. The cover quieted the pounding rain, giving Cat hope they'd make his house.

And then what?

There was a point when they could have headed over the bridge up SR 211 and maybe

made it into town. But the road half-mile from the bridge was a swirling mass of stream on steroids, and Case had turned right, heading up into the foothills. "Are we close?"

"To what?"

"Your place?"

Case shifted gears into park but didn't turn off the engine. Cliffy made some kitten noises from the backseat. Her rabbit, of course, said nothing. "Yes. I hope you're okay that we opted out of crossing over to highway two-eleven. You know I didn't take this route as some sneaky way to get you alone, seduce you, or that sort of thing."

"Spoken a bit too matter-of-factly."

"Damn it, Cat. I'm not a bad guy."

"I know that." She turned, the seat belt restricting her movement, and tried to read his features in the dark.

"Well, you don't act like it."

She felt the shift of his weight in the seat and assumed he too was trying to read her features. "I guess I'm a little intimidated. Plus, you stole my monkey."

"I didn't."

"Well, no, you didn't. When I think about it, we wouldn't be on this romantic first date if you hadn't."

A deep chuckle filled the cab of his truck. "If this is your idea of romance, maybe I should take you hunting."

"That would be cool." She paused, wanting, no needing, to touch Case. Maybe a brush against his shoulder. "Can we use Nerf guns?"

He was quick. Somehow, he released the shoulder harness and slid across the bench seat in the dark. He held Cat's arms below the shoulders in a strong, but painless grip. "You are the single most infuriating, aggravating, sexy..." Case didn't finish the sentence. Instead, his mouth came down on hers, hungry, devouring, and she melted into the caress.

***

Dangerous, and impractical, but Cat didn't resist. She yielded to his assault, and it could be considered nothing less, which made disengaging from the kiss impossible. The unlikeliness of a relationship ran through his head as if he watched a movie. While it reeled frame by frame, his fingers were wrapping strands of her hair around and around, his lips moved down her neck, nibbling, wanting, nipping, back up to her mouth.

Case felt her arousal through the cotton shirt. The poncho she'd worn lay tossed on the backseat. With the heater blasting in the cab, neither needed extra layers. A loud crack outside shook Case back to reality. They were under a grove of old redwoods: sturdy, yes, but undermined roots due to possible soil erosion signaled a recipe for toppling. If that didn't happen, the weight of rain and near hurricane-force winds could split branches at the trunk, sending huge and heavy limbs down on the truck.

Cat gasped when he pulled away. Still, he forced urgency into his tone. "We can't stay here." He slid back to his seat, re-clipped the seat belt, and put the truck in gear. Too late. A flash of lightning revealed their circumstances: a huge trunk forty feet or so up the hill completely blocked the road.

"Wow, when did that happen?"

"Maybe earlier, or, about the time we were making out. That was quite a kiss, I reckon."

"Really? You still doing the reckon thing after that kiss?"

"Ms. Morgan—"

She cut him off. "So, it's serious."

"What gave it away?"

"Two things."

He didn't speak. Instead, he counted to ten under his breath. The woman he'd fallen for also made him crazy. "Only two?"

"One, the *Ms. Morgan* bit. Two? There's a giant tree in our path, a wobbly trailer hitched to your truck with dependent animals in the back, and the river of mud running down the hill isn't drying up."

"That's either four or five things depending on whether we count your trailer as an ark, ergo a single unit."

"I'm sorry. It's my fault we're stuck."

"No. A tree fell. But we can't stay here. My cabin is about half a kilometer more."

"I don't know kilometers from widgets."

"Sweetheart, it's over a quarter mile."

"That's practically nothing."

"Uh, right. Consider we have to go uphill in a torrential downpour, get around a fallen tree that on my estimate extends out over both sides of the road, and deal with your menagerie." Case didn't expect her to sacrifice the pets, but he did need to capture her attention.

"Shit."

"Well spoken, as always." Cat punched him in the shoulder, which he ignored. "I have a plan."

"Is there a treasure map?"

"This is serious, Cat."

"You say that a lot. Sorry, give it up. The plan that is."

***

Fifteen minutes later, Cat stood under a broad canopy of pine trees to the right of the truck. She'd retrieved her poncho and shoved two bottles of Chardonnay in the outside pockets of her backpack. If they were going to die, it might be better to go tipsy. But, with the plastic-wrapped laptop and charger, the pack was cumbersome. She bit her tongue because Case would probably make her leave something behind if he knew. Like the wine. The pet carriers remained in the back of the vehicle, while the trailer, now unhitched, sat secured between multiple trees by a series of ropes and cables, and Case had used blocks to wedge the truck's rear tires.

When he completed the work of securing the trailer, Cat's animals, and his truck, he headed to her at the side of the road.

Cat could worry all she wanted about Bess and Topsy, but the fact was, neither truck nor trailer could go anywhere until the storm cleared out. At least, with luck, the big animals could survive. The kitten and rabbit had been recently fed and still had water. So, unless the truck somehow washed away, they'd be safe. As a final measure, the vehicle's windows were cracked for fresh air, but not enough to let in predators.

She watched as he came slipping and sliding in her direction.

"Do you have your cell phone? It won't matter here, and I have mine, but up at the house, different carriers might come in handy if my landline or the cable are out."

"It's in my backpack."

"Okay, then let's go."

"I'd say lead the way, but that would state the obvious." A flash of his smile showed simultaneous with a small break in the clouds. "Wow, I forgot about the full moon." Somewhere off to their right, an owl hooted as if nothing unusual had happened. Maybe they wouldn't die after all.

Case's hand found Cat's, and he tugged her to the center of the road. "Gravel between the tracks from tires. Try to walk on it. Water runs off it quicker than in the ruts, so it's less likely there's mud and slippage. But stay cautious, you can slip on the gravel too."

The downpour had eased to a drizzle, at least for the time being. Cat looked up to see the moon drift out from behind clouds again. The beauty of it seemed surreal under the circumstances. "Seems a bit like, damned if you don't, damned if you do." He released her hand, and Cat immediately missed his touch. "Hey. Can I call you Tarzan?"

"Sure, Jane. Watch where you're going and try not to fall on your ass." Then he was off, up the hill. Cat worked at calculating the math. Less than a half, but more than a quarter mile uphill in the rain. Yeah, sure. She'd make it.

Chapter Eight

Case's hand grabbed Cat's, and though it felt like her arm might rip out of the socket, the downward slide stopped. They'd been climbing around one end of the big tree that blocked the truck's path, and where, as he had said it would, the road dropped off on both sides.

She had been prescient when she'd called him Tarzan. Case had used a sturdy but grab-worthy branch to swing around the base of the tree. Following his lead, she tried the same method for making it around the ragged end of the pine, but the difference in their height meant her feet didn't clear the berm. The weight of her pack cinched it, and those few seconds of maybe dying had rocked her to the core.

With one foot wedged against a big limb of the fallen tree, he had lunged, grabbing hold of her loose hand until she managed to lodge her feet against the same branch.

Rain fell, though not with the intensity of earlier. The renewed torrent had begun within moments of their heading for the downed tree. Now, as an inevitable consequence of being retrieved by her handsome game warden, Cat lay prone across his hips and chest. She felt it when his lungs filled and expelled air. Beneath his jacket and despite her poncho, Cat could also feel the pounding of his heart. She didn't want to move, and waited for a few beats, listening as the rate eased.

"How did you put it earlier? Looks like you saved my bacon yet again, Deputy Gallagher." Joking about it was the best way for her to get past the terror.

"All in a day's work, ma'am."

Though the position was awkward, she managed to prop one elbow against the trunk of the big tree and raise her head from his chest. He stared at her, although she couldn't read his expression. He reclaimed the flashlight from the mud, but the beam pointed down, leaving his face in shadow.

"I don't mind. Saving your cute ass, that is. But, sexy and inviting as this position is, we should keep going."

Her reaction to Case had to wait. "I suppose."

"That's an order, Morgan."

"Okay, okay. How?"

He said nothing, and instead wiggled into a sitting position and leaned against the tree, Cat sort of in his lap. "Can you get your legs under you and use the tree for support?"

"I think so." But she hadn't anticipated the slickness of the mud, and her knee slammed into his groin. The oath and following moan sounded agonizing. Supported by the tree, she tried to comfort him. "God, Case. I'm sorry, are you okay?"

He hauled himself up from a near fetal position, grabbed a limb, and stood beside her, his breathing ragged. "Let's go," he ground out.

She got it. He was in pain. Or maybe he was using the pain to hide the possibility they wouldn't make it. Search and recover teams would find their bodies miles down the Eel banks, perhaps even on the rocks at the river mouth. She'd be a statistic. Any obituary would be limited to the two-line legal notice in the town paper. There was nobody to mourn her passing. Everyone was gone.

Unsure of how far they'd trudged since the near-death experience at the tree, Cat stopped, ready to cave. "I'm sorry." She knew he couldn't hear the words as rain continued to pelt down, the gods no doubt getting even with her for her reckless teen years.

A cropping of boulders jutted into the road. One downward-sloped stone screamed for her to sit, and she did. The rock was wet, but the rough granite held her butt in place. "So long, Case." She watched him move onward up the road, knowing she couldn't stay put, but she was too tired to take another step.

Lightning flashed to the north—she thought that's where the storm was coming from—but with all that happened, she could get turned around. And if she couldn't see her deputy, she might end up lost. And injured. And maybe eaten by bears.

Exhausted, suddenly every bush hid an ominous creature ready to gobble her up.

She patted her pocket. At least the inhaler was still there.

***

Case was good at being in the woods, good at keeping his bearings. Being a Marine had helped, and he'd spent his childhood in the Sierra Nevada. His position as a game warden had reinforced those skills. Weird how a happy youth, kind and attentive parents didn't necessarily equate to contentment in adulthood. For all the things he might be adept at, he was a failure when it came to women.

Except Cat was mostly girl in a lot of ways. Naïve, uncertain of herself. And that was odd because she was beautiful, smart, and funny. He sneezed and cursed the fact that he might be dealing with the flu on top of almost losing the woman he now accepted he could love. His groin had recovered from the accidental kneeing incident, and so he decided to let her off the hook.

Case turned to take her hand.

"Cat?"

They were barely two ticks from his cabin now, the marker for his driveway reflected in the flashlight beam. What was that adage? So close but yet so far. Panic wouldn't help, but the fear that something had happened to her welled up anyway. He shouldn't have been short with her. He should have turned around to check on her progress.

Running was dangerous given the mud and loose gravel, so he started slow, deliberate steps down the hill, focusing the flashlight beam at the curve in the road. Cat came around the bend, wet and bedraggled, but despite the darkness and the rain, her determination was apparent.

The storm lessened, and clouds shifted enough for the moon to offer temporary illumination. He covered the ten or so steps and pulled her into his arms.

"Hi, Case."

"Hello back, Catherine." He buried his lips in the mat of wet hair, recalling how it looked in the sunlight. Impossible that less than forty-eight hours had passed, an in that short time he'd managed to fall in love.

In that same timespan, he'd almost lost her, not once, but twice.

She mumbled into his neck, "Sorry, I hurt you."

"You didn't."

"Did so."

It was becoming habit, tilting Cat's chin up to get her attention. "Did not." His mouth pressed against hers, and he parted her lips with his tongue, needing to feel the heat between them. She grabbed his jacket, bunching fabric in clenched fists, clinging as she returned the kiss. He moaned with pleasure when she nibbled on his lower lip, opened and closed her hands against his chest.

"Sweet Jesu..." He scooped her up in his arms, determined to carry her the rest of the way home. She softened in his hold, wrapping one arm around his neck, and laid her head against his shoulder.

Chapter Nine

The time it took to get to Case's cabin might have been all of five minutes, yet Cat had almost drifted off in his arms. His steps had been rhythmic enough, and she was exhausted. There'd been outside stairs, some kind of deck, a key hidden at the top of a doorsill, and she remembered thinking to lecture him on security.

Then she'd stood numb and unmoving when he propped her up against a counter. Dazed, she'd surveyed the house. The A-frame was all windows facing southwest. There were narrow steps to a loft that ran halfway into the room from above. The kitchen, including the counter she'd leaned against, occupied the space beneath the overhang. Overstuffed furniture seemed the focal point of a massive stone fireplace.

Case hunched building a fire. The room filled with a soft glow from the flames. He removed his jacket, and if she hadn't been frozen, worried, nervous, emotions tumbling through her head and heart like pebbles tossed along a stream, she'd simply admire the physique stretching against his shirt.

As he approached, the look on his face telegraphed his intentions. And damn, the kissing thing *had* been hot, too hot. But, at the time, she kind of thought they might die. Reality tended to set in when she had a roof over her head, and interior warmth had begun to melt the chill. Still, she didn't back away. She couldn't really, he'd set her down gently, and the counter that had held her up now acted as a barrier to escape. The only effort she'd taken in ten minutes was to push out of her soaked shoes.

"Cat."

"Deputy." The quip sounded unlike her own voice, and far away.

"Knock it off." His hands came up and unzipped her jacket. She thought he meant to toss it away and ravage her, but instead, he laid it over a barstool to dry. Fingers pushed wet strands of hair off her forehead, and he planted a kiss there, then on her shuttered eyelids.

Brushing his lips across a cheek, he hovered over her mouth. He traced an earlobe, slipped his hand along her neck, to rest at the apex of her breasts. He tapped the top pearl snap of her shirt. "Your clothes are wet, Ms. Morgan."

The heat of his breath against her chest melted away any resistance. "Is that bad, Officer Gallagher?"

"Well, it's not good." With a flip of his thumb, the top snap of her shirt popped open.

"So, you have experience with wet cowgirl shirts, do you?" When she spoke, the vibration of his closeness made her tremble. An involuntary chill zipped along her nerves.

"None really. But I'm a quick learner." Another snap popped, and she quivered at his touch. "See? You *are* cold."

"I'm anything but, deputy." Case leaned his forehead against hers, and she felt the grin that she had learned caused dimples on either side of the mouth she wanted to devour her.

"I believe you purred. You know, technically, you're still under arrest. Be best you didn't try to bribe your way out of it."

"Cuff me then." She hadn't meant to play into a pseudo-fantasy, but all the parts of her body capable of reacting hummed at high velocity.

Like the lightning, he had her shirt unsnapped and off her shoulders in a flash. Her hands were stuck in the sleeves so she couldn't react. In truth, all she would've done was tug his head down to hers and kiss him. Against the silence, the sound of the cuffs of her shirt unsnapping at his touch seemed like thunder.

"I have to take you, Cat."

"You can't take something that's already yours, buster."

Case searched her face only for a moment. She knew willingness showed in her expression. It had to. If he didn't make a move soon, she'd be a puddle on the floor. Her musings proved unnecessary because he was carrying her to the sofa. He set her down gently, appearing once again to need her approval.

"Officer Gallagher. I'm going to explode if you don't..." She didn't have to finish the sentence. He bent and unbuttoned her jeans, and she helped push down the wet fabric past her ankles. No care taken this time. He threw the pants toward the front door.

"You were right, Morgan."

"How so?"

His grin paled behind the mischief she saw in his eyes. "The underwear I bought you— turns out it is important later. Like now. It's cute."

Cat glanced down and laughed. The panties were sexy, at least in cut and design, but the pattern of small pink ducks wasn't exactly conducive to foreplay. "What? You don't like ducks?"

"On the contrary, Ms. Morgan, I love ducks." Case sat himself beside her hips and ran a finger from duck to duck. His touch against the lacy fabric was unbearable.

"OMG."

"Really? We're going to do this in acronyms?"

Cat was beginning to adore more than his physique. She couldn't help but fall for his brain and the way he made her laugh. "I don't like to swear."

"Well, you're gonna."

"Make me?"

"My pleasure, ma'am."

Put her on an iceberg and her body would become the sole cause of global warming. His tongue traced her lace underwear, and then the panties were somewhere with the bra and his clothes. He brought her to orgasm with his mouth, and he'd been right, she swore. A lot.

But she stopped him at his second effort. "You next, deputy."

"Aw, come on, Cat. I'm having such a good time." He was lying on top of her, a layer of sweat and heat cushioning her from the outside cold. He was hard, and she knew it had to be near torture for him, which was why she pushed him back. Sitting up, she reached back and tied her long hair into a knot at the base of her neck.

"It's your turn to swear."

His laughter filled the cavernous space but ended abruptly when her mouth slipped over his erection. "Holy…" Any swearing he might have expressed fell away to a low moan.

Cat felt possessed, needed, loved. She looked into his eyes for only a moment, tracing the scar on his belly. She'd ask about that later. Her hands moved slowly up and down his shaft, her tongue working in tandem to heighten his pleasure. Though she wanted to do this for him, he stopped her.

"Not this way, Catherine. Not this way. I have to be inside you. I have to…"

She shushed him by covering his mouth with hers and straddling his hips. Pulling back long enough to take in the smoldering look on his face, she slid down, guiding him inside her.

"By all that is holy, Catherine Morgan..." She kissed him into silence.

Cat rode him to the exquisite moment of his release. He tugged on her ponytail, rubbing her most sensitive area with one thumb for the few seconds it took her to cry out at coming again.

They collapsed onto the sofa, joined, holding each other so tight neither could breathe until crooked against his chest, his arms around her, she slept.

***

Cat awoke as the logs in the fire were snapping a message of exhaustion. She wished she'd been a Girl Scout because then she'd make a snappy new fire and impress her man. Was he her man? She questioned whether hot sex created a bond strong enough to maintain a relationship, if the sex was that hot because they might have died in the storm.

Okay, maybe that was too dramatic.

She had to be rank in body aromas, not to mention her hair. She remembered enough of Case's house to know there'd be no sneaking into the bathroom for a shower. The restroom was by the front door. She'd have to walk naked to get there.

And where was he, anyway? Cat turned on her side to survey the big room. "Oh, hi."

"Ms. Morgan," he teased. He'd showered, shaved, and put on clean jeans. No shirt. Yummy.

She sat up, next-day-shy, and pulled a blanket up to her chin. The covering had found its way to the sofa somehow. "Hey, the sun's out." A fact she found annoying because any expression on his face was backlit and in shadow. He sat with a foot resting on his knee, coffee mug in one hand.

"Yeah, and believe it or not, it's almost warm outside. It doesn't change our situation, though. When I called in to dispatch, they informed me of the road conditions. We'll be stuck for a few days. Both of us are safe. I have food and supplies. I told the department to put us on the bottom of the list. We don't need rescuing. Besides, it's likely going to take heavy equipment to get that monster redwood out of the road."

"But what about Bess and Topsy? Clyde? Heathcliff?" At his name, the kitten came scrambling over the top of the couch and landed in Cat's lap. "Cliffy, you're here." She cast a questioning glance at Case.

"Clyde is fine. The hutch is out on the porch. Which reminds me you're going to have to explain to me how a rabbit gets named Clyde."

"I'll do that right after you tell me how you got that nasty scar on your belly."

"Deal. And before you ask, Topsy and Bess are going to be taken to the animal shelter outside of Fortuna. A work crew can get to the trailer before they get to the tree. For now, I checked, your pets have enough food and water for a day."

"I guess that's a relief."

"Then what's bugging you, sweetheart?"

"You."

"What'd *I* do?"

"Well, I think you're sick and hiding it."

"Took," he swallowed from his cup, "aspirin, and I don't feel bad. You know the flu doesn't hit everybody the same way. I don't usually even notice I have it. I promise. I'll stay in bed all day. You want to help me with that? The bedrest, I mean?"

"I don't want to catch anything."

"Nice try. You already *had* the flu remember?"

"Oh. Yeah. I guess I did."

"That's settled then."

"I need a shower."

Case nodded his head toward the restroom. "Clean towels on the rack. Guess you'll have to use manly soap."

"No problem." She nudged the kitten to the floor and dashed toward the bathroom wrapped in the blanket. Once again, the hunk who had taken over her life proved to be faster. His foot came down on the corner of the covering, and when Cat spun away, she stood stark naked.

She closed the door on him, shouting, "I need to pee for crying out loud."

Hearing his laughter through the wall didn't faze her. After she flushed, she unlatched the lock.

No matter how hard she tried to fight it, she had fallen head over heels for the bossy deputy.

***

Cat sensed him, and opened one eye, despite having shampoo in her hair. It was sheer joy to watch him studying her, especially as he stepped out of his pants and boxers while heading for the shower.

Case cupped her breast as water poured over her head, rinsing away shampoo. He pulled her against him. There could be no question of his motives.

"Cad."

"It's Neanderthal, brute, etcetera to you, Morgan. Now shut up. You owe me. I saved your life. Twice." He nibbled at her ear, her neck, then dropped to her belly button.

She gave up on any snappy comeback. Her deputy game warden was also an EMT.

He could save her anytime, anywhere, and any damned way he pleased.

MARCI'S CO-STAR
A Durango Street Theatre Story

Emily Mims

This story is dedicated to all the health-care professionals putting their lives on the line for us right now. We love you!

Chapter One

Jake sat on a barely tolerable chair in the almost deserted lobby of the Durango Street Theatre Academy and tried not to squirm. A dull ache in his lower back reminded him that the big four-O was in his rearview mirror and that his days of tolerating discomfort patiently had come to an end.

Dust motes danced in the bright sunlight shining through the plate glass window of the Academy lobby next door to the Durango Street Theatre. The former Art Deco movie house now held a live theater and offices and children's Academy attached to the theater. The October sun was still hot but rode low in the sky. Idly he wondered how much longer it would be hot this deep in South Texas. Another two weeks, at least. Another month, possibly. Maybe into December. He didn't know. Despite long years in the military, he'd never lived this far south.

And wouldn't be now if he'd felt he had a choice. He wouldn't be living in San Antonio, Texas, and he sure wouldn't be sitting here on a high-backed armless chair in this artsy-fartsy acting school waiting for his daughter to finish her dance lesson.

Given his druthers, he would still be stationed at Fort Lewis in Washington State, or at an Army buddy's cabin in the crisp cool mountain air of western Colorado, cleaning his deer rifle and planning a hunt in the morning. But that choice and a lot of others had vanished three months ago when his ex-wife, Valeri—with-an-"i"—had called him and dropped her bombshell. "Jake, I wanted to let you know that Zoom Daddy's going on tour as of the first of next month," she'd trilled excitedly. "We've finally, *finally* gotten our chance. The chance of a lifetime! I am so excited." He could only imagine the excitement on his hippie-dippie ex-wife's face as she danced around the living room of the house she shared with their daughter, Angela, and two other like-minded free spirits.

"What about Angela?" he'd asked, not liking what he thought was coming.

"She's coming. I can homeschool her on the days we don't have a show, and she'll be able to do her schoolwork on the tour bus between gigs. The bus is big enough for her to travel with us."

Haul his precious daughter around the country on a tour bus full of pot-smoking musicians? Jake didn't think so. Instead, he managed to call in a couple of favors and took leave. He then put in for retirement and got to San Antonio mere hours before the tour bus was scheduled to depart.

Valeri had been more than happy to leave Angela with him and wave to her daughter from the window as the tour bus pulled out. So here he was, out of the Army and raising the daughter he loved dearly but barely knew. Currently, he'd gone past patience while cooling his heels in the Academy lobby waiting for her to get finished so they could go somewhere for dinner.

He considered the acting and dancing lessons a complete waste of time, but for the joy they brought his daughter. Coming here was about the only thing that put a smile on Angela's face these days. His daughter didn't smile nearly often enough. If learning to dance across a stage singing "I Gotta Crow" made her happy, he wasn't about to deny her that.

He wiggled again and checked his watch. Fifteen more minutes and they would be out the door. He hoped she was good with dinner at the coffee shop close to the house. He still had a ton of work to do to polish the resume he planned to send to a long list of doctor's offices and med clinics.

Officially, he'd detached from the Army last week, but he was not a man inclined to sit around when he could be working. Thank God he had a skill that was marketable in the civilian world. He'd gotten tired of dodging bullets a few years back and the Army had been happy to send him to school to train as a physician's assistant.

His specialty was emergency medicine, which produced the adrenaline rush he craved while taking him, for the most part, out of the line of fire. He'd hoped to land something similar in San Antonio, but the positions here seemed to be mostly diagnosing colds and strep throat and stitching up cuts in a doctor's office or an emergency clinic. Not much adrenaline involved, but he could take care of his child and make a house payment.

The door opened and a couple of moms strolled in, chatting a mile a minute. One looked like she had money to burn and the other like she'd just finished a shift waiting tables. But the ladies were talking like old friends, excited about the upcoming children's production of *Peter Pan.* They greeted him with warm smiles and cheerful "hellos."

Valeri had mentioned the friendliness of the Academy parents. "Nicest bunch ever. Everybody likes everybody else. I feel right at home. Not a snob in the bunch." Jake smirked to himself. Valeri was right. If they'd accepted his ex with her iridescent green hair, black and orange striped leggings, and maroon lipstick, they would accept anybody.

Even a tight-ass military type like him.

At least he hoped they would.

The door whooshed open for a second time and another mother walked in with a girl about Angela's age. She greeted the other mothers with an enthusiastic squeal and hugged them both. Jake resisted the urge to roll his eyes. Hoo boy. Another hippie-dippie type like Valeri.

The woman was probably in her early thirties. Small, petite even, and was cuter than pretty, with an elfin face and a sprinkle of freckles across her nose. Her smile was wide, her chin was pointed, and her nose was turned up on the end. Hazel eyes twinkled from behind heavily done-up lashes, and short hair an eye-popping shade of fuchsia feathered around her face.

She wore a loose t-shirt tie-dyed in a half dozen vivid colors, and an equally bright pair of jeans that matched her hair. Around her neck she wore a kukui nut lei painted in red, yellow, and green to match the shirt. The little girl was a mini-me of her mother and dressed as outrageously in a pink sparkly short set and cowboy boots. Jake stared in fascination for a few seconds before turning his eyes away. *God Almighty.* This one and her kid could out-hippie-dippie his ex-wife any day of the week.

Which wouldn't explain why he had the sudden urge to kiss that great big smile right off the pixie's face.

He rubbed his hand down his cheek. That was the problem with him and women. Always had been. The women he should have been attracted to, either soldiers like himself or serious no-nonsense ladies who would have been good military wives, held no appeal whatsoever. The free spirits and flakes rang his bell.

Valeri had not been the first to catch his eye. It had been a pattern since college, when his date to the ROTC ball had shown up looking like something out of the summer of love in a purple muumuu and love beads. After being the butt of more than one joke from his fellow Army Rangers, he'd kept his social life and his professional life strictly separate and dated the flaky girls on the DL.

After Valeri's accidental pregnancy, and the two-year marriage from hell, he'd given up on relationships together. These days he limited himself to the occasional one-night stand. Which pretty well ruled out the mother of an Academy student, no matter how much she might appeal to him.

Besides, she didn't look all that impressed with him. She'd glanced his way one time and a shutter went down over her eyes. Probably preferred long-haired types with sandals and floppy t-shirts sporting peace signs. Not that he cared. He fought back a smirk. Definitely not a match made in heaven, him and the hippie mom.

He leaned his head back against the wall and shut his eyes. And popped them open a moment later when the door flew open and a handsome young man barreled in. "We need help," he gasped. "A man has collapsed in the lobby."

The hippie-dippie woman leapt to her feet and dashed out the door. Jake stood up, bouncing the chair off the wall. "Which way is your lobby?"

"Next door." The man gestured and Jake flew out the door and down the sidewalk to the double doors of the Durango Street Theatre. He shoved the door open and ran inside, only to find the hippie mother already bent over the patient, a man in his sixties whose face was turning blue. She'd already loosened his tie. She bent over his chest and put her hands together and pumped like she knew what she was doing.

But this needed a professional, not a well-meaning amateur. He got down on his knees and tried to gently move her to one side. But she raised her elbow and none too gently shoved him away. "I've got this," she snapped. "Let me work."

"Move over," he shot back. "He doesn't need a well-meaning hippie-dippie theater type, he needs a medical professional who knows what they're doing."

The woman spared him a *fuck you* glance as she bent over. "I *am* a medical professional," she ground out. "And I know what I'm doing. Now either do something to help me or *get the hell out of my way.*"

***

Marci Lark ground her teeth and bent over to administer the requisite life-giving breaths. The idiot next to her was a jerk of the highest order, pushing aside a nurse administering CPR. He might be in the business himself, but he sure as hell wasn't a nurse practitioner with training in emergency medicine or trauma.

She blew into the patient's mouth and listened. Damn. Still no breaths. She moved over and resumed pumping his chest. One, two, three, four, five. But this time when she went to breathe, the soldier bent over the victim's mouth. To her surprise, he handled the breaths perfectly, shaking his head afterward and motioning for her to continue.

Maybe he knew what he was doing after all.

But he was still a jerk.

They fell into a rhythm. Pumps, breath, pumps. She prayed for the EMTs to hurry. She and Sergeant Army could keep this up for a while, but the sooner the EMTs got a paddle on the patient and his heart going, the better off he would be.

Josh Goldstein, the young man in charge of the place, said he'd called and the fire department had dispatched an ambulance. But long minutes had passed and she was starting to flag. The soldier lifted his head and looked at her. "Want me to spell you?"

She nodded and wordlessly they traded places. He placed his hands in position and almost effortlessly pumped down on the man's chest. She leaned back to give him room. Now that she wasn't concentrating on applying pressure, she could take a minute to look at the man who'd misjudged her.

Definitely a soldier, even if he had on jeans and a t-shirt stretched tight over a pair of broad shoulders that tapered to a trim waist. His hair was cut high and tight and his face wore the I'm-a-soldier-don't-fuck-with-me expression career military all seemed to develop sooner or later.

His face was all hard planes and high cheekbones with a chiseled nose, square jaw, and steel-gray eyes that were piercing. He was big, six feet at least, and had the hard, fit body of a younger man despite the lines between his brow, around his lips, and fanning out from his eyes that put him on the high side of forty. Large, square hands effortlessly performed the needed compressions, and a shiver ran up her back as she wondered if they would caress a woman's body with the same expertise.

Jerking her mind away from those musings, she breathed again for the patient, feeling immense relief when she heard a siren coming down the street. A moment later the lobby doors burst open and two San Antonio Fire Department paramedics came through the door, one of them carrying a defibrillator.

She and the soldier moved away in unison, making room for them. They watched silently as the paramedics hooked up the defibrillator and paddled the man. Once, twice and then their patient coughed and gasped for breath. The EMTs held up their thumbs to her and the soldier and Marci was surprised by the sound of applause coming from around them.

"Great job, you two," Josh crowed as he clapped along with the rest of the audience they'd managed to garner.

Marci shrugged. "It was nothing."

"No big deal," the soldier added.

"Still, I'm grateful," Josh said. "Eloy Solomon is the theater's attorney and one of our most ardent supporters. We love him to pieces. He's a good friend and has funded I don't know how many scholarships for the Academy."

A scholarship her daughter didn't need, but plenty of other kids did. "I'm glad I...no, we're glad we were able to help him," she said, smiling broadly.

"Likewise," the soldier murmured. "Looks like we were the show this afternoon."

Josh huffed. "You sure were. Drama at its best."

She looked around. Wow, everybody in the Durango offices must have come over to watch. And a number of the Academy students and their parents as well.

She spotted her daughter Monique standing with a solemn-faced little girl dressed in jeans and an Academy t-shirt. The child had a sweet face and steel-gray eyes the same color as the soldier's. She looked at the man and her eyes lit up. "Told you my daddy's a hero," she said to Monique.

Monique shrugged. "He was doing the same thing my mom was. Doesn't make him a hero."

"But he is. He saves lives on the battlefield."

"Mom does it in the emergency room. Tell her, Mom."

Marci glanced over at the stone-faced soldier. "Actually, hon, there are those who think of me more as a hippie-dippie theater type," she said dryly.

She wasn't sure what devil made her say that. But it was gratifying to see a pink stain creep across his cheeks.

"But Mom," Monique protested. "You're a nurse practitioner. You don't do theater at all."

His cheeks got even pinker and she stifled a grin.

The paramedics continued to work on Mr. Solomon and the crowd began to disperse. The soldier and his daughter headed out, and she and Monique went back to the Academy. Monique went to her singing class and Marci sat down in the same chair the soldier had occupied earlier. She leaned against the wall and shut her eyes the same way he had.

God in heaven, she was tired. She had run her legs off at the clinic today. Everybody in town had the flu and they had been lined up out the door for most of the day. Maybe relief was in sight.

Dr. Esquivel was interviewing for another nurse practitioner tomorrow. The clinic had been understaffed for the last month. But she knew better than to get her hopes up. Dr. Esquivel was notoriously particular when it came to hiring. He could very well pass on every candidate, leaving everyone in the office overworked for the foreseeable future. Not something she was looking forward to.

At least she could sit here and meditate while Monique was in class. She tried to summon the calm that usually came so easily to her, but rather than the usual tranquility she conjured up, a certain gray-eyed soldier popped into view, disapproval and disdain radiating from every pore.

Tight-assed and judgmental, exactly like Monique's father. She'd suffered through five long years of having everything from her choice of wardrobe to her herbal tea to her perpetual cheer criticized before she told Aaron Lark to take his tight ass and shove it.

"Is it so bad that I like to wear color?" she'd demanded during their last epic fight. "Is it so bad that chamomile tea rings my bell? Is it so bad that I like to smile? *Is it so bad that I do things that make me happy?*"

Apparently, it was. They filed for divorce a month later.

She'd sworn off soldiers in general, and tight-assed men in particular.

Which was a shame in San Antonio. The city was full of eligible men in uniform. But once burnt, twice shy.

These days, when she took her precious time to date at all, it was looser types who were free spirits themselves. She wasn't particularly drawn to them, but she was safe from judgment.

A little shiver ran down her back as she thought of the soldier's piercing gray eyes. Thank goodness she wouldn't have to have anything more to do with him.

Even if he was the most attractive man to cross her path in a long time.

Chapter Two

Jake pulled his Ford F-150 into the parking lot of a small, freestanding medical clinic on the edge of downtown and parked next to a yellow Volkswagen with a "Love on Board" bumper sticker. This was his second interview since beginning his job search. The number of responses his resume garnered had been gratifying. But a lot of the jobs were in areas like orthopedics or obstetrics, or other areas out of his field of expertise.

This position was in a primary medical care clinic, and the office manager he'd spoken to this morning had explained they provided primary care and minor emergency care to an older neighborhood in the inner city. It sounded like something he could handle. So here he was.

The building was a no-nonsense structure of gray cinder block. He suspected he would find the same kind of practical austerity inside. Which was fine with him. He hated to see patients pay a premium to sit in a professionally decorated waiting room. He'd bet his first paycheck the staff would be no-nonsense as well. Unlike the tie-dyed nurse practitioner who'd administered CPR with him the other night.

He dismissed her from his thoughts, grateful he'd not be seeing her again, and strode into the office. The waiting room was as institutional as he'd expected and packed with patients of every age group. He cringed at the sight of small children with coughs and runny noses sitting together at a small table sharing books and crayons.

The middle-aged receptionist smiled at him out from behind oversize glasses. "I'm Rhonda Ramirez and we're really glad you came today. If you'll give me a minute, I'll come around and take you to Dr. Esquivel's office."

She appeared a moment later and escorted him through a maze of exam rooms and past an on-site laboratory to an office in the back, across the hall from the employee break room. "Dr. Esquivel is in with a patient right now, but he should be here in a couple of minutes."

Jake nodded and she left him waiting in one of the two chairs across from the desk. Things were quiet this far back, but he could hear voices coming from the exam rooms and the sound of an unhappy child making a loud and vocal protest to something. "A few minutes" became more than a few, and Jake pulled out his phone and was checking emails when a flash of color disappeared into the break room. Shrugging, he went back to his emails until a chubby man in a rumpled lab coat appeared. The man looked tired, but his smile was warm.

Jake leapt to his feet and offered his hand. "Dr. Esquivel? I'm Jake Pierce."

"Major Pierce, I believe it is. Thank you for your service."

They shook hands. Dr. Esquivel sat down at his desk and gestured for Jake to be seated. "Your resume is impressive," the doctor said. "Would you tell me a little more about your clinic experience in Germany?"

Which was logical since he'd be doing the same work here. "We took care of the soldiers mostly. But it got busy, as we saw their families as well. They used me wherever they needed me, but the two things I did the most often for the Army was primary care and emergency medicine, including battlefield."

"Not much call for battlefield expertise, although we've done a few gang-related gunshot wounds over the years," Dr. Esquivel said dryly.

After another half-hour of discussion, it was evident to both men that Jake possessed the exact qualifications and experience Dr. Esquivel was looking for. "I don't know about you, but I'm ready to offer you a job right now," Dr. Esquivel said. He named a salary that Jake found generous.

"I'm ready to accept that offer," Jake said. "Thank you."

"The pleasure is mine. And I'm sure the rest of my staff feels the same way, Ms. Lark in particular. She's run her legs off the last few weeks. I know she'll welcome the help. Come on. I'll take you around and introduce you to everyone."

Jake followed him around the clinic. He was again introduced to the receptionist and the scheduler who worked with her. Dr. Esquivel then took him by the lab and introduced him to the two lab techs and then to everyone in the business office.

When they entered the breakroom, they found the three LPNs eating lunch. He was introduced to Vickie and Marlene and exchanged a few words with Darnell Jones, the young, tattooed veteran who would be working with him. Darnell's smile was huge in his ebony face. "Man, am I glad to have another soldier around here." He looked around. "'Cept for Dr. E, it gets downright girly. Ya know. Pink and girly."

"Aw, come on, Darnell. You know you love us," a cheerful voice trilled from the hall. "Pink and all."

"And you'd know all about that, wouldn't you, Marci? That pink business," Darnell shot back.

Jake froze. He knew that voice. It was the same voice that had parroted his comment to his daughter. It was the same voice that had ordered him out of the way. It was the same voice that had informed him in no uncertain terms that she was a medical professional.

His mind protested that it couldn't be, that of all the medical clinics in San Antonio, he'd walked into the one where she worked. But a vision in pink stepped into the room and he groaned inwardly. Here she was, in the flesh. His hippie-dippie nurse from the theater. The one who had expertly saved a man's life. The one who'd so effectively put him in his place in front of his daughter.

The one he'd daydreamed of kissing more than once.

The room suddenly felt brighter, as though the sun was shining inside. Or maybe she was the sunshine. Her exceptionally pink scrubs, festooned with green dinosaurs, certainly contributed to the extra illumination.

Her athletic shoes were sturdy but flowered, and the rubber in the stethoscope around her neck was bright blue. No kukui nuts today, but her Apple watchband was rainbow colored and she wore sparkly beads on her other wrist.

She stopped in her tracks, as surprised to see him as he was to see her. The smile slid momentarily from her face but reappeared a second later, and she looked from him to Dr. Esquivel with a question in her eyes. Jake wondered how she was going to handle this and made a quick decision that whatever she did, he would follow her lead.

Dr. Esquivel turned to her with a big smile. "Got you some help, Marci." He gestured toward Jake. "I'd like you to meet Major Jake Pierce. He's a PA fresh out of the Army and starting tomorrow. Jake, this lovely lady is Marci Lark. Marci, with an 'i.'" Dr. Esquivel winked at the young woman.

Of course, it would be Marci with an "i." He groaned inwardly. She had to be as flaky as his ex-wife.

He stifled the urge to make a face. Working here was going to be so much fun.

Marci extended her hand. "Pleased to meet you, Jake. Glad you're on board." Her smile was broad, but not particularly sincere. Jake wondered if anyone besides him noticed.

"Likewise." He shook her hand and made himself smile. So that was how she was going to play it. Fair enough. Their first meeting had been inauspicious in the extreme and if she wanted to sweep it under the rug, he would be happy to help her do it.

Dr. Esquivel smiled broadly. "I think you will enjoy working with Ms. Lark. She's by far the best nurse practitioner I've ever had. Her experience mirrors your own to a great extent."

"Combat wounds?" He wasn't sure what devil made him ask that.

"I used to work in the emergency room at the public hospital. We saw two or three gunshot wounds a week," she said diffidently. "And a car wreck almost every night."

Okay. She had him there. Probably more trauma experience than he had.

"The only reason we were lucky enough to get Ms. Lark was that she needed regular hours," Dr. Esquivel said. "Our gain. The patients love her."

"They sure do," Darnell enthused. "Especially the kids." The other LPNs nodded.

"Speaking of, I need to get back to work. We have a waiting room full of little ones. If you'll excuse me," she said.

She ducked out of the room, taking the sunshine with her. Dr. Esquivel turned Jake over to Darnell, who spent over an hour showing him where supplies and such were stored and how to navigate the computerized medical records. Then Jake spent the better part of two hours wading through all the employment paperwork.

He'd had the foresight to get his Texas paramedic license secured, so he was ready to go when he showed up in the morning. He handed over the papers, thanked Rhonda, and made his way to the truck, staring for a moment at the yellow Volkswagen parked in a sea of nondescript sedans and crossovers. He could see a child-size backpack and a pair of small cowboy boots on the backseat and grimaced.

The car should have been his first clue.

Maybe it wouldn't be so bad, he assured himself. She obviously enjoyed the confidence of her boss. Darnell and the others seemed to hold her in high regard. For now, at least, she deserved to be given the benefit of the doubt, and that's what he would give her. Only time would tell if she deserved it or not.

He climbed in his truck and headed into the traffic. Yes, he would give the cute, appealing sprite the benefit of the doubt. Again, he wondered why he was so attracted to her. Why he found her so enormously appealing. Why he wanted to rip off her clothes and lay her down and do all sorts of naughty things with her.

He was disgusted with himself. It was always like this, him lusting after the free spirits. He wished that once, just once, he could be interested in a regular woman. Someone who wore simple clothes and drove a white car, and whose hair was blonde or brown. Someone who knew how to dress and do a conservative makeup job. Someone who could be relied on.

He would give Marci-with-an-"i" the benefit of the doubt. But it was beyond him how someone that damned flaky could be any good at medicine.

***

Marci swallowed the last of her Earl Grey and put the mug in the breakroom sink. She'd barely eked out time for the break, but she'd been tied up with patients since stepping in the door three hours ago and was on the wane. With the sugar she'd added to the tea, she ought to be good for another couple of hours before she needed to eat.

Breakfast had been a big bowl of oatmeal and that would hold her a little while longer. She caught a flash of an increasingly familiar blue lab coat hustle around the corner and her lips tightened.

She was getting thoroughly tired of the man wearing that blue lab coat.

Her next patient was waiting in exam room three. Marci took a quick look at the workup on her iPad screen. Lila Washington. Eighty-seven years young, as she liked to say. Five feet tall. One hundred sixty-five pounds. Blood pressure one-sixty over ninety-nine. A1-C of seven point five. Uh-oh. Lila was as sharp as a tack but suffered from a variety of health issues, many of which were exacerbated by her refusal to take care of herself. Marci would need to sit down and address these issues this morning with the hardheaded old lady. She stifled a sigh, plastered on a smile and opened the door.

This was going to take a while.

Thirty-eight minutes, to be exact, during which Marci explained yet again why indulging in guacamole was okay but the salt on the corn chips wasn't, that Lila needed to stay away from German chocolate cake and sticky buns, that sodas were bad news on many levels, and that chicken could be cooked with other flavorings besides salt. Marci encouraged Lila to get out and take a walk as weather permitted, and answered the elderly lady's questions as best she could. Lila asked if her prescriptions needed to be changed and Marci shook her head. "Not at this time. I'd like to give these diet and exercise improvements a chance to work before we tinker with your meds. Does that work for you?"

It did. Marci was smiling as she escorted Lila to the exit counter. "I want to see you back here in three months," she said as she wished the old lady well.

"Three months? As much time as that took, it ought to be three years," a gruff voice growled in her ear.

Marci's smile faded and she glanced up at an aggravated-looking Jake Pierce, dressed in his usual outfit of a lab coat thrown over khakis and a black polo shirt. His version of a civilian uniform, she guessed. She forced herself to look back at him calmly. "Some visits take more time than others. You know that as well as I do."

"I saw three patients in the time you spent with one. We have a waiting room full. Sometimes we simply don't have a lot of time," he went on impatiently. "We need to take care of whatever problem's in front of us and move on. Just sayin'."

"Woo-hoo. Conveyor belt medicine. In and out in ten minutes. And if we miss something big? We were by-God efficient." She didn't even try to hide her sarcasm.

Jake nodded. "Military efficiency. Quick and sweet. I pride myself on it."

"Civilian efficiency. Thorough and careful. All the time, not only when it's convenient. I pride myself on that." She raised her eyebrow. "Was there anything else?"

"No." He turned on his heel and stomped toward the exam rooms.

Asshole.

A sexy, mouthwateringly good-looking asshole, but still an asshole.

She saw four more patients in an hour, and then had another one that took a lot of time. She peeked out at the waiting room on her way to eat lunch. Jake was right. They were slammed. But she'd be damned if she hurried anyone along for the sake of efficiency and possibly miss something relevant. She'd rather put in an extra hour at the end of the day.

But today that would be problematic. Monique was due at the theater at five-thirty and at this point Marci was supposed to drive her there. Her daughter was in the running for the part of Wendy in the elementary level production of *Peter Pan*. It didn't help that Angela Pierce was also in the running, along with a couple of others.

Marci could always call Monique's grandmother to help, but then Monique would be subjected to an afternoon of snide remarks from Aaron's mother, a situation Marci would like to avoid if she could. She cut her lunch to ten minutes, barely taking time to bolt down a sandwich of roasted chicken and bean sprouts on wheat.

She was swallowing the last of her sandwich when Jake sauntered in with a delicious-smelling bag from the local hamburger joint. He had taken off his lab jacket. The polo shirt fit tightly over his broad shoulders and the khaki pants outlined a delectable ass that Marci was tempted to reach out and pat. A six-pack was outlined beneath the knit shirt. Damn. Once again, she was attracted to a soldier with a cob up his butt.

She would never learn.

Darnell followed Jake into the breakroom. Jake sank down in a chair with a contented sigh and unwrapped a huge cheeseburger.

"Gonna enjoy every bite of this one. Darnell, the other one's for you."

"Thanks, man." Darnell unwrapped the second burger. "Marci, you eat that usual healthy shit you like so much?"

"It's all I had time for." She smiled sweetly. "We have a waiting room full of patients. Or so I was told. Those burgers are gonna take forever to eat. Enjoy your leisurely lunch." She waltzed out before either of them had a chance to reply.

The crowd began to thin about three and she thought she might be close to catching up. She did a couple of routine well-geriatric exams and stitched up a kitchen accident. Her next patient, Betty Jo Wilson, was new to her, although she'd visited the clinic a couple of times in the past. Marci glanced over the intake information. Blood pressure was a little high but not too bad. Labs normal, even good for a seventy-year-old. Not a follow-up, and she wouldn't tell the LPN why she'd come. "I'll talk to the doctor and nobody else."

Hmm. She wasn't the doctor, but maybe the lady would talk to her anyway.

She stepped in the room and shut the door behind her. Betty Jo was a big, raw-boned woman with work-roughened hands, chapped lips, and cheeks. She wore jeans and a work shirt and her expression was blank but for the pain that filled her eyes. Her eyes flicked over Marci. "You're not the doctor."

"No. I'm the nurse practitioner. But I can treat you the same as Dr. Esquivel can."

"Does that include prescriptions?"

"It does."

"Then I want a prescription for an antidepressant. I'm depressed and tired of it. I have a farm to run and most mornings can barely get out of bed."

Whoa. It sure did sound like she was depressed.

The question then became why.

"Okay. When did the depression start?"

"Two months ago." Betty's face twisted.

"I see. Did anything happen at that time that would make you depressed?"

"Dub died."

"Dub?"

"Dub Wilson. My husband."

It was like pulling teeth, but Marci finally got the story out of her. Dub had keeled over from a heart attack while out on his tractor one afternoon. Betty Jo hadn't found him in time to do CPR. They had no children and she was faced with either keeping the farm going by herself or selling a property that had been in the family for over a hundred years.

It was enough to give anyone a walloping case of depression.

Still, Marci didn't think medication was the answer. The woman needed support, not pills. It took Marci the better part of an hour, but she finally made her case and sent Betty Jo out with an appointment with a therapist for the following week and a list of grief support groups in her small town south of the city.

Marci glanced at the intake list and groaned inwardly. No way was she going to get out of here at a reasonable hour. She made the dreaded call to her former mother-in-law and was coming out of the restroom when she almost ran into Jake. He raised his eyebrow. "Some more of that civilian efficiency?"

She forced herself to remain calm. "Something like that. A lady came in asking for antidepressants. It took me awhile to convince her she didn't need them."

"Was she depressed?"

"Big time."

"So why didn't you give them to her?"

"Her depression's situational, not chemical."

"And you know this because?"

She sighed. "Because any woman who's just lost her husband and is trying to manage a farm by herself is going to be depressed. She doesn't need pills. She needs counseling and a grief support group."

"She might not need them long term, but meds right now would help her a lot."

"Grief? You want me to write a script for grief?"

"Grief. Anxiety. Depression. Same ingredients as PTSD. Meds would help. At least get her over the hump."

"So will a caring counselor," she said through clenched teeth.

"Fine. Send her to a counselor. Send her to all the grief support groups you can find her. *After* you've addressed the anxiety and depression with medical help. Works with PTSD."

"Grief isn't PTSD."

"They're first cousins involving the same kind of brain changes."

Marci felt her temper snap. "Damn it, I'm not Nurse Feelgood. I don't offer a pill for everything." She pointed to the prescription pad in the front pocket of his lab coat. "That sucker's not the answer to all that ails them." She leaned forward. "You need to quit pushing me to hurry and questioning how I do my job. I've been working her for the last three years and have kept the boss happy the entire time. *You're* the newbie, Major Pierce. You would do well to remember that."

She felt his angry gaze on her as she walked away.

Chapter Three

Marci Lark was going to be the death of him. If he didn't strangle her first.

Jake ran his hand around the back of his neck. He was trying. He really was. More than once he'd reminded himself that he *was* the newbie in this office and that apparently Dr. Esquivel was pleased with her work. But it was like she was trying to get on his nerves. Thirty-minute appointments that should have taken fifteen. Counseling. Tea and sweet talk. Any minute now she'd probably pull out a candle and recommend aromatherapy. Why couldn't she simply make a diagnosis and send them out the door with something that *worked*?

And if he'd been guilty of questioning her work, she was sure as hell guilty of questioning his. Oh, not out loud. But the smirks and the eye rolls said more than words would have. Yes, he believed in using medication. Because it worked. And it wasn't his job to be everybody's buddy. He was being paid to deliver health care. So that's what he would do, deliver the best health care he knew how. They could find good buddies on their own time.

He made his last entry into the file and checked his iPad. There were a couple of patients waiting, but he was due a break and Marci was coming off hers. Dr. Esquivel was holed up in his office doing a pile of paperwork required by the state. Which was considerable with a PA and a nurse practitioner working for him.

Texas had yet to grant the same kind of autonomy to PAs and nurse practitioners that they enjoyed in most of the rest of the country, and Dr. Esquivel had to sign off on their prescriptions and such. Jake chafed under the restrictions, but it was what it was. He'd half expected the doctor to question some of his decisions, especially with Marci's style being so different, but the doc hadn't questioned anything yet, and Jake hoped he wouldn't.

He wandered into the breakroom and popped a coffee pod in the machine. Marci was rinsing her mug at the sink. She glanced over and murmured a quick greeting before she walked out.

She'd found time to change her hair color last night. Instead of the eye-popping fuchsia, it was now cotton candy pink. Her lipstick was pink as well. Today she paired the pink hair with lime green scrubs with orange hippos, a combination that should have clashed, but remarkably went together well. It was downright cute on her. In fact, he found everything about her downright cute. The hair, the eye-popping scrubs, everything.

Which irritated the hell out of him. For the thousandth time he wished women like her didn't appeal to him so much. He wished that *she* didn't appeal to him so much. But the attraction had been growing since that afternoon at the theater. And it damn well wasn't one-sided.

He hadn't missed the veiled peeks at him when she didn't think he'd notice. Her interest she tried so hard to hide was evident, even when she was treating him to a curled lip or sarcastic rejoinder. The bottom line was that they were interested in one another, yet neither of them wanted to be. And with their medical philosophy so different, it made for a working environment that was interesting, to say the least.

He enjoyed a short break and headed to his next patient. Joel Ramirez. Forty years old. Five-seven, two hundred twenty pounds. A1-C of seven point five. His pants and shirt were paint-spattered, and his shirt sported a pocket patch proudly proclaiming "Ramirez Painting Company." Jake shook his hand and sat down across from him. "You're diabetic. Full-pop. Family history?"

Joel shrugged. "Pretty much every one of us, sooner or later. My father lost his leg to it last year. Nurse Marci said Pop probably went ten years without being diagnosed."

Jake winced inwardly. "So you know you have to take care of yourself from now on. Eat right, exercise. Get some weight off. Test your blood sugar twice a day." Joel nodded. "I can send you out of here with a glucose meter and a thirty-day supply of test strips and a prescription for a highly effective oral medication. I'll also send you out with a pamphlet explaining what you should and shouldn't be eating. I want to see you back here in a month, sooner if your sugar levels don't drop significantly. Understand?"

Joel nodded. Jake found one of the complimentary meters left by the sales rep and took a few minutes showing Joel how to use it. He wrote a prescription for the oral medication and took Joel out to the exit desk where Marci was helping an elderly man check out. She and Joel smiled at one another and she shook his hand. "So what brings you to see us this morning?"

Joel ducked his head. "They found out I have diabetes. The new doc fixed me up with a meter and some pills."

Jake stiffened as Marci's eyes narrowed. "What about your diet? Did the new doc talk to you about it?"

"He gave me something to read. I'll be fine." Joel got out his wallet and started counting out his money.

Marci opened her mouth and then shut it. She shook her head and gave Jake a withering look before stalking down the hall toward the breakroom. He stared after her. What the hell was wrong with what he'd done? He'd talked about diet and exercise and shown the guy how to use the meter. He didn't know what else she expected him to do. But if he followed her into the breakroom, he'd bet he'd find out.

She whirled on him the minute he got to the breakroom. "A pamphlet? You sent a newly diagnosed diabetic out the door with a pamphlet? Was that the best you could do?"

Jake felt his teeth grind together. "I sent him out with a glucose meter I demonstrated to him, a prescription, and a damn extensive description of a proper diet. And that was after we talked about diet and exercise."

"Let me guess. You told him to get some exercise and eat right. One sentence. Did you explain what eating right involves? Did you take the time to tell him what he can and can't eat safely?"

"Why should I?" He hated the defensiveness in his voice. "It's in the pamphlet. He can read it. Besides, with a family full of diabetics, surely he knows something about a proper diabetic diet."

"No, he can't," she said. "Joel can't read worth a damn. His wife's from Mexico and can't read or write English at all, so she can't help him with that. The family has no idea what a proper diabetic diet consists of or his father wouldn't have lost his leg last year." She stopped and took a breath. "He needed to have detailed instructions given. Spelled out in a professional voice of authority that he might listen to."

"You mean in a giggling trill along with instructions on making chamomile tea?" Jake shot back.

He heard a gasp behind him and turned around. To his horror, Darnell and Marlene were standing there with horrified expressions on their faces. And behind them stood a pissed-off-looking Dr. Esquivel. Jake felt his face flame. He'd been caught denigrating a colleague in front of her coworkers.

He'd be lucky if he still had a job.

Not that Marci looked any happier. Her face was beet red and she looked like she could crawl through the floor.

Dr. Esquivel motioned for the LPNs to go. He stepped in the room and shut the door behind him. Jake's heart pounded in his throat. He knew what he would do if he were the one in charge. But he wasn't. He didn't know if Dr. Esquivel was a hard-ass or not. But he had a feeling he was about to find out.

The doctor looked from him to Marci and back to him. "Professional disagreement?" They both nodded. He looked at Jake and his expression hardened. "We don't run our colleagues down in this office. *Ever.* Do you understand?"

"Yes, sir."

He looked at them both and shook his head. "Professional disagreements happen. I get that. And sometimes they need to be addressed. I get that as well. But they are always addressed privately. Not in front of patients, not in front of the LPNs, and not in front of me. Do you both understand?"

Jake swallowed. "Yes, sir."

Marci nodded. "Yes, Dr. Esquivel."

The doctor turned on his heel and left the room. He and Marci stared at one another for a minute, then she glared at him and left him alone in the room. A part of him breathed a sigh of relief. The doctor could justifiably send him packing. But he'd been given a reprieve so to speak. A reprieve he would make good use of. He would steer clear of Marci. Keep his mouth shut. Avoid her as much as possible.

He hoped she had enough sense to do the same with him.

***

Marci breathed a sigh of relief as she walked toward exam room three. Unless an emergency walked in the door in the next fifteen minutes, this would be the last patient for the day. It was almost six, and the office had pretty much cleared out. Dr. Esquivel had left for the hospital thirty minutes ago, and the office staff and LPNs had drifted out as well.

She thought Jake might still be somewhere with a patient, but didn't know for sure and didn't particularly care. She had no intention of talking with him or interacting with him in any way, shape, or form. Not if she could help it. After the other day when they'd had their clash and got a talking-to from her boss, she had no desire to deal with Major Pain-in-the-Ass.

She'd been horribly embarrassed by the incident, even if Dr. Esquivel had seemed more upset with Jake than with her. As far as she was concerned, Jake could do anything he damned well wanted and she'd keep her mouth shut. The medicine he practiced was between him and Dr. Esquivel. He could poison them for all she cared.

She wasn't speaking up again.

She glanced over the intake information on the iPad. Loretta Camillo. Forty-five years old. Five-seven, one hundred thirty. Blood pressure one twenty-seven over seventy-two. Temperature of one hundred one. Sore throat from hell. She looked a little further in the medical records. Preschool teacher in a daycare center. Marci nodded. She would bet her license Loretta had picked up strep throat from one of the kids.

She breezed into the exam room. Loretta was sitting on the exam table wearing a sweater over her red pullover even though the room was warm. Marci greeted her with a smile. "Still working at the daycare?"

"Yes, and half the kids are down with sore throats. Why the parents send them when they're sick is beyond me."

Marci winced. "Having been there, but tried not to do that, they may feel they can't miss work. Which isn't fair, because now you're sick and have to miss work." She got out a tongue depressor and examining light. "Open up."

Loretta gave Marci access. Yep. Classic strep symptoms. White patches on her tonsils. Red spots in the back of the roof of her mouth. Marci gently palpitated her throat, and found her lymph nodes swollen. "Gonna give it to you straight. Strep. A nasty case of it. I'll do a throat culture, but I'd like to get some antibiotics started. Are you allergic to penicillin?" Loretta shook her head. "I'd like to start with that. I'll write the script for a two-week supply, but if you don't start to feel better in a couple of days, let me know and we can amp up the meds."

"What about the pain? It hurts like hell."

"You can start by gargling with salt water. That has the added benefit of destroying bacteria. Tea with lemon. Your favorite romance novel."

Loretta laughed. Marci wrote a prescription and they walked toward the exit desk. Jake was standing there updating his iPad. "Call me if you don't feel better in a couple of days. And remember, the tea with lemon and the saltwater gargles do wonders for strep."

Jake's eyes widened. Loretta trudged toward the door. When she was out and the door shut behind her, he whirled on Marci, his eyes blazing. "Of all the damned-fool things you've done since I came to work here, that has to take the cake. You sent a strep patient out of here with tea and fucking salt water? *What the hell is wrong with you?*"

Marci gasped. She took a step back, but then marched up to him and poked him in the chest. "I also sent her out of here with a two-week supply of penicillin and instructions to call me if those don't work so we can switch her to a med that does. *What the hell was wrong with that?*"

Jake blinked. "Nothing, I guess. But—"

"But nothing," Marci spat. "That fucking salt water destroys bacteria. Or is that too low-tech for you? The tea with lemon juice is soothing. Oh, and I guess you're going to object to the romance novel I recommended. It's sure as hell low tech, but she might enjoy it. I gave her antibiotics. First damn thing I did. So tell me. What's wrong with any of that?"

"*Fine.* You gave her what she needed." He turned back to his iPad.

"And why would you assume I wouldn't?" she asked icily.

"Because too many times you haven't. You've sent them out with a diet change or counseling when they needed medication."

"No, you've sent them out with a damn pill when they needed advice and counseling. But you know what? You've had a cob up your ass about me ever since you laid eyes on me in the theater. You thought I couldn't perform CPR. You took one look at me when you walked in here and decided I didn't know what I was doing. I was at least willing to give you the benefit of the doubt. So tell me, what's so damned bad about me that you automatically assume I don't know how to do my job?"

He looked her up and down. "I guess we could start with the pink hair and the cutesy clothes. They're unprofessional. Then there's that damned herbal tea you love to recommend. The touchy-feely medicine you practice. You're a flake, Marci-with-an-'i.' Just like my ex. A flake nobody can take seriously. If you expect me or anyone else to take you seriously, you have to look the part."

"Actually, I don't." She glared across the room at him. "Nobody else has any problem whatsoever taking me seriously. My boss. My coworkers. My patients. They have enough sense to know that the hair and the clothes have nothing to do with my professional competence. The only one who ever had a problem with it was Sergeant Aaron Lark, the asshole soldier I was married to for way too long. Two-foot-long cob up his ass, that one. Exactly like the cob up yours. No, wait. I think yours is a little longer."

"I don't have a damned cob up my ass," he shot back, "because I think dressing appropriately is important."

She looked him up and down. "Yep. You wear the costume well. Bet you're something else on Halloween." She took a step closer. "But as far as I'm concerned, a costume is all it is. It's not what you wear, Major Pierce. It's the job you do. And the job you do is sorely lacking. Unprofessional as hell. You plow through patients like you're on the damn battlefield. Get 'em in, write a script, get 'em out. Never mind treating the whole person. And you're cold and unfeeling on top of that. You couldn't give a damn about your patients. And that, my friend, is the definition of unprofessional."

"There's nothing unprofessional about being efficient." The muscle in Jake's jaw bunched. "And those scripts were developed for a reason. To make my patients' lives better. You're damned right I write them. And I'm going to keep right on writing them because you know what, Nurse hippie-dippie? *I'm right.*"

"The hell you are. You're nothing more than a Doc Feelgood-uh-what—"

Her next words were blocked by Jake's mouth crashing down on hers. Hard. Marci's lips ground together with his as he jerked her up against his hard, trembling body. Too stunned to fight, Marci stood frozen for a moment as the warmth of his chest and thighs seeped through her scrubs.

Against her will her arms crept upward, anger mingling with passion as she pulled his face even closer and deepened the kiss, her lips opening and her tongue snaking out and teasing his.

Strong arms were like steel bands crushing her to him, his chest rock-hard and the evidence of his desire poking insistently into her stomach. Her nipples hardened and she felt warmth between her legs. In a corner of her mind she knew this was the last man she should be kissing like this. She had no business wanting him so badly or desiring him so much. But she didn't care. All that mattered now was the feel of his lips on hers, his arms holding her close, his hard body trembling beside hers. All the pent-up desire she'd felt for him for the last two weeks poured out, and she willingly gave herself up to the attraction she, no, they, were finally acting on.

They clung together for long moments. Marci willingly lost herself in the sensation, not a slave to her desire but not entirely in charge of it either. All too soon Jake lifted his face from hers. Marci looked up at him, dreading the smirk she was sure was on his face. But there was no smirk. Instead, he looked at her with a dazed expression that slowly morphed into shock. He released her and stepped back while they stared at one another wordlessly.

Oh. My. God. What had they done?

Marci stumbled back a step or two. She looked at Jake in horror before running to her desk and grabbing her handbag and her keys and leaving everything else.

Nothing for it but to beat a hasty retreat. She fled to her car, her hands trembling on the wheel as it took three tries to get it started. It took the entire drive across town before her fingers no longer shook.

She pulled into her driveway and laid her head on the steering wheel. Sex. Hormones. Forbidden attraction. That's what all the sniping had been about. There wasn't a damned thing wrong with the medicine Jake Pierce practiced. It was dispassionate and impersonal, but it was solid.

Her overt hostility had been all about her fighting his appeal. Wanting to distance herself from the disapproving but all-too-alluring military man. Trying to protect herself from another soldier who would hurt her as Aaron had. From the kiss that had flared between them, he had to be as attracted to her as she was to him.

And from what he'd said about his ex-wife, he had the same kinds of ghosts she did. She reminded him of his flaky ex, who was apparently the last kind of woman he wanted to tangle with again. Which was fine with her. She didn't want to tangle with his kind again either.

They would do well to stay away from one another.

If they could.

Chapter Four

Jake checked his iPad and headed down the hall to exam room three. It had been a long day, but the waiting room was almost empty and he had one patient, two at most before he could make his escape and take Amanda to the theater. She hadn't gotten the coveted role of Wendy, that had gone to Monique Lark, but instead was playing Tiger Lily and eagerly learning her lines and her songs.

The rehearsal schedule had added another evening to Amanda's theater obligation, and not for the first time he wished he were on better terms with Marci. Amanda said they lived one subdivision down the road from his recently purchased home, and it would be nice to have another parent to help with the transportation. But he'd blown any possibility of a détente, or even a truce, when he'd grabbed her and kissed her silly last week.

Foolishly, he'd given in to the attraction he, no, they, felt for one another and laid the kiss of a lifetime on her, and ruined any friendship or any other kind of relationship they might have developed down the road.

Directly after that scorching kiss, she'd fled like a scalded cat, and had done her best to avoid him since.

He sighed inwardly. It wasn't the first time his stupidity had cost him, and it wouldn't be the last. He wished he could forget how good she felt in his arms. Despite everything, he would love to kiss her again. To kiss her and strip off those cheerful scrubs and lay her delectable body down on his king-size and enjoy her all night long. He wondered if she still felt the same, or if kissing her the way he had destroyed any desire she might have felt for him.

Joel Ramirez sat in the chair clutching his glucose meter in his hands. "You said to come back if my numbers were bad. I showed this to my next-door neighbor and he said they were bad."

Jake reached for the meter. "Let's see how bad."

He took one look at the numbers and groaned. "Joel, have you been eating a proper diabetic diet?"

"I guess. My wife and my mom do the cooking. I eat what they fix."

Marci's words popped into his head. "Joel, what have you eaten for the last three days?"

Joel ran him through it. Marci had been right. The family had no idea what a proper diabetic diet consisted of. Even though it was going to make him late, he spent twenty minutes explaining exactly what Joel could eat and why. Something he should have done in the first place. Joel thanked him and headed out the door.

Jake stared after Joel. Marci had been right about him. Maybe she was right about some of the rest of it as well.

He swung by the house to collect Amanda and made it to the theater with seconds to spare. He sat down in the mostly empty waiting room. Amanda had warned him the rehearsal could last as long as two hours and suggested he go home and come back. But he was tired and didn't feel like fighting the traffic any more than he had to. He'd wait.

He called up a novel on his iPhone and was deep into James Patterson's latest when Marci wandered in an hour later. She sat down as far away from him as she could and got an iPad out of her voluminous handbag.

From the small grocery bag in her hands, he guessed she'd been shopping. She removed a chilled bottle of chamomile tea and unscrewed the lid.

He returned to his book, determined to ignore her. But he was conscious of the little peeks she kept sending his way. *A-ha.* She was still interested, even if she didn't want to be. The question then became whether they would do anything about it.

He dragged his attention away from Marci and was getting back into the story when he heard the screech of tires, followed by the god-awful sound of crashing metal and breaking glass and the reverberation of terrified screams. He was on his feet and out the door in a flash, Marci close on his heels.

The sight that met them had them both sprinting into the street. Two twisted, tangled, misshapen vehicles had come to rest right in front of the theater doors, their chassis deformed beyond recognition. Jake quickly scanned the passenger compartments. An elderly couple was trapped in the front seat of an old Buick, and a carload of injured teenagers filled a Dodge Charger. He and Marci looked at one another as the Academy students poured onto the sidewalk, Amanda and Monique among them. He dug his keys out of his pocket and Marci pulled hers off a wristband as their daughters ran up to them. "Get my bag," they shouted almost in unison as they handed their keys to the girls.

The girls took off running. He and Marci quickly assessed the situation. "You take them and I'll get the kids," she said as she gestured to the elderly couple and ran toward the Charger. He approached the old Buick and groaned. The passenger compartment was pushed forward, almost but not quite trapping the woman. The steering wheel had the man pinned. Gasoline pooled under the car. *Crap.* He had to get them out of there before the damn car blew.

He reached across the woman and turned off the engine. "Ma'am, can you feel your hands and feet? Does it hurt to move?"

Her eyes were dazed as she shook her head. "Take care of my husband. I'm fine." Blood ran down her face and dripped onto her shirt.

No, she wasn't fine. But the husband was worse. Jake made a quick assessment. She could move her hands and feet and didn't appear to have a back injury. But you never knew. He turned to the theater director. "Do you have any boards we could put these people on?"

The young man nodded and snapped orders to someone behind him. An SAPD officer pulled up and quickly assessed the situation. He gestured toward Jake. "Do you have any training for this kind of thing?" he asked curtly.

"Physician's assistant. Army field hospital experience. Pink hair over there is a nurse practitioner with extensive trauma experience in the ER."

The officer's face cleared. "Carry on."

Amanda returned with his medical bag and a moment later a couple of young men returned with two flat boards that would serve nicely as makeshift litters until the EMTs arrived. Jake enlisted the help of the policeman and together they eased the lady onto the first board and laid her on the sidewalk.

The husband was more problematic. He was obese and would be difficult to lift. Moving him could exacerbate his injuries, but that pool of gasoline was growing by the minute. "How much longer before EMS gets here?" he asked the officer.

"There's a crash on the freeway with multiple injuries. It has traffic at a standstill and is tying up a bunch of ambulances," he replied grimly. "They routed one here, but it'll take a few minutes."

Jake muttered a curse under his breath. He made a quick decision and glanced over at Marci, hoping she wasn't doing her usual hand-holding routine, and was surprised to find all five occupants of the other car lined up on the sidewalk. She had patched one up already and was working on the second. He blinked as she swiftly applied a makeshift bandage on a bleeding forehead and moved toward the third. "Marci. I need you over here for a minute. Officer, I need you as well."

She took one look at the situation and came running. "See if you can get the seat to move back," she said.

He leaned down and pushed down on the lever. It took a mammoth shove but Jake managed to get the seat moved back far enough that he and the cop could ease the elderly man from the car and lay him on the board Marci put into position behind them. Together the three of them hoisted the board and carried it away from the potentially deadly car and laid it on the sidewalk next to the old lady. "You take care of them," she said as she sprinted down the sidewalk to the kids.

Jake spent the next few minutes examining the old man and taking his blood pressure. He had a lump on his head and was in shock. A couple of his ribs were broken. Jake's main concern was possible internal injuries, but he had no way to assess that. The old man was conscious but dazed, and in considerable pain.

Jake wracked his brain for something he could do for the pain, but heard a siren, and a moment later a fire truck and an EMS unit came around the corner, coming to a stop in front of him. The paramedics hopped out and began triage. "BP seventy over forty and he's shocky," Jake said. "The wife's blood pressure is one-forty-five over eighty and she doesn't appear to have any serious injuries."

The paramedic glanced down at Jake's bag. "Thanks, man. We got this."

Jake started toward Marci and the kids but stopped when he heard the wife cry out. "Don't leave me alone, please," she begged.

He stopped in his tracks and glanced down the sidewalk. Marci appeared to have everything under control so he sat down beside the frightened woman. She thrashed around and grabbed for his hand. "I'm scared."

"I know that," he soothed. "But the paramedics have everything under control. Your husband will be fine."

The paramedics did an examination of both the man and his wife and determined that the guy's needs came first. Carefully, they put the man on a stretcher and into the back of the ambulance. "*No,*" the woman protested when they shut the doors. "I need to go with him. Harvey will be terrified."

The paramedics ignored her. "Ma'am, your husband is in the best of hands. And you need an ambulance yourself," Jake said soothingly. Her face was getting redder. She was about to go into full-blown hysterics. "What's your name?" he asked.

"Helen. And my husband's Harvey. We were on our way to get Mexican food for dinner."

"That's good. What's your favorite Mexican food?" he asked as he surreptitiously glanced over to where Marci was working. He was prepared to draft someone to stay with Helen while he assisted Marci with her remaining charges, but she had things well under control. More than under control, if her brisk, efficient care of the last banged-up teenager was anything to go by. *Well, if that didn't beat all.* She'd been brisk and efficient. She'd handled her patients like a pro. No, she handled her patients like the *pro she was.*

She was a professional. She knew her job and did it well. It was time he remembered that.

***

Marci couldn't believe her eyes.

Jake was sitting on the sidewalk, holding the old lady's hand and murmuring soothing words to her. The woman had been frantic and on the verge of a meltdown and Marci had feared they would have a case of hysterics to deal with. But Jake had taken her hand and gotten her talking about Mexican food, of all things, and was doing a splendid job of keeping her calm until a second ambulance arrived.

But the next paramedics determined that one of the teenagers needed transportation next, and it was over twenty minutes before another ambulance came. Jake sat patiently, talking softly the whole time and keeping the terrified woman occupied. Exactly the way Marci would have done. She stared at him, hoping her astonishment didn't show. *Son of a bitch.* He was perfectly capable of the caring and compassion she thought was so important. He was as kind and caring as he could be tonight.

She had completely misjudged him.

The paramedics took the old woman away as the rest of the EMS units lined up to transport the remaining teenagers. Marci packed her stethoscope and her blood pressure cuff into her bag and walked down the sidewalk to where Jake was getting to his feet. They stared at one another for a long moment. He had surprised her tonight. And from the look on his face, she had surprised him as well.

"Nice job," she said softly.

"Likewise." A hint of a smile played around his mouth.

Monique and Amanda rushed up to them. "Everybody's talking about how great you and Amanda's dad were tonight," Monique enthused. "You're a hero. So's Mr. Pierce."

"Oh, sweetie, it would take a lot more than what I did tonight to make me a hero," she said.

"Hey, if they want to call us heroes, let 'em." Jake put his hand on Amanda's shoulder. "Are you still rehearsing or are you done for the night?"

"We're done and I'm hungry," Amanda said. "Pizza?"

Jake nodded and they took off down the sidewalk. Marci retrieved her handbag from the lobby and she and Monique headed for the car. They picked up Chinese at the drive-through and Marci took a quick shower while Monique set the table.

Her daughter was wired and talked nonstop through dinner. Marci tried to listen but her mind kept drifting back to the sight of Jake Pierce sitting cross-legged on the sidewalk holding a terrified old woman's hand and murmuring soothing words to her. Engaging in pointless conversation to take her mind off her fear. It was the last thing Marci would have expected of him.

And that had been wrong, so wrong of her.

So maybe he wasn't the most touchy-feely health-care provider out there. But he still cared and was capable of enormous kindness. She had erroneously lumped him in with her unfeeling ex, assuming that because Aaron had been cold and uncaring, all soldiers were. It hadn't been true of Jake. He'd proven that tonight.

Monique helped her clean up and disappeared into her room to do her homework. Marci poured a glass of wine and was settling in to read a romance novel on her iPad when the doorbell rang. She turned on the porch light and peered out the peephole.

Jake Pierce was standing on her front porch. His hair was damp and his jeans and t-shirt were fresh, and he clutched a bouquet of daisies in front of him.

She loved daisies.

She opened the door, hoping she didn't look as confused as she felt. "How did you know I love daisies?"

Jake smiled. "Recon. You have daisies taped to all your pens and have at least three sets of daisy scrubs. And I might have had my daughter text your daughter and ask. Same way I got your address."

She smiled and pushed open the screen door. "Come on in."

He stepped in and handed her the flowers. "I figured with the ass I've been it was the least I could do."

"I've been no better. Let me put these in water. They're absolutely lovely. Thank you."

She made quick work of putting the flowers in a vase. "Can I offer you anything? Wine? A soda?"

"Got any beer?" he teased.

"Actually, I do. It's a craft out of Fredericksburg. Will that do?"

"I'm sure I'll love it."

She handed him the beer and they sat down together on the sofa. "I misjudged you," he said abruptly. "I misjudged you badly, and I'm so sorry."

"I misjudged you just as badly." She took a breath. "I lumped you in with my ex-husband. He's a sergeant in the Army and about as cold and unfeeling as they come. I assumed you're like him. But you're not. I mistook military-style efficiency for not caring. I shouldn't have."

"I misjudged you based on the clothes and the hair. I equated you with my ex-wife, who has a similar sense of style. Valeri is as big a flake as they come."

"What does she do that's so flaky?"

"Well, for starters, her band got a touring gig and she was going to take Amanda along with her on a touring bus full of musicians.

Homeschool her from the bus. Was perfectly happy to sign custody over to me and wave good-bye to her daughter from the bus window."

"Ouch. That would be the textbook definition of flaky."

"And it wasn't only her. I seem to be attracted to ladies who like, well, uh—"

"Hippie-dippie types?" she offered helpfully.

Jake blushed a deep shade of red. "I guess free-spirited would be more like it. Unconventional. Marching to the tune of their own drummer. Every woman I've wanted in the last twenty years has been a free spirit. And yes, there were some flakes sprinkled in." He looked her in the eye. "You turned me on the minute I laid eyes on you. It scared me to death. I was afraid you were another one."

Marci thought a minute. "I am a free spirit. The clothes, the hair, I look like this because it makes me happy. It reminds me to be cheerful with my patients. It reminds me not to let my responsibilities as a single parent weigh me down. It reminds me that by being happy I can make the world around me a happier place."

"Which is probably why you turn me on the way you do. You do make the world a happier place. You make your patients happier. You sure as hell make me happier."

"But Jake." She laid her hand on his arm. "I am not a flake. I promise you that. Underneath the clothes and the hair and my endless cups of chamomile tea, I'm as rock-solid as they come. A serious practitioner of medicine and a responsible single mother. And underneath all that military efficiency, you do care about your patients."

"I do. Very much."

"I'm thinking we need to be more tolerant of our different professional styles."

"We do. You practice solid medicine, Marci. Different from mine, sometimes, but solid."

"You do too, Jake. Absolutely solid."

"Glad that's settled." His eyes danced.

She smiled impishly. "Now what about...?"

"You mean the fact that I've lusted after you since the minute I laid eyes on you? That I would love to sit down over dinner and get to know you better? That I would give anything to strip you out of those outrageous clothes you love and have my wicked way with you? That I would like to spend lots of time with you and see where things might go? That? Come here, Marci."

He held out his arms and she melted into them, her lips seeking his. They came together gently this time, touching and caressing ever so tenderly, his lips barely grazing hers as she wound her arms around his neck. He put his hands around her waist and effortlessly lifted her onto his lap. "You're as light as a feather," he breathed against her lips. "Like lifting a pixie. You're adorable, you know that? Cute, sweet, and as sexy as they come."

"And you're the hottest soldier I've ever known."

He put his hand behind her head and held her close as his lips closed in on hers. The kiss started out gentle, but passion claimed them and he held her closer.

Marci's breath grew ragged as she ran her fingers down his shoulders and chest, reveling in the hard, warm muscles under his tee. She breathed in the fresh soap and shampoo and the unique essence that was Jake Pierce. Her nipples pebbled and grew even harder when he slipped his fingers down to her chest and caressed her breast, cupping it in his big hand with room to spare. He touched her greedily, like he couldn't get enough of her. Which worked. She couldn't get enough of him either.

Her fingers eagerly explored his chest and abs and she wondered what he looked like with his shirt off. Wondering if he was slick or had a chest full of hair. Wondered if he had a happy trail that went down to his cock, which was at the moment poking into her backside. Wondering if he was as wonderful to make love to as he was to kiss.

Wondering how soon she would find out.

They clung together for long minutes. He finally released her lips and she raised her head. "Still hot?" he asked with a smirk.

Marci stared at him. "You have dimples."

"Yeah, I do."

"Then you have to smile for me all the time."

"You want me to smile? Let me take you out on a date this weekend. That would really make me smile." His smile faded. "Or would that be a problem with us both working for Dr. Esquivel?"

"I don't see why. We're co-workers and neither of us is in a position of authority. Besides, Dr. Esquivel would rather have us dating than fighting any day."

Jake's smile returned. "Saturday night. Seven. Wear something, uh, colorful."

They both laughed. A date. Saturday night. With Jake Pierce. Wearing something colorful.

She had a feeling it would be the start of something wonderful.

LOVE IN THE TIME OF HANTAVIRUS

J.K. Winn

To my grandson, Nero, and my granddaughter, Olena, for being the lights of my life.

#

I'd like to acknowledge Boroughs Publishing Group, and especially Michelle, for all their support and encouragement.

Acoma, New Mexico
April 1993

As medical director of the Acoma/Laguna Indian Health Service Hospital in New Mexico, Marc knew the cost of a love that wouldn't last. So why the hell was he allowing himself to fall for one of the Harvard medical students on rotation through the hospital for a three-month training program? Here he was dating Amanda Fisher against his own medical advice, and in violation of hospital standards. His better judgment told him to break it off before he became too involved with the beautiful, strong-willed, exceptionally gifted woman, but reason was losing the war to his overwhelming attraction to her.

He extracted a file from the rack while thinking back to their coffee break earlier in the day. Amanda had looked especially flush although less animated than usual when she took her seat across from him in the cafeteria. He couldn't help noticing the pink on her cheeks, which was so appealing. "What are you up to today?"

Amanda smiled her serene Mona Lisa smile. "I heard from a friend at Harvard last night. There's an internship opening up at Mass General and they're seeking out a Harvard med student. She suggested I should apply."

Marc grunted. The last thing he wanted to consider at the moment was the imminent loss of Amanda from his life. They had only begun to grow closer. He would be losing her before he had a chance to get to know her well. "Sounds like an opportunity for you."

Amanda glanced down. "I hate to think about leaving here so soon." She raised her eyes to his. "But I will have to do my internship and residency first before I return to work for the Indian Health Service."

"Of course you will," he said, although he had his doubts she would ever return.

Most of the students who rotated through New Mexico expressed a desire to work there one day, but few followed through. He understood. While the beauty of the endless skies and miles of sunlit crimson and peach-colored mesas stunned them, the isolation and remoteness often proved prohibitive. Besides, big city hospitals and private practices sought these superior students and offered so much more than he and the IHS could ever give them.

While the thought of Amanda leaving the hospital in a month was unbearable, in a way, he looked forward to her return to Harvard to escape from his inner turmoil. There was too much to be done with the recent outbreak of hantavirus on the Pueblos to let her take up so much time in his mind. It had been distracting him from other more critical priorities.

Lost in thought, he jerked to alert when he heard the static of the overhead speaker announce his name. "Dr. Sanders to the ER. Repeat. Dr. Sanders to the ER."

Marc placed the patient chart back in the rack and scurried down the hospital hallway to the emergency room. He rushed up to the nurses' desk. "What's going on?"

Beverly Espinoza pulled him aside. "Looks like we might have another case of hanta on our hands. Just came in with the same symptoms as the last one. High fever, cough, shortness of breath, possible edema in his lungs." She handed Marc the patient chart. "He arrived a few minutes ago and I knew you would want to be notified. We've ordered labs, but they might take a few hours."

Marc glanced over the chart. "I'd like to see him."

"Sure, Amanda Fisher is with him in cubicle three."

Amanda? His Amanda? He had to stop himself from thinking about her that way.

Of course, Amanda would be the first one on staff in with the patient. Her dedication was impressive.

"Good. I'll return the chart once I have a chance to check on Mr..."

"Anthony Siaw."

"Thanks." Marc took a deep breath before entering the cubicle. Inside, a middle-aged man reclined on a gurney, his eyes closed, his breath shallow and rapid. Amanda stooped over him holding a stereoscope against his chest, her long, silky, wheat-colored hair cut off his view of the patient.

Marc cleared his throat and Amanda looked up. "Mind if I step in between you two for a moment?"

"Not at all." Amanda stepped aside, allowing him to approach the patient.

One look at Anthony Siaw and it was immediately obvious how sick he was. His sclera were lipstick red as though capillaries had burst in his eyes, and his skin had been bleached yellow, patchy and unhealthy. He gasped for air then coughed up phlegm.

"What's his fever?"

Amanda looked at her notes then up at him with those alluring amber-colored eyes. "One hundred and three."

"What's the plan?"

"I'm waiting for the respiratory therapist to intubate him. He needs to be on a vent. His oxygen levels are below ninety. The sooner we get him ventilated, the better."

Marc nodded. "Good. Then?"

"We're going to move him to the ICU. They're preparing a bed for him." Amanda met his eyes and he could see the trepidation in hers. Even as a fourth-year medical student, handling a complex case like this one was terrorizing. A tremor of her hand as she brushed hair away from her face further indicated her anxiety.

While the patient was Marc's first concern, he felt an obligation to put Amanda at ease. He had been a student once upon a time himself and he knew the stress of dealing with a critically ill patient for the first time. "You're doing a good job. Keep it up."

"Thanks, Marc...I mean Dr. Sanders," she stuttered. "I appreciate the boost of confidence."

"No problem. Do your best." He heard the coldness in his voice and adjusted it. Why was it when he felt most determined to be supportive, the fear still snaked through? "I assume the family is outside. Will you take the time to talk to them?"

"Sure."

"I'll see you later at rounds."

Before he left the ER, he checked in with the nurse to make certain the respiratory therapist was on his way over for the intubation. After confirming that he was, Marc took a look at another patient's chart. He signed off on an order, then handed the chart back to the nurse.

All the while thoughts of Amanda ran through his mind. What an incredible person she had turned out to be. She was always available at the hospital and willing to do whatever was required.

While the other students could often be found in the coffee room when they weren't busy, Amanda was usually somewhere on the floor. In the past he had found the medical students immature or less motivated by the menial tasks they had to perform, but Amanda was heads over and above the others in self-confidence and maturity.

That's one of the main things that drew him to her. He saw her as having the makings of an extremely capable doctor, but one with compassion and ambition. If the main sign of maturity was being able to hold two opposing things in your head simultaneously, then Amanda fit this definition.

She had been strong in the face of his conflicting feelings about her, and she had to be somewhat conflicted herself but never showed it. Against his will, she had won him over and it had become a daily internal struggle not to succumb to her appeal.

He went directly back to his office from the ICU to report the new patient to the Centers for Disease Control (CDC).

The state as well as the Feds would need to be informed about the case, as was protocol with this disease. Records were being compiled. Cases followed. While this was the first outbreak of Hanta Respiratory Syndrome in the United States, it had been found in other areas around the world, including China and Korea. The main vehicle of transmission to humans was deer mice through their blood, urine, or feces.

Insect bites or inhaling infected dust or dirt were the main vehicle of delivery to the human host. The origin of these three new local cases had yet to be revealed until an epidemiologist had a chance to research the recent outbreak.

A call had been placed to the University of New Mexico. Help was on the way.

***

An hour later, Marc checked in on Mr. Siaw and was surprised to see so many people congregated outside the ICU. He approached the group who stood close to the door and introduced himself to them.

A middle-aged woman stepped forward. "I'm Tony Siaw's daughter, Anna. And this is my mother, Constance."

Marc shook both women's hands.

"How is my father doing?" Anna asked.

Marc didn't wish to frighten the family, so he couched his words in as much kindness as he could muster. "He's sick, but he's in good hands. Our staff is top-notch and they are taking good care of him. We think we caught this disease early enough that we are hopeful we can reverse its progression."

Anna pointed at a man standing nearby dressed in slacks and a white shirt with a turquoise squash blossom necklace and turquoise bracelets. "This is our medicine man, Daniel Ortiz. We would like to have a few minutes with my father so Daniel can do his part to remove any old spells or bad vibes that might stand in the way of his recovery."

Normally only one or two family members were allowed in the ICU at any one time, but it wasn't unusual for the family to bring a shaman along for a healing ceremony. Since Marc knew how important this was to the patient and his family, he almost always agreed to the request unless the patient had a communicable disease, which wasn't the case here.

"Sure, but since we've only moved him into the ICU an hour ago, could you please keep it a bit short today so the nurses can get him set up? I will leave an order that all of you can return tomorrow if need be."

Constance grabbed his hand. "Thank you, doctor. Thank you. This means so much to us."

How could he ever turn away such gracious and grateful people? "Go ahead in and I'll check on Tony after you're done."

Marc went over to alert the nurses of what to expect. When he turned around, he saw Daniel standing on one side of Tony's bed, across from the family. He could hear the medicine man chanting. While he watched, Daniel passed prayer sticks over the stricken man and shook a rattle above his head. Marc had seen this done before, and the soothing and healing nature of the ceremony mesmerized him. If anything could help his patient out, in addition to modern medicine, it was this ritual.

When the group quietly completed the ceremony and left the room, Marc checked in on Tony and another seriously ill patient before leaving to prepare for afternoon rounds with the students.

***

After rounds, Marc had agreed to take Amanda to dinner at a Mexican restaurant in Grants, their go-to spot after work to catch a bite. Whenever he thought of spending time with her, his pulse would race and he would feel slightly flush. He tried his best to deny his feelings for her, but his body wouldn't cooperate with his brain. No matter what he told himself, he couldn't calm the anticipation. He wished this would all go away.

Aside from how twisted his insides were—all self-inflicted—he could see the pain his ambivalence was creating for her. While she always seemed genuinely pleased to see him, it didn't take long for him to find some way of alienating her. Whether it was by criticizing her work or letting her know he was too busy for her, he couldn't control the unconscious cruelty that he perpetuated upon her. The agony in her eyes at his biting remarks served to remind him of the power he had over her, and the pain he could inflict upon her. While this should have made him feel strong, it only made him feel wrong, and he was often left disappointed in himself afterward.

He couldn't help comparing his relationship with Amanda to the one he'd hoped to have with Susan Jaffe six years earlier. Susan had been a beautiful teacher on the nearby pueblo of Laguna, and had been his first major romantic interest after finishing medical school and moving to the area from the east coast. The moment he'd met her, he'd been drawn to her. They seemed to have so much in common. He'd been devasted when she chose to marry another teacher at the same school over him. The pain from that blow lasted a long time.

When he'd started to come back to life, he'd dated a couple of the nurses from the hospital, but the first one didn't work out well because she was still pining for another lover, and the second left the area before the relationship had a chance to develop into something stronger. A year later, when he received her wedding invitation and saw in that short time she'd found another doctor, gotten engaged, and was getting married he figured he'd throw in the towel.

Getting involved wasn't his forte.

Living far outside of an urban area had put a crimp in his ability to meet women. While he had considered pulling up stakes and moving into Albuquerque or another large city, the bond he had with his patients and staff, and the connection he felt with the local community, kept him anchored in Acoma. Moving still sometimes drifted through his mind, but never seemed to develop into anything real. His true alliance lay with the Pueblo people.

He ran a hand through his hair and thought about Amanda and their attempt at lovemaking a couple of nights earlier. They had left the hospital together and had an after-work drink in Grants, then proceeded to Marc's house in the foothills of Mt. Taylor. Once settled in on the sofa, they both reached for each other at the same moment.

Prior to this night, Marc had kept their physical contact to little more than a few kisses and a little fondling, but their hunger for each other had been slowly simmering to a boil over the past couple of weeks. He had known it was only a matter of time until it bubbled over.

Without a second thought, he sought Amanda's lips with his. The kisses were tentative at first, and grew deeper, wetter as they pressed up against one another. He rejoiced in the feeling of her in his arms, the taste of her lips, the scent of her. His hand traveled slowly down her torso and she responded with even greater urgency to his touch. Everything inside of him ached for her. He wanted her more than he had wanted anyone in a long, long time.

Then she pulled back and began to cough. This interruption allowed him to get a handle on himself. Was he really ready to open his heart to her when she would be leaving in less than two weeks? Surely, this would only cause both of them heartache, and he'd had enough of that to last him a lifetime.

He sat back, trying to get his body to stand down. Easier said than done when his erection was hard as steel. "Are you all right?"

She coughed again, cleared her throat, and sputtered, "Fine...fine."

"Let me get you a glass of water." He felt as though they had just experienced coitus interruptus in advance. He went over to the sink and turned on the faucet, knowing her coughing fit had probably saved them both a great deal of torment in the long run. As much as he desired her, his logical mind conceded to the futility of following through with that desire in light of their impeding long-term separation.

After she'd regained her breath, and him his composure, he drove her home, returning to another night of tortured sleep.

Now, Marc glanced down at his watch. Time for nightly rounds. He met the medical students in the hallway outside of room 106 and proceeded to lead them from patient to patient, room to room, detailing each presenting problem, the course of the pathology, and the measures being taken to address that particular affliction. He took questions when asked as part of a teachable experience for the students.

When the group finally reached the ICU and approached Anthony Siaw, he asked Amanda to describe what she had learned about the hantavirus to the other students. As usual, Amanda had done her homework.

She started by telling the other students that they didn't have to worry, the disease wasn't contagious and they wouldn't become infected by contact with the patient. She followed up by describing Anthony's symptoms, but her description quickly eroded into a coughing fit. With tissue in hand, she coughed for a good thirty seconds before another student handed her a water bottle and she took a sip. This quieted the cough and she continued with her understanding of the mechanisms of Hanta Pulmonary Syndrome, addressing the progression of the disease and the reason Siaw had been transferred to the ICU. She explained the early symptoms of HRS included fatigue, fever and muscle aches, sometimes followed by headaches, dizziness, chills, and abdominal problems, such as nausea, vomiting, diarrhea, and stomach pains.

If the disease progressed for about four to ten days after the initial phase, the late symptoms of HPS appeared. These included coughing and shortness of breath, with the sensation of tightness in the chest and difficulty breathing as the lungs filled with fluid. The students reacted with a mixture of shock and fear upon hearing about the severity of the late-stage symptoms, and one of the young men asked about the morbidity of the illness.

"About thirty-eight percent of all cases end in death," Amanda explained, with a strained look on her face.

"Wow," another student exclaimed. "Scary disease."

Everyone nodded their heads in stunned silence.

At their reaction, Marc took charge. "This is a deadly disease, but we're doing all we can for Mr. Siaw, and will continue to do our best to keep him alive. Okay, since this is our last patient today, let's disband and meet again tomorrow morning at nine. Have a good evening."

All the students said their goodnights and departed the room except for Amanda. She put Siaw's chart back in the stand and waited for Marc to finish his directions to the night nurse. When he was done, he escorted her into the hallway.

She turned to him. "Are we still on for dinner tonight?"

He studied her, noting how flushed she looked. Her eyes were bloodshot and watery. "Before we shore up our plans, I'd like to know more about that cough of yours."

She shook her long wheat-colored hair. "It's nothing more than a little congestion. Been going on for a few days."

He glanced down at the tissue in her hand and could swear he spied blood spatter. He really didn't want to be her doctor, but given her symptoms, he could do no less. He pointed at her hand. "Let me see that tissue."

"Yuck. No way. It's only a snot rag."

Silently, he held his hand out until she gave it to him. The blood was obvious, and he held back from scolding her as he began to worry about her condition. "This is more serious than you've been telling me. Have you had any insect bites?"

She frowned. "Not that I know of."

"Could you have come in contact with any dirt or dust?"

"To tell you the truth, I had to move into a new room in the house where I've been staying because Grandma moved into my old one. The new room had been closed off for some time and hadn't been cleaned awhile. Why?"

Concerned, he raised a brow. "You know as well as I do that hantavirus is transmitted through droppings mixed in dust. I assume you swept the floor and wiped down the counters and furniture."

She looked down at the ground for a long moment. "So you think I might be infected with the hantavirus?"

"We're going to find out. I'm taking you right over to the laboratory for a serology test. Antibodies of HPS in the blood are indicative of the disease. We should know more in a few hours. The quicker we know and get you help, the more likely you won't be one of the thirty-eight percent."

At his dire pronouncement, Amanda began to cough again.

Fearing the worst, Marc clasped her hand and led her directly to the lab where he asked the technician to draw her blood immediately for a diagnostic test. He had to know the truth as soon as possible. Once done, he checked her into the hospital, where she was given a regular room and placed on a respirator while he awaited the report. Even though she resisted his instructions, and begged him to let her go home, she was too weak to fight back with any real intention.

***

Three hours later, Marc entered Amanda's room to find her gasping for air. He read her pulse oximeter. Her numbers didn't look good. She flailed about, restless and feverish. He took a seat on the bed next to her. "I'm sorry to have to do this, but I'm afraid we're going to have to intubate you. I'm having you transferred to the ICU."

"Noooo," she groaned. "I'll be fine."

"No you won't without intervention. We will need to help you breathe."

Amanda reached out to him, but another coughing fit stopped her from grasping his arm. He elevated her head enough to help her catch her breath. "I'll be right back." He lowered her head and rushed over to the nurse's station. "We need to move the patient in room one-ten to the ICU stat. Also, please alert the respiratory therapist, we need another intubation."

"Is that Amanda, the medical student?" one of the nurses asked. "I was talking to her only about fifteen minutes ago and she said she was feeling much better."

Marc cocked a brow. "Wishful thinking. This damn thing is progressing much faster than I hoped. She's probably been feeling lousy for days and didn't say anything. All we need is a martyr around here. Just have her moved, stat."

He turned away from the bustle and noise of phone calls being made and nurses racing down the hall to Amanda's room.

Preparations needed to be made to move her. He had to ensure there was a bed available and awaiting a new occupant in the ICU.

***

Marc tore himself away an hour later after making certain that Amanda had been moved to the ICU, sedated, and started on a ventilator. Her breathing had deteriorated significantly over the few hours since she was admitted to the hospital and her fever rose rapidly. At over 104 degrees, her beautiful face was flushed scarlet red and her soft skin felt hot and dry to the touch. He prayed the medication would reduce her inflammation and make her more comfortable.

He'd quit her side long enough to catch a bite to eat and clean up before returning to her room to sit in a chair alongside her bed. Her condition had stabilized, but he was reluctant to leave. About one in the morning he knew if he didn't lie down and get at least a few hours' sleep he wouldn't do her or any of his other patients any good. His home was close to the hospital, and he left strict orders to the staff to wake him immediately if anything changed. The nurses nodded, understanding the importance of his demands.

Once home he was restless. He tried to sleep but couldn't quite quiet himself down and spent much of what was left of the night on edge waiting for the phone to ring. When it didn't by four in the morning, he finally dozed off to have a nightmare where Amanda didn't recover and he saw himself standing at her grave, crying. He awoke in a sweat, stunned and worried.

He got back to the hospital around six-thirty. A hospital-wide page stopped him before he could even make it to Amanda's room. "Dr. Marc Sanders to the ICU." He bolted down the hallway, heart in his throat, sure he'd find Amanda coding. Instead, he saw nurses and the doctor on duty around Anthony Siaw's bed, working on getting his heart to re-start. After the third go with the defibrillator, Marc shook his head and told the doctor to call time of death.

This was their first fatality: their first victim who succumbed to the hantavirus in Acoma. Someone turned off the monitors, and a blanket of sorrow fell over the room. Everyone stood around looking lost and bereft. No one made a move for the longest time.

When Marc felt they'd had enough to process what had happened, he cleared his throat. "I know how disheartening this is, especially for those of you who knew Anthony and his family well, but we can honor Anthony by doing what needs to be done to treat our other patients. This is a sad moment for all of us, but we have to use this to motivate us to do our best to save other lives. Take a minute, then let's get back to work."

One by one the nurses moved from Anthony's side and one of them murmured that she'd make the requisite calls to the morgue and his family. No one anticipated the hours ahead with any enthusiasm, but they all recognized the necessity of taking care of their patients.

Marc watched the progression of his staff as they went from close to comatose from the shock of losing Anthony back into action. He sighed a breath of relief. He had to be grateful for the amazing people who worked with him in Acoma. Residents and outsiders alike, they were dedicated professionals with a true sense of purpose.

A nurse tapped him on the shoulder. "The patient in the room next door wants to speak with you."

He thanked the nurse and went where he intended to go when he got to the hospital: Amanda's room. The moment she saw him, she reached out for him. He took her hand as he sat beside her bed noting her color was still off, and her breathing was ragged. "I hope you're feeling better this morning."

Amanda looked at him through half-shut eyes and nodded, but he saw how she held her body, and the fear was emanating off her. He couldn't show how frightened he was for her, and he wrapped his professional cloak around him to keep his feelings hidden.

"Don't be afraid," he said, reaching for her chart. He checked out her oxygen levels, which were lower than they had been earlier. "Let's turn up that oxygen for a while to see if that makes you feel better."

The corners of her mouth turned up ever so slightly in what he interpreted as a smile. She was as weak as a day-old kitten and equally as helpless. Her vulnerability touched a nerve in him. He wanted desperately to do anything he could to make her better, but there was nothing more that he could do beyond comfort measures. No medical intervention aside from keeping her hydrated, nourished, and trying to maintain her oxygen levels would be of any use at the moment.

Amanda struggled to say something, although it was impossible with the vent in place. He leaned over and told her, "Don't try to talk. Write in my hand." He held up his palm for her to trace letters in.

She pointed at the wall that separated her from Anthony Siaw's room.

He wanted to shield her from the heartbreaking news, but being as smart as she was, he knew she'd figure things out soon enough. "I'm afraid he didn't make it."

Even with the sedative in her system, her eyes opened wide. Then she closed them. A tear trailed down her cheek and he wiped it away with his thumb.

"Sorry to have to be the bearer of bad news. But we're doing all we can to make sure you have a different outcome."

He heard a footstep behind him and turned to see the hospital administrator, Emily Boling, striding over to Amanda's bed.

"Mind if I look at that chart?" Emily asked, holding out a hand. "I'd like to see how our patient is doing."

He handed her Amanda's chart, wondering about her interest. He'd never seen Emily take an active concern in any of his patients except to determine how much the treatment would cost and when a patient needed to be discharged. This was unusual, and intrusive.

Emily leafed through the pages, then handed him back the chart. "Can you tear yourself away for a few minutes because I'd like to speak to you in the hallway."

Marc looked at Amanda and smiled. Whatever Emily wanted, he needed to make sure Amanda was reassured. "Okay, I'll be right out." He turned back to Amanda. "Don't worry, I'll be back right away. Get some rest."

Outside her room, Emily turned to face Marc, and he made a motion to walk down the hall so Amanda and the nurses didn't hear whatever Emily had to say. "I have bad news for you. Your patient is not native born and cannot be treated in our facility."

"But," Marc was fuming, "she's a student training at this hospital and she's in critical condition. There's no way we could or should discharge her now."

Emily placed hands on hips. "She can be transferred to UNM hospital or Presbyterian in Albuquerque. We can order a Medivac if needed."

Marc couldn't believe his ears. The thought of transferring Amanda, in her current condition, to another hospital, especially one that hadn't treated many hanta cases, would be murder. "There's no way that's going to happen. She'd never make it to Albuquerque." He leaned in and Emily looked surprised. "You're worried about money, yet you'll pay for a Medivac, and you'd risk the life of a patient. If her health is compromised or, worse, she doesn't make it, are you willing to take on the lawsuit that is sure to follow? Think again. And don't forget, as medical director, I have to sign off on the transfer of a patient. Medivac won't transport someone without medical approval, which you don't have. I'm sure you can find resources to pay for her stay."

Emily gnawed at her lip. "Do you have any idea what it will cost to keep her here on the ICU? We really don't have the money to foot the bill."

"You find a way to make it work and I'll do my best to have her off the vent and moved out of the ICU as quickly as possible."

Emily raised a skeptical brow. "I'm no doctor, but I can see the condition she's in."

"Exactly my point. You do what you have to on your end, and I'll do what I have to on mine, including footing the bill."

Emily gasped. "She must mean a lot to you for you to commit yourself to that kind of expense. I know you're a doctor, but you work here, not in LA. You'll be paying that bill off for some time to come."

Marc drew a deep breath. Amanda meant the world to him and he wasn't going to let her die to spare the hospital the expense of keeping her. "I'll figure it out."

"Okay," Emily muttered. "I'll look into our alternatives funding wise, but be advised, if we have to make other financial arrangements, I know where to send the bill." Emily rotated on her heels and strode down the hall toward the administrative office.

Marc watched her go, and considered taking his anger out against the wall. Even if he didn't feel the way he did about Amanda, he would've fought for her. What kind of idiot would move a patient from the ICU? He didn't have the kind of money to cover a long hospital stay, but he had a house he could sell, and he would if that's what it took to keep Amanda under his care.

As he turned to head back to Amanda, he saw nurses rushing into her room. He ran down the hall, and called out, "What's going on?"

The charge nurse stared up at him with a strained expression. "Amanda started gasping for air. We'd like to increase her oxygen levels some more."

Worried, Marc took his stereoscope to Amanda's chest, then looked at her heart monitor and pulse oximeter. "Let's double the dose. Her levels are too low and she's wheezing. She's not getting enough air. Also, call the respiratory therapist. Let's make sure there isn't any obstruction in the endotracheal tube."

"Okay, doc. Will do." Not quite a professional response, but not unusual for Barbara Mason, the charge nurse. Barbara was still a hippie at heart who gravitated toward work in areas where her expertise was needed most. She was good at her job and he knew he could trust her. She went to work following his orders.

Marc stood back and watched the activity around Amanda, knowing her condition was deteriorating, and real fear gripped his chest. There was nothing more that he could do than was already being done, but watching her suffering made him want to scream. He never wanted to lose any patient, but this was Amanda, and he had to find some way to make her better. He'd never felt quite so helpless.

After all the nurses had cleared out of the room, he approached Amanda again. She looked up at him through half-lidded eyes, wearing an expression of pure gratitude. She took his hand and squeezed it.

Her gesture hit its target and pierced his heart. The heart that he had been hardening against her not long before. He wanted to take her into his arms, but he had to stay strong in the face of her condition. Her health was his first concern. Their hearts was next.

At the nurses' station, he caught up with Barbara Mason. "Let me know the minute Amanda Fisher's condition changes. Don't hesitate to call me immediately if you notice anything."

Barbara sent him a knowing look. "No problem, doc."

He knew she'd cottoned on to how he felt about Amanda, and he didn't care. For years he'd kept his emotions in check and had been the picture of professionalism at work. He was a flesh-and-blood man with needs, and right now, a heart that stuttered at the thought of losing Amanda.

He nodded and left to take care of his other patients so he could return to Amanda's side. He had just finished up with a kidney patient who had become jaundiced and needed dialysis right away, when he heard the call from Barbara Mason to come to the ICU. He turned the patient over to the nurse who was arranging a ride to the closest dialysis unit in Gallup and tore off toward the unit.

Barbara met him outside Amanda's door. "She's not doing well. Her fever has spiked to one hundred five degrees. She's less aware of her surroundings and is restless enough to pull out her IV tube. What do you want us to do?"

"Come with me." He led her into Amanda's room. Not surprisingly, Amanda looked at him through clouded eyes. She flailed her arms and kicked at her covers. He took her hand and for a second she focused on him. Then her eyes floated off to the corner of the room and he could no longer gain her attention.

He pulled Barbara aside. If he didn't take a risk with Amanda's treatment, he'd lose her, and he wasn't going to let that happen. "Best to increase her sedation for now and let her rest. She'll never recover this way. I'll write an order for a stronger sedative. Start it as soon as possible."

Barbara nodded. "No problem. But aren't you worried about suppressing her breathing?"

Of course he was, but without a vaccine or drugs that would cure the underlying virus, he had to take whatever strong measures he had to give Amanda a chance.

"We'll need to monitor her closely. Give her the lowest dose we can start with to quiet her without suppressing her oxygen levels. We'll be walking a fine line, but I trust you to watch this and let me know if we need to make any changes. I'll be in on a regular basis, but you're the front line. I know you can do this."

Barbara blanched. "Okay, doc, I'll do my best, but I can't make believe that this isn't scaring the hell out of me."

He patted her on the shoulder. "You're a damn good nurse and I'm glad you're working with me. But I want you to know, if anything should happen, I'll be the one responsible. I promise you that."

Her face looked drawn. "It's not the responsibility that concerns me, it's the idea that we all will have to live with the consequences. Write the order. I'm ready."

"Thanks. I couldn't do this without you." He made the note in Amanda's chart and left her room weighted down by the situation he found himself in and the decision he had to make.

Marc ordered a couple of pizzas delivered to the hospital and shared with the nurses. He ate at Amanda's bedside, listening to her every breath. Even exhausted, he could barely close his eyes for fear he'd fall asleep and not be there for her.

The ramifications of what could happen to Amanda were too overwhelming to contemplate. She'd found her way into his heart, and now he might lose her to a disease he had no cure for.

He didn't mean to, but he drifted off and had disturbing jumbled dreams of being in the hospital and fighting through a thick cloud of smoke to reach Amanda. Obstacles kept getting in his way and he had to push aside Emily Boling, who held onto his lab coattails while a huge gale wind blew him in the opposite direction. The closer he came to Amanda's bed, the farther he found himself from her. He fought hard to move toward her, but the more effort he put into it, the farther he was pushed back. Frustration and rage consumed him along with a feeling of total helplessness.

Sounds from the hallway woke him from his stupor, and he shook his head to clear the groggy as the last of the dream left him. He couldn't shake off the anger he felt at not being able to do more for Amanda. The closer he came to helping her, the further he found himself from success, and any chance of them finding a way to be together.

He got up to use the bathroom. The halls were deserted, but the machines in all the patients' rooms beeped and whirred, making an odd symphony of noises while helping the patients in the ICU. After he'd washed his face, he stared at himself in the mirror and asked his reflection, "What more can I do?"

On his way back to Amanda's room, Barbara stopped him at the nurses' station, holding Amanda's chart. "I know you saw this, but she's almost comatose. Her temp has decreased by half a degree, but otherwise she's hanging in there. She's fighting, doc."

He handed back the chart and went into Amanda's room to resume his vigil by her side. After a while, he took his stereoscope and leaned over to listen to her breathing, which was still ragged and uneven. Every breath she took sounded like a death rattle. Her body heaved with the effort. He lowered himself into his chair and began talking to her.

"You probably can't hear me, but I want you to know that I'm here, and I'm not going anywhere. Fight, Amanda. Fight and come back to me."

She didn't respond verbally, but the hand lying on the side of the bed closest to him shifted ever so slightly.

An hour later, nothing had changed and it was nearly one-thirty in the morning. He had another busy day tomorrow. Before he dragged himself home to sleep, he gave instructions to the nurses to call him immediately if anything changed. Once home, he shed his clothes and left them on the floor, collapsed onto the bed, and drifted off to sleep with thoughts of Amanda weighing on his mind.

***

Marc woke at five a.m. surprised he had slept that long. As soon as he took a shower and poured a cup of coffee down his throat, he drove his pickup over to the hospital. Inside the hospital was like a morgue. He winced at his own analogy and headed straight for the ICU.

Amanda slept fitfully, still sedated. Her fever had dropped a couple degrees, but that was expected in the morning. Otherwise, her breathing still sounded labored. He knew the course of the disease, and now blood had seeped out of her capillaries and into her lungs. If the fluid filled her lungs, it would be impossible for her to breathe on her own. He prayed with all his heart that he could remove her from the respirator by later that day or the next morning, but it didn't look good. Unless she made a major turnaround within the next twenty-four hours, he feared she would succumb.

He brushed the hair off her face. Her lovely face. How he wanted to take her in his arms and comfort her, but given her condition, it was out of the question, and might be forever if she didn't improve. He ached with the thought of losing her. She looked so vulnerable, so tiny, dwarfed by the equipment surrounding her that was keeping her alive. He wished he could do more. Wished he had loved her more while he had the opportunity. All his life he'd waited for a love like this, and caution had prevented him from having what they both had wanted.

He wished he would be given a second chance.

Would fate be that kind?

He did all he could to make her comfortable, wiping her face and arms with a wet rag, drying her off and covering her. When he glanced over, the nurses were watching him intently. He had taken over their job and they didn't know what to make of it.

At the nurses' station, he thanked them for their diligence, then left to do rounds. He could feel their eyes on him as he walked out of the ICU.

***

Later, after meeting with the medical students and going over procedure and protocol with them, he was heading back to the ICU when he heard the intercom call for him. He jogged the rest of the way to the ICU, his heart thundering in his ears, but slowed when he saw a well-dressed couple who looked like typical New Englanders. He should know. He was raised in Connecticut. The woman had the same wheat-colored hair as Amanda so it didn't surprise him when she stepped in front of him and extended a hand.

"Dr. Sanders?" she asked, shaking his hand. "I'm Amanda's mother, Kim, and this is her father, Mike."

Marc shook Mike's hand. "I'm glad you're here."

"It's quite a shock to see our beautiful, animated daughter in this condition," Kim said. "Can you tell us what's happening? Help us understand what's going on with her."

Marc asked them to take a seat and he gave them an overview of the illness and his understanding of what had contaminated her. He conveyed the progression of the disease but refrained from worrying them with the prognosis. As a virus that could convert to a hemorrhagic fever, causing bleeding into the lungs, and end in such a high percentage of deaths, he knew no good would come from scaring them more than they were. They'd traveled over two thousand miles to see their beloved child fighting for her life. There was no reason to say more unless Amanda took a fatal turn. Only then would he be forced to tell them the worst.

Kim paled while he spoke. When he finished, Mike reached for her hand. "It's okay, honey, we'll do what Emily Boling suggested and move her to a hospital in Albuquerque. They are more equipped to handle her."

At that, Marc's heart stopped. What a conniving witch. How dare she usurp him, insert herself into treatment issues, and prey on these poor people, "I apologize that Ms. Boling had that conversation with you, particularly since moving Amanda will not be in her best medical interests."

Kim had tears in her eyes when she looked up at him. "Why's that? Wouldn't a big city hospital have more resources than you do?"

"In general, yes. But they haven't had many cases of HPS and I'm afraid they don't know as much as we do about treating it. There are not as many problems with deer mice in the big city so we're the front line for this disease. We've been forced to become experts on it quickly."

He drew a breath while observing the flicker of doubt in her eyes, and he knew he had to be blunt to make her understand what was best for her daughter. "I'm afraid in Amanda's present state, moving her could be dangerous, maybe even deadly. We have her stabilized at the moment. That's not to say she's improving, but her condition is no longer deteriorating like it was when she was first admitted. I'd hate to throw off her equilibrium."

Mike put his arm around Kim's shoulder. "We've never seen her like this. She's in dreadful condition. Wouldn't anything be better than this 'equilibrium' as you call it?"

Marc shook his head. "If there were alternate treatments, we'd have them. There's nothing else any medical facility can do for her. As her doctor, I advise strongly against moving her. The little strength she has while fighting the disease will be compromised by any trip out of ICU, especially one as taxing as being taken to Albuquerque."

What he wanted to say, but knew it would skew the way they viewed his ability to remain professional, was that he loved their daughter and would fight with all his knowledge and strength to keep her from dying, to make her well and whole again.

Kim nodded. "We want to visit with Amanda now for as long as you'll let us. After we have time with her, we'll process what you've said. Thank you for taking the time."

Marc led them through the ICU doors onto the unit. "I'll let the staff know that you're from out of town and should be allowed to visit with Amanda as long as possible. Please know that we're keeping her sedated and she may not be actively responsive, but she'll know you're there."

Mike shook his hand. "We appreciate that."

***

Later that afternoon, Marc circled back to the ICU, but bumped into Emily Boling leaving the unit.

"Can I speak with you for a moment?" Emily asked.

Suspicious of her motivation, he nodded. "Sure, but only a moment. I'm here to look in on my patients."

"Like Amanda?"

"She's certainly one of them. Why?"

Emily frowned and Marc wanted to walk away from this soulless person who saw numbers, not people.

"I made sure the matter was taken out of your hands. As her closest relatives, her parents have the final say regarding her treatment. I'm certain they're going to move Amanda to Albuquerque."

Her smug satisfaction made Marc want to scream. Instead he gave her a small smile and said, "You can't truly believe they'll take the word of a number cruncher over that of the hospital's medical director. I'm looking out for Amanda's survival, and you're looking out for a fiscal advantage. Remember, Emily, my say-so is the one that matters."

Before he had to hear one more of her arguments in that irritating voice of hers, he turned and walked into the ICU.

He went straight to the nurses' station to speak with Barbara Mason about Amanda. After consulting with Barbara, he wrote an order in Amanda's chart that he would be reducing the oxygen levels to test out her responsiveness.

Standing at Amanda's side, he listened to her breathing, palpated her abdomen, and did a general exam. Damn. While Amanda's breathing didn't seem any less labored than the day before, even with the vent doing most of the work, she was a shadow of her bright, charming self, and his insides clenched at the prospect of the outcome.

He had to find out if the sedation was suppressing her body's ability to breathe on its own, but the idea that it could seemed ludicrous. He knew he had to try to give her the chance to recuperate, doing this seemed so drastic. Medically, he knew it was sound thinking, but the man who loved Amanda did not want to experiment with her well-being.

On the way out of the ICU, he ran into Amanda's folks, who were probably waiting to be told when they could go back in and spend more time with her.

Mike stood when he spotted Marc. "We've been talking things over."

Noting the expression on Mike's face, Marc didn't feel too hopeful. "What have you decided?"

Kim stood beside her husband. "We considered what Ms. Boling has to say…"

Marc could feel the boom lowering. "And?"

"But we are convinced Amanda needs to stay put," Mike said. "We want to keep her here."

Relief rushed through Marc's body, making his limbs weak. "Good. Have you conveyed your wishes to Ms. Boling?"

"Yes, we did," Kim said.

Mike shook his hand. "Thanks, doc. We know you're doing all you can for our daughter."

Marc only wished he could do more.

***

Later, when Marc returned to the ICU and Amanda's side, he placed a syringe in her wrist to extract blood from her radial artery, which would give him a direct measure of the oxygen levels in the blood. She groaned, indicating she'd become more alert. At the same time he drew the blood, he kept his eye on the oxygen tracing on the heart rate monitor, which would tell him if she was receiving enough oxygen.

Slowly, he lowered the dial on the ventilator to reduce its oxygen flow. When he had reduced the oxygen by slightly under fifty percent, her levels had dropped so precipitously that he rushed to raise them, but not all the way.

Fantastic. She could take a little less oxygen. She was growing stronger. A good sign.

He decided to reduce the level of her sedation a bit more to encourage her to recover. The more she was able to breathe on her own, the more likely she would recover.

He made a final note in the chart and left the ICU.

***

When Marc returned that evening, Amanda watched him through partially open eyes. The sedative had been decreased enough for her to be partially conscious. Time to test out her response to lowering the oxygen even more.

He smiled at her as he took her hand. "I'm going to lower your oxygen level a little more. Squeeze my hand to let me know if you understand me."

Amanda gave his hand a squeeze of acknowledgment.

"Good. Now, squeeze if it becomes difficult to breathe. I'm starting slowly by reducing the levels a little bit at a time." He turned the dial down ever so slightly and consulted the heart monitor. Levels looked good.

"Okay. A little more." He continued this exercise, until he had lowered her oxygen to the lowest possible setting. Suddenly, he felt a squeeze. "I'm raising the levels now."

He raised the level slightly and she loosened her grip. Another good sign. To confirm oxygen levels he took blood from the artery. "Better?"

She nodded slowly.

"Great. We'll keep the levels here for a while, but we'll try another round in the morning." He felt hopeful for the first time since admitting her to the hospital. "You're young, healthy, and determined." He winked, and she gave his hand a squeeze. "You're responding well. Let's try to get you off this vent soon."

Amanda indicated her assent with a limp thumbs-up.

After he finished his work, he went back to her room and sat with her again until about one in the morning. Before he went home to catch a few hours' sleep, he went to the nurses' station and the charge nurse said, "I know. Call you if anything changes." She smiled, and he nodded.

He couldn't hide how he felt about Amanda if he tried, and he had no intention of trying.

***

Marc slept fitfully that night. He must have been up and down a half dozen times, unable to get Amanda out of his mind.

As much as he had convinced himself it was better to let her go before her illness, knowing he could lose her—really lose her— unleashed the banked fire he'd been carrying around inside of him.

He hated to watch her suffer, and feelings he didn't know he was capable of enveloped him. Protective and territorial had never been part of his character. But when it came to Amanda, he didn't want anyone else to touch her, comfort her, and he would never allow her to be taken away from Acoma.

***

He'd gotten up early and was out of the house by six. As he walked into the ICU, he noticed the nurses huddled near Amanda's room. He made his way to them, and they parted so he could get to her doorway. When he saw two orderlies preparing to move Amanda onto a gurney, his blood ran hot in his veins.

"What's going on here? This is my patient and I never gave anyone orders to move her."

One of the orderlies pulled out a sheet of paper. "Emily Boling in administration ordered a Medivac to move this patient."

Marc didn't even bother to look at the form. "Stop what you're doing immediately. As the hospital's medical director, I order you to stop what you're doing right now."

"Sorry, boss, but we didn't know, and, you know...we didn't want to get in trouble with administration," the other orderly said.

"You won't," Marc told them. "Leave. I'll handle this."

He could see the flicker of gratitude in Amanda's eyes.

The orderlies looked at each other. "Okay, boss. If you need us, let us know."

Marc knew these men needed their jobs. They both lived on the pueblo and had families to feed. "You're covered. Promise."

Marc watched the two men go, then turned back to Amanda. "You're almost off the vent. You're doing so much better. Don't worry about going anywhere. I won't let that happen." Amanda gave his hand a squeeze. "Now we'll do as planned and see if we can lower the oxygen enough to remove you from this vent later today."

With trepidation, he again turned down the flow of oxygen to its lowest level. He could hear Amanda gasp for air and was about to raise the level, but she stopped him with a hand on his arm. What an incredibly brave woman she was, and clearly an inspiration as he found his inner alpha.

Her heart monitor showed her oxygen levels were low, but not excessively so. "Okay, we'll try this, but if you have any problems breathing, I want to know right away. Understood?"

She sent him a faint smile and gave him another pat on the arm.

He stayed by her side for the better part of an hour listening to her breathing and monitoring the oximeter. She continued to struggle for air for a number of minutes, but gradually her respiration slowed to a normal pace.

When he felt satisfied she was stable, he said, "I have some business to tend to this morning. I'm going to give you a little bit more time before we attempt to remove the vent. We don't want to be forced to put it back in. Rest now and I'll return in a bit to see how you're doing."

Again, she tried to smile. Her tenacity amazed him. The more he came to know her, the more he admired her, and the more certain he was that she was "the one."

He informed the head nurse of what he had done and made a notation in the chart. Then he took a deep breath and marched out of the ICU, headed directly for the administrative office.

Inside, he announced to the secretary that he wanted to meet with Emily Boling immediately. The woman informed him that Emily had only arrived a couple minutes earlier, but she would let her know he was waiting.

Rather than give Emily warning, he rushed past the secretary and went straight into Emily's office. She was seated at her desk and jerked her head up as he entered.

"What are you doing here?" she asked, looking shocked at his unannounced presence.

"The real question is what are you doing with my patient." He stepped up to the desk, towering over her. "How dare you try to circumvent hospital procedures and my orders. I had to stop two orderlies from moving my patient to Albuquerque after I had informed you she couldn't be moved without my authorization."

Emily sprung from her chair and faced him. "I was only doing what would be in the best interest of this hospital. I told you we couldn't afford to keep this patient. We're tapped out."

"And I told you I would move this patient out of the ICU as soon as possible, but you're trying to sabotage her treatment in an underhanded and irresponsible way."

"I had no choice."

"Bullshit," he growled. "You could have allowed me the time to work this out. You didn't need to go behind my back to move her without my permission."

She placed her hands on her hips. "I was only doing my job."

"That is if your job includes medical director. But since it doesn't, you decided to take things into your own hands and do what you thought was good for the bottom line rather than what was medically indicated for the patient, and, as I told you, the ultimate financial well-being of the hospital."

"But I was protecting IHS resources."

"By threatening the life of a patient and creating a potential legal nightmare for the IHS. I doubt they'll support you when the medical and legal facts are laid out." He ran his hand through his hair. "As of now, I forbid you from any other intervention with this patient or any other patient in this hospital. You're going to turn in your resignation and step down. FYI, I'll be dealing with the regional administrator in Albuquerque. If you don't get out of here pronto, I'll file a report with Washington."

Emily blanched. She tried to speak but only stuttered.

He raised a hand. "I've heard enough from you for this lifetime." He turned on his heels and strode out of her soon-to-be ex-office, not even glancing back when she regained her voice and called after him.

***

Marc went straight back to Amanda's room. When he arrived, she was resting comfortably and her oxygen levels were within the low-normal range. When the level moved a little higher, he'd remove the vent. In the meantime, he lowered himself into the chair alongside her bed and waited for her to wake.

He was busy studying her lovely features when her eyes fluttered open. For a second she looked stunned, but quickly focused on him.

"Good morning, beautiful," he said and took her hand in his. "Your oxygen level is looking better. I think we'll be removing the vent any time now."

Her eyes opened wide and she squeezed his hand. He shifted his weight to lower himself to the edge of her bed. He took her hand in his. "I know how difficult I've been these last few weeks and I truly regret my behavior. I've been so afraid of losing you once you moved back to Boston and went on with your busy life that I did everything in my power to push you away even when I wanted with all my heart to hold onto you."

Her amber eyes filled with tears. How could he have done so much damage to her when what he really wanted to do was make her life better?

"I'm so sorry. I know I caused you pain."

She struggled to say something but couldn't speak.

He opened his palm to her. "Can you write it? We'll have plenty of time to talk once I extubate you."

She lay quiet for a long moment, as though she needed to think through what she wanted to say, then scratched out I Love You onto his hand.

He watched as she drew out the words and lingered over the sensation once she was through. Then he took her hand, turned it palm side up, and wrote with his finger, I Love You Too.

And although they were stymied by the machine from holding one another, the look they exchanged said it all. They would seal their love with a kiss once the vent was removed.

***

Later that afternoon, Amanda's oxygen level had improved enough for Marc to remove the ventilator. He recruited Barbara Mason to help him with the procedure. Barbara gave Amanda a small dose of muscle relaxant to quiet her, but not knock her out, then Barbara stood to the side while Marc slowly removed the vent.

While it was always easier to extract the endotracheal tube than insert it, the withdrawal still needed to be done carefully to avoid damage to the trachea or the throat.

When Amanda began to choke, he had to stop and let her catch her breath.

"Sorry, baby."

She blinked twice, then reached out and touched his hand.

He nodded and squeezed her hand before finishing the job.

Once the ventilator was out, Amanda took a breath and coughed repeatedly while massaging her own throat. He checked the oximeter and breathed a mental sigh of relief. The procedure had gone smoother than he had anticipated, and much of that had to do with Amanda herself.

With a scratchy, weak voice, Amanda whispered, "Thank you, Marc."

At hearing her voice, he lit up.

***

While Marc made notes in Amanda's chart, Barbara sidled up to him. He glanced up at her and she had the wide grin on her face of someone who had pulled off a major coup. "What's going on?"

She pulled up a chair alongside him and leaned in close enough so their conversation couldn't be overheard. "I caught wind of the fact that you've had some…what should I call it…disagreements with Emily Boling."

Marc cocked a brow. "Is there anything sacred around here?"

Barbara chuckled. "Not much."

"And?" he asked.

"I overheard Emily's secretary tell one of the nurses that Emily has requested a transfer to another hospital."

Marc sat back, letting the relief run through him. He had made his point. She would no longer be around to create the kind of problems he had with her. Whether he let her boss know of her behavior was a matter he'd contemplate later. He didn't want to be passing along a problem to another hospital.

"Is that so? I hope she finds what she's looking for."

Barbara gave him a knowing look. "Me too, Marc. Me too."

***

Later, after Marc had a chance to complete a number of tasks he had put on hold, he sat at the edge of Amanda's bed while the nurses bathed Amanda and changed her hospital gown. She had been asleep since he withdrew the vent, but she roused when he touched her face.

"I know you're weak and probably don't feel like talking, but I never finished what I was saying earlier. I don't want you to leave this hospital without me letting you know how much you mean to me."

Marc could barely go on. His mind told him it was too late to fix what he had broken. That even though she'd told him she loved him, she didn't necessarily want the same things he did. But he couldn't live with the regret he'd feel if he didn't share what he felt before it was too late. He took a deep breath to fortify himself.

"I love you, Amanda, and I'd like to see where this relationship will lead. If you still want me, I'm ready to do what's necessary to have a future with you. I'm tired of holding back. I want to be with you and to make this work."

Amanda's large, luminous eyes fixed on him. She tried to speak, but not much came out. She still sounded slightly breathless. Then she cleared her throat a couple times and said in a scratchy voice, "I know…" She stopped to cough, then reached out her hand to take his. "I know you've been with me this whole time in the ICU. And I know it hasn't been easy for you, but you took care of me."

Marc smiled. "Always."

Amanda smiled. "No." She cleared her throat once more. "I know you fought to keep me alive. Since actions speak louder than words, you showed me how much I mean to you in spite of anything you said or did prior to my illness."

Tears sprang into her eyes, and with his thumb, he wiped away an errant drop that drifted down her cheek.

She took his hand to her lips and kissed it. "If I'm well enough, I'll be leaving for Boston in a little over a week. What do you think we can we do about that?"

Time to share. "I decided to apply for a leave of absence from the IHS for one year to move to Boston. I have a friend from med school who lives there, and he's told me repeatedly that I can come work with him at any time. I plan to find us a house in the city where we can live together."

Amanda gasped. "Really?"

Hell yeah. In his head he'd pictured the two of them remaining in Boston until she finished her internship and could arrange a transfer to the University of New Mexico for her residency. That way they could return to Acoma and be within an hour's drive either way. Since it seemed premature to mention it now, he planned to bring it up once they were securely hunkered down together in Boston.

Amanda tried to sit up, but she couldn't do it on her own so Marc put a hand behind her back and levered her to sitting with his support. Once up, she threw her arms around him and held him closely. "I knew you cared about me, but I had no idea I meant enough for you to plan a future with me."

He could feel the dampness of her tears on his shirt. "Baby." He squeezed her gently. "I want more than anything to share my future with you." He held on, never wanting to let her go. He could feel her fatigue, and gently lowered her down to the bed.

She glanced at something behind him at the same time he felt a tap on his shoulder. He turned to see Barbara Mason.

"Amanda's parents arrived and are waiting to see her."

"Okay," he said. "I'm almost finished here."

Barbara checked Amanda's vitals, then left to fetch her parents.

Marc rose slowly, looking down at Amanda. "Sounds like you have company, but I'll be back in a bit to talk more about our plans."

She took his hand one more time. "Don't worry. I'm not going anywhere…without you."

He bent over her, and they sealed their love with the long-awaited kiss.

HEART MURMUR
Elle Wright

To all the medical professionals and mental health professionals who have sacrificed their well-being during this crisis—thank you. We are forever indebted to you.

One

Brett stretched out on the stainless-steel table and prayed no one would find him for fifteen minutes. Twenty if he was really lucky. He was past exhausted, and knew this operating room was free for about a half hour because he was scheduled to perform the next surgery: a ruptured spleen that should've been repaired hours ago. The ED was backed up to the point of overflowing. A 6.5 earthquake had hit LA at 8:15 this morning, smack-dab in the middle of rush hour. Freeways had buckled, buildings had collapsed, and the steady stream of patients had been unrelenting for the past fourteen hours.

His first surgery had started at 7:00 that morning. Scheduled. When he'd gotten to the hospital, the world was quiet and his day was planned. He'd had two consults later that morning, then lunch with his brother, and after he was expected in his office where he had a full afternoon of patients. He'd been in the middle of a bowel resection when the earthquake hit. The building shook mercilessly for nearly a minute. The good news: no structural damage, and they hadn't lost power. The bad news: everything else.

"Brett, wake up." He knew that voice. She'd said those words to him five thousand times if she'd said them once. "Brett." She shook his shoulder.

"Go away, Ange."

"You have a surgery in here in ten minutes."

Shit. He lifted his phone from beside his head to see he'd actually slept for seventeen minutes. A miracle.

He swung his legs over the side of the operating table and straightened. Stretching his arms behind his back, he locked his fingers together, then leaned forward and pushed his arms in the air. Angie stood silent. Waiting. For what, he could only imagine. A half a minute later the surgical staff was pulling out the disinfectants before bringing in the trays and supplies. He walked out to go to the bathroom and change his scrubs. He was surprised when Angie followed.

"What?" he asked without looking at her.

She was scurrying to keep up with him. "I thought you'd want to know Bruiser and Callie are okay."

"Knew that. Spoke to Victor earlier."

"You called the house?"

He stopped outside the locker room and looked down at his soon-to-be ex-wife, and the best surgeon he knew. "It's my house too, Ange, and they're my dogs too. Do you honestly think I wouldn't've called to find out if everything was all right?"

She sighed. "Of course not."

"What do you really want to say?"

"We need to talk."

"Talk as in through our lawyers?" She shook her head. "Work? A surgical consult?" She shook her head again. "Listen, I have a ruptured spleen in a few minutes and I've got to get my head in the game. Spare me the drama and spit it out."

Her head dropped and she looked at her electric green Crocs. "Never mind," she muttered.

Before he could respond, she turned and walked away.

Goddammit. How the fuck had they wound up here?

Brett had met Angelina Nuñez the first day of medical school. It took him fifteen seconds to cross the student lounge and ask her out. They'd been together ever since. Well, until four months ago when he'd come home to find divorce papers sitting on the kitchen counter along with a note telling him she was staying with her sister in Pasadena.

He wasn't a clueless husband. He loved his wife. No. He adored her. Wanted to spend his entire life with her. Wanted to have kids with her. They had date nights. They went away to Santa Barbara for long weekends. They visited her family in Mexico every year during the winter holidays, staying with her grandmother for Christmas, and they went to his family in Philly every year in the spring, making sure they spent Passover with them. They had a house in Pacific Palisades, two rescue mutts, and a housekeeper/chef/butler/gardener/dog-sitter named Victor.

Every day for the past four months Brett had been trying to figure out what the hell Angie meant by "irreconcilable differences."

After she'd dropped the bomb on him, she wouldn't talk to him directly for a month. They had to talk through their lawyers. He hated that he had a divorce lawyer. Hated more that his lawyer couldn't get an answer from her lawyer what the fuck this was about. Six weeks ago he moved out of their home, and she moved back in.

He was staying in an apartment in Century City that his brother's friend owned. Brett hated high-rise buildings. He missed his house. He missed his dogs, and he missed his beautiful, stubborn, brilliant, pain-in-his-fuckin' ass wife.

Twelve minutes after his wife had confounded him yet again, he said, "Ten blade," to his surgical nurse, and then all he could think about was repairing the tear in this fifty-three-year-old man's ruptured spleen so the guy could get back to his life with his spleen in place.

Two

Angie didn't run on emotions. That didn't mean she didn't feel things. She did. Deeply. But her decision-making process was practical, organized, and thoughtful. She understood why she'd spent the only thirty minutes she'd had free that day to track down Brett. She'd needed to see him. To actually lay eyes on him to make sure he was okay. Sure, she'd heard a few of the nurses talking about how Dr. Shapiro had been doing back-to-back surgeries. She knew he was alive and functioning.

But...she'd needed to see him.

Be near him.

Take in his scent.

Her visceral reaction to the earthquake and all the pain and suffering she'd seen throughout the day had been she needed her husband. In truth, she always needed Brett. Like air. It'd been that way for nine years. Since day one, when he walked his six foot two long lanky frame across the lounge and said, "Dinner tonight. Thai. I know a great place around the corner."

Confident. Smart. Unbearably handsome, and too sexy for his own good, he was funny and sweet.

And a liar.

For the past two years, he'd been lying to her, and it shook her to her core. She'd suspected something was off with them and had tried to talk to him about it. Many times. He'd laughed and told her she was "off her mind" or "imagining things." But she had proof. No, she hadn't hired a private investigator. She'd trusted her husband. She couldn't put her finger on what was going on that she felt they weren't "right," but never in her wildest dreams would she have believed he'd cut her to the quick.

Quite by accident, she'd seen him coming out of an elevator in a hotel in Santa Monica, his hand resting possessively on a beautiful young blonde's waist. Angie had been there for a Heart Association conference. He'd been there for the blonde.

The next day she went to a lawyer, three weeks later, she learned she was pregnant. Brett had gotten the divorce papers the night before, and she was already at her sister's. She hadn't intended to stay there long—Lila had three kids under the age of five and a husband—but once Angie knew she was pregnant, she couldn't go back to the house in the Pacific Palisades. It would've killed.

She loved that house. They'd researched neighborhoods with an eye on schools and proximity to their offices and the hospital. For years, they'd lived in a tiny apartment in North Hollywood to save as much money as they could for a down payment on a house in a nice area. They'd gone to fifty-seven open houses and twenty-eight private viewings before they found their home. When their offer was accepted, they'd bought a bottle of tequila, splurged and got a room at the Beverly Hills Hotel, and partied like college freshmen.

When the morning sickness started, she knew she had to stay away from Brett and their home or he'd find out, and she wasn't ready to deal with him and being pregnant.

Since medical school, they'd played a game: How many kids? Three. Two years apart. When would they start? What would be the kids' names? Who'd take family leave when? Both their families had twins, and even though they knew it was her genetics that mattered, they agreed the odds were good they'd get two for the price of one, which, if it happened, meant they'd try for four kids.

Brett had always wanted children. Unlike her family—her father had left them to go live with his three kids by his mistress he'd been keeping on the DL—Brett came from a great family. Loving, noisy, close, and happy. His parents were inner-city public school teachers, and had been their whole lives. Original hippies who'd stuck to their ideals. Brett was the oldest and his brother and sister—fraternal twins—were three years younger. His brother had followed in his footsteps and came out to California to go to college and stayed. His sister went Ivy League—UPenn—which made their parents happy that one of their kids was closer than three thousand miles away.

Now, Angie had to talk to her husband. Time was ticking and she had a pronounced baby bump. God bless scrubs. Shapeless by design, recently she'd switched to a much larger size, and until now, no one had a clue. But the day of reckoning was coming, and she'd decided she had to talk to Brett today. She wasn't going to tell him about the pregnancy minutes before surgery, but she wanted to get him to agree to meet for lunch the next day.

She couldn't imagine anything worse than some staff member speculating about her being pregnant and saying something in front of him. True, they worked in a big hospital and they had different surgical specialties, but the gossip mill was active and virulent. He had to hear about the pregnancy from her, and she'd set aside time later in the afternoon to go to his office to speak to him.

Then the earth had shaken, rattled, and rolled, and after 8:15 this morning, no one's life in LA, and the hospital, was going according to plan. The ED had been a madhouse. Emergency triage procedures were put in place, and people on gurneys were lined up in hallways like containers at the port. Not until now, nine-fifteen at night, had things started to slow down.

She had another surgery scheduled in twenty minutes to implant a pacemaker. Typically, the procedure wouldn't last more than two hours. But going home after her last surgery wasn't an option.

All the surgeons were on call. She'd talked to Victor and knew the house and the dogs were fine, so she decided it was best to sleep at the hospital tonight. If she were called back after she'd driven home, she'd be too wiped to be effective.

She'd find a cot somewhere and pass out. With any luck, she could get four hours sleep, which would hold her.

The pregnancy was kicking her ass, and she got tired sooner than usual.

She couldn't keep up this pace for more than another couple of days.

Three

Immediately after he'd showered and brushed his teeth, Brett went looking for a cot. He'd been able to repair his patient's spleen, and had stayed in the post anesthesia care unit, PACU, until the guy started to show signs of consciousness. Then Brett went to the waiting room and told the guy's wife and kids that he came through surgery well, and that Brett expected the guy to recuperate fully. As had happened many times before, the wife—although almost all spouses did this—hugged him and thanked him about fifty times. The kids shook his hand, except the youngest daughter. She hugged him too and told him she was going to college next year and she was thrilled her father would be alive to see it.

Yeah, that's why he became a doctor. Not for the accolades, though they were great, or the gratitude, which made him feel like a better human being, but for the families who would get to keep their loved ones for years to come and share all of life's events, big and small.

Which brought him back to his wife. Now that he had the time to think about it, she'd been pale, and looked defeated before she trudged off without telling him why they needed to talk. Defeated wasn't his Angie. She'd argue she wasn't his Angie anymore, but that was bullshit, and she knew it.

For the first couple of months after she'd dropped the divorce papers, he'd been so angry he couldn't speak to her civilly. He'd missed her so intensely he had a hard time concentrating on anything else. When they did start to talk, she seemed so sad that his heart broke every time he saw her. If she didn't want this, why the fuck was she doing it?

Since he'd left their home, he'd started strategizing. They were going to mediation next week, and he planned on making her lay it all out for him so he'd find out what was going on in that brain of hers that she'd split them up. Then, whatever the fuck it was she'd conjured, he'd fix it. Make it right. Undo whatever it was she thought was wrong. She couldn't make him sign the divorce papers, and he had no intention of doing it.

Angie was his wife. When he slipped that wedding band on her finger, he'd promised to love her for the rest of his life, and he'd meant it. And he knew she had too.

Now, though, he needed sleep. Four hours should hold him through tomorrow, but tomorrow night he'd need at least six hours' sleep to keep functioning at this pace. His work required precision and brainpower. Brainpower required rest and nutrition. His stomach growled, reminding him he'd missed too many meals today.

The residents' rooms were packed. The resident lounge was packed. Brett had been a resident at this hospital and knew a few of its secrets. He went up to the psych ward, sure he'd find an empty bed, only to learn all the rooms were full, mostly with patients brought in because of the quake. Before he was forced to sleep in a storage room on what Angie called a *tendido*—a bed made of layers of blankets on the floor—he went down to the long infusion unit for cancer patients where, in the cavernous room, there were huge reclining chairs separated by curved half walls. There were also a dozen private spaces with beds and curtains that created a full partition between the room and the ward.

Dammit. All the curtains were drawn. In the hope that one of the rooms might still be empty, he went down the row, sticking his head around each curtain. In the next to last room, he stopped, and his heart thunked against his rib cage. There was Angie, fast asleep.

She lay curled up, the pillow stuffed under her chin, her spikey dark brown hair a mess of points going in all directions. When he'd met her, she'd had hair down to the middle of her back. Thick and wavy, the mane made her already sultry face, with its pouty lips, wide dark eyes, and pronounced cheekbones, even more enticing. He'd loved when her hair had cascaded over his chest when she collapsed after riding him like Secretariat. Or when he'd fisted the silken length to control a kiss, or get her worked up when he was behind her.

He shook his head. Exhausted to the point of feeling woozy, he was hard as a rock thinking about the pure heaven of sinking his cock into her slick, hot channel.

She'd started to cut her hair halfway through their second year of medical school. A few inches at a time, she'd settled on a shoulder-length bob until her internship. Then off it came, and over the years she'd had various stylish short cuts. He understood the practicality of it, but he missed her long hair.

He missed her.

So bad it choked him when he woke alone in his bed, went to sleep alone at night, and, pretty much, every waking hour in between.

Quietly, he bent to undo his laces, then he toed off his sneakers and climbed onto a bed that wasn't made for couples. Wider than a twin, as hospital beds were, but certainly not suitable for a tall man and his wife. Brett didn't care. He'd done this a hundred times before when they were interns and residents. He knew how to contort his body to wrap around hers while leaving enough room for him not to be pretzelized when he woke up. He also knew when he stopped moving around, the small light over the bed would cut off.

Brett lifted the edge of the blanket and rolled up behind Angie, careful not to disturb her rest. He was so wiped out, his hand got as far as her shoulder before he fell asleep.

He could've sworn he'd been out for no more than ten minutes when a phone rang. Shaking himself awake, he knew it wasn't his because he'd put it on ring and vibrate, and its light weight was still tucked into the front pocket of his shirt and wasn't moving.

Angie reached over to the bedside table and answered, "Nuñez."

It must've been instinct or habit that had her scooting her ass back into the cradle of his groin. Sure, she was dead tired and probably still half asleep, but he took it as a sign that her body knew where it belonged, and he was happy to start with that bit of encouragement to work at getting them back together.

"I'll be right there." She put the phone down and looked over her shoulder. "Hey."

"Hey." He smiled.

"Gotta go. A firefighter's a few minutes out. He was extracted from a collapsing building. His chest's badly injured. The EMTs think a rib punctured his heart."

Brett wanted to kiss her so badly he could taste her on his tongue. Instead, he dropped his arm over her waist to give her a hug.

She stiffened in his arms and began scrambling off the bed, but not before his hand had rested on her rounded, protruding abdomen.

She'd shot up so quickly she was beside the bed and shoving her feet into her Crocs before he could lean over to grab her. When she moved a couple of steps out of his reach, he growled, "What the fuck, Ange?"

Her eyes were wide and her mouth was fish jawing. She shook her head as if she were repositioning her brain, then she swiped her phone off the table and turned to leave. He managed to tag her wrist as he was untangling himself from the bed.

It took everything in him not to holler. Yell. Scream. Break something.

Through gritted teeth, he said, "I asked you a question."

Her chin dropped to her chest and she turned her head enough for him to see the tears pooling in her eyes. "I...can't." She sucked in a deep breath. "Not now." She tried to pull away. *I don't fuckin' think so.* "I *have* to go."

In that moment he wanted to tell her he didn't give a shit and the ED could get someone else. But he knew better.

His body was shaking, but he released her wrist. For a moment she stayed where she was and it seemed as if she was about to say something. The moment passed, and she took off, leaving him decimated and half-hanging off the side of the bed.

***

Of the two of them, Brett was the more volatile and outwardly expressive of his emotions. He never saw the point of keeping important shit bottled up. He also knew if he didn't let the steam out of the kettle, his temper would spike, and he didn't like himself when he lost that kind of control. What he didn't expect, but obviously his body and brain needed, was to be sobbing into the pillow Angie had been sleeping on.

Everything came clear in the moments after she'd left the room. For the past couple of years, she'd been asking him *what's wrong* or kept saying something was *off* between them. He'd had no fucking idea what she was talking about. Sure, he'd been a bit stressed about the size of their mortgage payment—he could feed entire villages based on that monthly nut—and he worried they'd have to delay having children a couple of years to make sure they'd socked away more than a little something in the bank. But he'd talked to her about that shit, and as always, she had made him feel better.

Now he knew when she'd asked all those ridiculous "what's wrong" questions, she'd been talking in code. In a roundabout way she was telling him something *was* wrong between them. Something *was* off. She was having a goddamn affair, and now she was pregnant with that fucking piece of shit's kid. She must've filed for divorce when she found out she was pregnant.

Every time he said the word in his head he felt nauseous. He couldn't and wouldn't imagine another man touching her. He'd cut off his arm before he'd touch another woman. He belonged to Angie, and she belonged to him.

Apparently not.

When his breathing became erratic and he began to hyperventilate, he knew he had to rein it in and pull his shit together. He elbowed his body up and pulled out his phone. Huh. He'd slept for nearly five hours. And yet, he'd never felt worse in his life.

Before anyone saw him like this, he got out of the bed, put on his sneakers, and laced them up. He stuck his head out of the curtain, saw the hallway was empty, and made his way to the bathroom. Thankfully, no one was in there, and he grabbed a clump of paper towels, soaked them with cold water and took a few minutes holding the makeshift compress against his face. When his breathing began to return to normal, and his pulse rate started to lower, he tossed the wet towels in the trash, did his business, then washed up.

When he caught a glimpse of his face in the mirror, he shook his head at the disaster staring back at him.

Shit.

Angie could be practical, cool-headed, and focused, but he'd never thought her capable of being cold-hearted. Imagine, only minutes before a surgery, she wanted to talk to him about being knocked up by another man.

He shook his head and thought the earthquake was a metaphor for his relationship with his wife. The ground had shifted beneath his feet and everything was crumbling around him.

His phone rang, and when he saw the hospital's surgical number on the screen, he was grateful. How fucked up was that? He was glad he had to fix someone who was facing a life-threatening injury.

"Shapiro."

"We have three more traumas coming into the ED all from a collapsed building."

"I'm on my way."

Four

Angie ducked into a handicapped bathroom and locked the door. Yeah, she knew she shouldn't be in there, but she needed to pull herself together, alone, if only for a moment. If she lived to be ninety-eight years old, she'd never forget the look on Brett's face. His expression was the picture of devastation. At first, she couldn't process his reaction. He wanted kids. And sure, they were in the middle of divorce proceedings, but she'd never keep his children from him.

Then it hit her. He had no idea why she'd filed, and even though his lawyer must've asked her attorney fifty times, Angie refused to be more specific than the famous catchall: irreconcilable differences. Not knowing a specific reason, when Brett's hand had rested on her baby bump, his brain must've gone straight to unfaithful. On some level she was insulted he'd think that of her, but not having given him the truth, where else would his mind go? The mess their lives had become now veered into something akin to a multicar pileup on the 405.

She washed her face, took a deep breath, and rushed to the ED, pushing her fucked-up life aside as she focused on the firefighter hanging on by a thread.

Ten and a half hours later, the brave twenty-nine-year-old first responder was wheeled into the PACU. She couldn't talk to the family until she changed her scrubs. Blood had soaked through her gown, and had sprayed up onto her cap. Even though the nurses had cleaned her face shield, Angie had needed a replacement, the bleeder had been that bad. She'd lost the guy twice on the table, but she and her team, including an amazing third-year resident, hadn't given up. Neither had the firefighter. Strong, with an incredible will to live, he fought to stay alive so she could repair his decimated chest cavity.

She grabbed a new pair of scrubs in the locker room at the end of the hall, changed in a toilet stall—she couldn't let anyone see her body—then washed up and ran her fingers through her hair. When she came out into the corridor, her resident, a brilliant guy with a wicked sense of humor, was walking by and she stopped him.

"Kyle."

"Dr. Nuñez. Hey."

"Great work in there."

He grinned. "I was going to say that to you. He's alive because of you."

"He's alive because of all of us." She placed her hand on his forearm and squeezed. "Thank you."

Kyle turned his head at the same time Angie heard the squeak of rubber soles on the hallway floor.

"Hey, Dr. Shapiro. Your wife..." Kyle shook his head. "She's a magician."

Brett's jaw muscle jumped. "Yes. She is," he ground out.

Kyle couldn't have missed the anger wafting off Brett, and made a fast escape down the hall. Before Angie could open her mouth, Brett bulldozed her into the locker room holding her upper arms gently, but his size alone in forward motion made her walk backwards. "Anyone in here?" he hissed. She shook her head. "Is that him?" She blinked rapidly. "Is that," he looked down at her abdomen, "*your* baby's father?"

Four thousand thoughts collided in her exhausted brain, but only one feeling thrummed through her body. Regret. She hated seeing Brett like this. She'd never seen him like this, and, as much as her heart had splintered at his betrayal, she couldn't let him think the same of her.

"*Mi amado.*" He flinched at the endearment she'd said to him a million times. "There is no one else. We made this."

He gathered her in his arms and dropped his chin onto the top of her head. "That's..." his voice broke on a sob, "that's what you came to tell me yesterday?"

She nodded into his chest. "I...I tried to ask you to meet for lunch today. I didn't want to tell you about the pregnancy before you went into surgery."

"Are you all right?" He rubbed his cheek against her hair.

"More tired than usual, but otherwise fine."

"You eating well? Taking your vitamins?"

"Yes, doctor."

"You seeing Gayle?"

Gayle Stein was the best OB-GYN Angie knew, and a close personal friend. They'd gone to college together, but Gayle had gone to medical school in Massachusetts and did her internship and residency there before returning to California to a large, well-regarded practice. "Of course."

"Good." He sighed and held her tighter. "I have to go. Perforated bowel."

"Someone from the collapsed building?"

"Yeah," he murmured into her hair. "We need to talk, Ange."

"I know." She dreaded the conversation, but they needed to deal with so many things, and it made sense to do it now. They had mediation in a few days. Best if they were able to hammer out the particulars and get an agreement in place before she got too far along in the pregnancy. She swayed a little and Brett held her tight to his warm, hard body.

"You should plan on staying here tonight. You're too tired to drive home."

By the time she checked on her patient and spoke with his family, she would be too wiped to drive home. Sunset Boulevard would be packed with traffic at this time of day, and if she was called back in later, the thought of driving at night on a road that in places was serpentine was not appealing. "I'll think about it."

He grunted. "Why don't you stay at the condo?"

"Where?"

"The condo in Century City." It wasn't lost on her he wasn't saying *where I live now*. "It's about four miles away. Take a Lyft and crash there. I won't be done until midnight the earliest. I'll bunk here."

A real bed with soft sheets that weren't loosely stretched over plastic lining, a decent-size shower with large fluffy towels—Brett was a big guy who liked to wear his towel—and no noise. A kitchen with real food—she was starving—no hospital smell, no interruptions, except, of course, if her phone rang to call her back in, and the pillows would smell like Brett.

Yeah, masochistic, but she missed him so hard she could barely stand when she was near him. Wrapped in his embrace, feeling his love, knowing he cared about her—there was no way he faked his despair this morning—she wondered if she could learn to forgive him.

He was right. They needed to talk. She'd ask for the truth and hoped he'd tell her. Depending on what she heard, she'd know if they could find a road that led to them staying together.

"All right." Between the last surgery, the lack of food, the pregnancy, and not having Brett all the time to make her feel better, she caved. "I'll go to the condo."

He hugged her tighter then ran his large hands up and down her back. She loved when he did that. His touch had always been a bit of sorcery. A balm when she needed it, playful and light when he teased her, and a storm of want and need when he took her to sensual and sexual heights most women only read about.

"Good." His sigh was filled with relief. "I'll call building security and tell them you're coming. They'll ask for your ID, so take your wallet." She rubbed her cheek against his chest by way of a nod. "My stuff is in the locker room one floor down. Number seventeen, the usual combination." They'd agreed on a mutual combination when they started their internships in case they needed the car keys. For years, they'd had only one car—the one he'd driven across the country when he came to California to start college—a hand-me-down from his father. He moved her away from him by about an inch. His lips were a hairbreadth away. "There's food. Make sure you eat."

She swallowed the lump in her throat. "I will. Promise."

He leaned in and kissed her on the forehead, his lips resting there for a few moments. *Damn.* Every little thing, every stolen moment…she missed him so much.

"Gotta go." That look—she knew, she *knew* he wanted to say "I love you." Instead, his lids lowered for a few beats, then he told her, "Be safe, and sleep."

"'Kay," she managed to squeak out.

He let her go and walked out of the locker room.

She wanted to go into a stall, lock the door, sit on the toilet seat, and cry. She'd save that for the condo where she could lie in a comfy bed and sob her eyes out. Now, she had to go to PACU to see if her firefighter was conscious, then she had to talk to his family.

***

188

Angie knew Brett hated living in a high-rise. He'd chosen their little apartment in North Hollywood, which was in a two-story building that had been built in the 60s. There were twenty-four apartments in three buildings, eight apartments per floor that made a U-shape around an interior courtyard filled with bird-of-paradise, and at least six varieties of palm trees arranged around a small square of terra-cotta pavers where four lounge chairs were lined up opposite a picnic bench and a tiny grill. The owner, a retired stripper named Tanya, lived in a double apartment on the first floor of the building across from Angie and Brett, and spent a considerable amount of time in one of those lounge chairs.

When they gave their notice, Tanya wept, and told them they were the best tenants she'd ever had. They'd lived in that tiny apartment since their second year of medical school, had never been late with the rent, and were gone most of the time. No doubt, they were the best tenants Tanya ever had.

Compared to that place, which Angie had loved even though it was barely big enough for Brett alone, never mind two people, the condo was a palace. An open floor plan with two bedrooms, a full bathroom and a powder room, had to be about eighteen hundred square feet. The building was probably twenty years old, but the condo had been renovated into a modern, sleek design with high-end appliances. The furnishings were masculine. Black leather low-slung couches, a large flat-screen over a row of ebony bookcases, and a gray, black and white Miro-inspired pattern area rug sat beneath the sofas and large glass coffee table in the middle of the room softening the sheen of black marble tile.

This place couldn't be more different from their home if it tried. Brett didn't care so much about décor as space. Their house had five bedrooms, four baths, and was on a quarter acre of land, which in California meant s-p-a-c-e: a real backyard where kids and dogs could play, and Brett could hang out in his outdoor kitchen pretending to be a grill master.

They hadn't decorated much yet. The house was turnkey when they'd bought it, and hadn't needed any structural attention. So far, they'd had painters in to change out the bright white downstairs to a soft melon. They'd bought new furniture for their bedroom, a couple of sofas for the family room, a stupidly large flat-screen because it made Brett happy, a kitchen table and chair set, and a dining room table with comfy chairs.

Victor's room, the only bedroom downstairs, had its own bathroom, and was furnished with the basics. They let him do as he wished décor-wise in his own space. The kitchen came fully equipped with high-end everything, and they had been thrilled but cautious. They'd furnish the rest of the house as they could without breaking the bank.

Angie dropped her head on the black granite counter in the condo's kitchen and drew in a deep breath. She didn't want to sell their home. She didn't want to live somewhere else. She wanted to kill Brett for cheating on her and ruining everything they'd built together.

Opening the fridge, she thought, how could he be in love with her, and after today she didn't doubt he still was, and be with someone else? For the first time since she'd seen him with the blonde, Angie wondered if she'd gotten it wrong.

As unwilling as she was to revisit the memory that had run like a never-ending loop in her brain for weeks, she closed the refrigerator door, leaned against the counter, and replayed what she'd seen, breaking it down. When the elevator's doors had opened, Brett was looking straight ahead, as was the blonde. His hand was on her waist. Or was it? Angie closed her eyes and tried to be precise. Visualization and precision were critical in surgery, and she employed the muscle memory she used for work and applied it to those ten seconds of time that had changed her life.

Actually, his hand was at the blonde's back: her lower back.

Huh. Angie's lids snapped up. She'd been sure he was gripping the blonde's waist. She closed her eyes again and wrapped her fingers around the edge of the counter.

The elevator had dinged and they'd stepped forward, Brett slightly behind the blonde, his eyes on the lobby: his hand at her lower back. They'd turned left out of the elevator, and when the blonde walked a few steps in front of him, his hand had dropped to his side.

How could Angie have forgotten that?

To be fair, when she'd seen them her heart had dropped into her stomach, her knees had nearly given out, and she'd felt like she was going to vomit. When she'd replayed the scene months ago, she remembered what she'd felt in that moment as well as what she thought she'd seen.

It seems her memory might've been skewed by her emotional response. She'd been so sure he'd been seeing another woman, Angie hadn't considered any other possibility. And what did that say about her? All the years they'd been together he had never once given her any cause to doubt his love or fidelity. Why had she been so sure he was fucking around on her?

She remembered turning away and running to the bathroom as they'd headed for the front doors. That was it. A blip on the radar screen of her life that had turned her world upside down.

Okay. All right. She pulled in a deep breath, let it out, another deep breath, let it out…she had to give herself a break. There were a host of questions that remained unanswered. What was Brett doing at a hotel in Santa Monica in the middle of a workday? Who was the blonde, and why were they coming downstairs from room level?

Honesty required Angie to acknowledge there were two levels of meeting rooms below the guest rooms, and she'd never seen from which floor he'd come. But still.

If it was innocuous, why hadn't he mentioned it that evening? Every night, in detail, they recapped their day over dinner, or in bed, sharing medical information as well as hospital gossip. If either of them had a meeting or conference away from the office or the hospital, they shared. Especially since almost all their meeting/conference time was medically related. Even though they had different specialties, anything they learned from each other was good information to have.

The possibility she'd gotten it wrong made her nauseous. But she had to eat.

Back to the fridge.

***

She made a spinach and cheese omelet and inhaled a large cranberry muffin. After washing the pan and dishes, she pulled on one of Brett's t-shirts—yep, she was torturing herself—then grabbed a spoon and a pint of his beloved pistachio ice cream, wrapped it in a dish towel, and went into his bedroom. She plunked her butt in the middle of the bed and stared at the only thing, aside from his clothes, he'd brought here from their home: a silver framed eight by ten photo of them on one of their new sofas.

They'd had a small house party—about a dozen people—and Brett's brother, Nate, had taken that picture. In it, she was in profile, leaning into Brett, both hands wrapped around his upper arm. and his head was tipped down to hear what she was whispering. She remembered exactly what she'd told him that elicited the look of smug surprise on his handsome face: "They'll be gone in about an hour and before the last of them is pulling out of the driveway, I'm going to suck you off right here."

She knew Brett loved that photo as much for the intimacy of the moment as for the explosive sex they'd had on the couch. They'd passed out after and had slept the night there. She'd woken naked and sprawled on his chest, their legs entwined. Victor always had the good grace to go right to bed after guests left, and he didn't venture out of his room until ten on weekend mornings. They'd warned him they were "rather indiscriminate," and he made sure they never felt uncomfortable in their own home.

She longed for their life with every fiber of her being.

They had to talk.

Tomorrow.

Five

Brett didn't find a bed anywhere and was forced to sleep in one of the reclining chairs in the long infusion center. They were comfortable enough, but even as exhausted as he was, his brain wouldn't shut down.

Images of Ange in the bed in the condo had him sitting up debating whether to head over there and make her tell him what the hell was going on so he could slip into bed behind her, and sleep with his wife. But she'd looked worn out. Pale, drawn, and too thin for a woman who'd felt—he'd had his hand on her belly for a brief moment—about six months pregnant.

She'd always had a banging body. Five-five with big breasts and a nipped waist, she carried her extra weight in her fantastic ass and serious thighs. He fuckin' loved squeezing her tush when she straddled him, and simply adored grabbing hold of those thighs when his face was between her legs. He lived to make her moan while he teased her body.

Since he'd started getting laid at fifteen, this was the longest he'd gone without sex.

He missed everything about her, about them.

Their sex life was high on his list of things he craved to have back.

But his wife needed quiet time in a place where she could get a good night's sleep. Her health and stamina were more critical now than ever. As much as he wanted to hold her in his arms through the night, he wasn't going to jeopardize the fragile peace they seemed to have achieved.

Brett had nearly collapsed when she told him the baby was his. The thought of her being with another man practically laid him to waste. Now knowing they were building the family they had wanted, he'd double down any way he had to for them to return home together and reclaim their lives.

He leaned back into the recliner, stretched out his legs on the elevated footrest, and tucked the meager blanket around his upper torso.

This sucked hairy monkey balls.

***

Apparently his exhaustion was greater than his discomfort, which was why he groaned out "Fuck" when his phone rang and jiggled against his chest. He looked at the screen. Four-thirty a.m. He'd been asleep about four hours. Not as much as he needed, but enough to make do.

"Shapiro."

"Thirty-nine-year-old woman, severe hepatic trauma, penetrating injury. An overpass fell onto Olympic. Flying debris hit a cop car and shredded the door. Looks like shrapnel cut through the right lobe. ETA ten minutes. FYI, her partner sustained a broken arm and a few deep contusions. She's the one who caught the worst of it."

Brett shook his head. "On my way."

***

Angie was waiting for him in the locker room. He pulled off his blood-splattered top and threw it in the biowaste plastic lined bin, and then he sat beside her on the bench.

"Long one," she said.

"Grade four hepatic. Sliced into the right lobe."

She winced.

He got up.

"Where you going?"

He took in her slightly more rested face. "Baby, you shouldn't be sitting on this uncomfortable bench. I'm bringing a chair over."

She stood, tilted her head toward her left shoulder, and her thoughtful, questioning expression came over her beautiful face. "Actually, how about we go back to the condo, have lunch, and talk."

"Sure." He nodded, ecstatic she suggested it, and hoped with his whole heart this meant good things. "I'm gonna shower, change, check on my patient, and then talk to the family. You okay to wait for about forty minutes?"

"I'll be at the rooftop lounge."

Perfect: lots of comfy chairs and sofas there. "I'll find you." He leaned down and kissed her temple. Her hair smelled of her floral shampoo. "You sleep last night?" he whispered into her ear.

"I did. Great bed."

Lonely bed. "Good. You look more rested." He kissed her neck and drew in her scent, which had changed. Pregnancy hormones. Powerful stuff. "I'll be there as soon as I can."

"'Kay." She squeezed his bicep and walked out of the locker room.

His patient was a fighter. He'd learned she was a sergeant and he'd bet his house she was a hard-ass with attitude. This woman was not going to let a wedge of shrapnel ruin her day.

As expected, the waiting room was filled with cops and the sergeant's family. A husband who looked like an accountant, and two preteen kids who looked scared to death. Brett took the husband and kids into a small, private room with a couch and a couple of chairs and told them their beloved was going to recover, but it would be slow going.

As the husband pumped Brett's hand, the guy said, "She's not going to like that, but I don't give a shit." The man's bluntness surprised Brett. "We'll get her home and make sure she doesn't do anything stupid to fuck up her recovery."

Talk about "looks are deceiving." Brett had to ask. "You a cop also?"

The guy laughed and clapped Brett on the shoulder. "No, man. An orthodontist."

Brett smirked.

"I know," the husband said. "Everyone expects me to be milquetoast, but I met Amelia in the Army. Sniper. HHC, hundred ninety-ninth. She remained a warrior, I took the more sedate and profitable route."

Brett grinned before he said, "I have no worries about you keeping her contained while she recovers."

"Hell no. I'll threaten to shoot her and she'll know I mean it."

Brett laughed.

"Our kids." The husband threw his arm out and the kids came forward to stand in his embrace. "Shane and Sadie."

Both children shook his hand and wore serious expressions. Badasses already. "Pleased to meet you."

"Thank you for saving our mom," Sadie said.

"Joint effort. She put up a good fight," Brett told them.

"No doubt," Shane murmured, looking like a weight had been lifted off his chest.

"I'll let you go so you can share what you want with her brethren in blue."

"Thanks again, man. I'm Alejandro Cota. Most people call me Alex."

"Alex," Brett acknowledged.

"If I have to, I'm gonna call you to help keep her where she needs to be."

"Anytime. And I'm sure I'll see you while she's recovering, and at all the post-op appointments."

"Count on it." Then Alex leaned in to whisper, "Now I gotta go out there and tell those pussies she's gonna be okay."

Brett laughed and nodded. "Don't be too hard on them."

"Crybabies, the bunch of 'em."

The Cotas left and Brett knew that man was not going to let his wife be anything but one hundred percent all right.

***

Brett went to the rooftop lounge and found Angie sitting on a couch talking to another heart surgeon.

"Hey, Roseann."

"Hi, Brett. Crazy few days."

"Tell me about it." He looked to Ange. "Ready to go, baby?"

She nodded, then leaned in and gave Roseann a hug. "A promise. We'll hit the Norton Simon and do a Pasadena day soon."

"Can't wait," Roseann said.

In the elevator, Brett asked, "You hungry?"

"I could eat."

"Morning sickness?"

"A little for about a month, but fatigue is what's been kicking my butt. I eat, but a little at a time."

He hated that he'd missed the first months of her pregnancy. Everything about them being apart came into stark relief at the thought he wasn't there for her when she needed him most.

The elevator door opened and they walked through the building's main lobby, out the double doors, and turned left to head to the parking lot. Usually, he'd take her hand. It made him feel like they were teenagers, and something about that was a kick every time. Today, he didn't want to spook her, so he stuffed his hands in his front pockets.

"Actually, that's better for you, but you know that already." She looked up and gave him her side smile. The one that said, you're not the only doctor in the house, bud. He chuckled. "Did you get called in this morning?"

"No. I had a pacemaker scheduled for seven-thirty and that went off fine. I left the rest of my morning clear in case of an emergency, but so far there hasn't been any in cardiology. Did you see the operation manager's message?"

"I haven't checked my emails yet. What'd she say?"

"The mayor still has the city on shutdown while CalTrans, the fire department, and the city's public works department go around inspecting roads and buildings for potential collapses while tagging what needs to be torn down and what's quickly fixable. FEMA's on scene in the hardest hit areas, and the FAA is checking the viability of all the area airports. The emergency operations center said they expect the bulk of the emergencies have passed, but we're to remain on code orange until further notice since there are still a couple collapsed buildings that may have survivors."

They turned the corner and cut through a gap in the shrubbery to get to his car. "More than forty-eight hours has passed since the quake."

"You and I know the realities, but there have been survivors even after a week."

"And here I thought I was the optimist."

They stopped next to his car, and she leaned into him. He wanted to wrap her in his arms and never let her go. It'd been four months since she'd done that, and he prayed her outward sign of affection boded well for their lunch. He beeped open the locks and helped her into the car.

The first time he'd done that she'd said, "Such a gentleman." At the time, all he wanted to do was fuck her blind, so he begged to differ, but he didn't tell her that. Since she seemed to like it, he never stopped doing it.

Before he could start the car, her phone rang. He wanted to grab it, toss it out the window then drive over it.

"Nuñez." On paper she was Angelina Constanza Victoria Nuñez-Shapiro. They'd gotten married after their second year of medical school, and to minimize confusion, she remained Nuñez. "Yes. I'll be there. Thanks for checking."

He raised his brows as she stuffed her phone in her little backpack. "You have to go in?"

"No. That was Gayle's office. I have another sonogram this afternoon. I was going to ask you if you wanted to come."

Now he wanted to open his car door and dance around the parking lot. "Sure, baby. I want to be there. But why another one? Didn't you have one at eighteen weeks?"

"Twenty."

He frowned and she laughed.

"Gayle had been on vacation, and I had a tight schedule for a couple of weeks." She leaned forward and pressed her index finger on the deepening indent between his brows. "Nothing to worry about, old man."

He couldn't help himself. He grabbed her wrist and pressed his lips into her palm. When he released her hand, she was blinking rapidly. He hated this. The whole fucking thing. Their separation ended today. He'd make sure of it.

Right now, he'd do anything to keep her from crying. "Old man my ass."

It worked. She grinned.

"So why the follow-up?"

She looked into her lap and shook her head. He had a feeling he knew what was coming when she couldn't hide her smile. "Gayle wants to check on the twins."

A half-second after the word "twins" came out of her mouth, he didn't give a fuck if she thought they weren't together. They were more together than they'd ever been. She wasn't pregnant with one of his kids: she was pregnant with two of his kids. He leaned over, put both his hands on her face, and kissed her with everything he had. She didn't resist, and she wasn't "allowing" him to kiss her, she gave as good as she got.

They sat in his car making out like teenagers. She tasted so divine he wanted to drink her in for hours. He pulled back when he nearly broke off his dick from twisting in the seat while his hard-on was pressed against his jean's zipper.

She drew in a breath and looked at him with unfocused eyes. He had to get her horizontal immediately. Without a word between them, he started the car and got the fuck out of the parking lot.

Six

Thirty-five minutes later they walked into the condo. She went straight to the bedroom and he followed, stopping to lean against the wall when she disappeared into the bathroom. He toed off his sneakers and waited, staring at the bed, barely able to contain his need for her.

When she came out of the bathroom, she wore only her oversize scrub top. Her shapely legs an invitation to start at her toes and work his way up her body. There wasn't an inch of her he didn't know by heart, but every time he had her naked there was something new he learned, tasted, or touched. She was his endless dream, made for him to love and treasure until time ceased.

He pushed off the wall and she looked at him like he was her favorite appetizer, entrée, and dessert. Oh yeah. He could definitely work with that.

As he took his first step toward her, she whispered, "Stop."

He froze, cursing that he hadn't picked her up and taken her mouth the moment she came out of the bathroom. She'd had too much time to think. Between their quiet and burning-hot tension-filled car ride, and her few minutes in the bathroom, she had rearranged where they were heading. But not quite. She was half-dressed, and she wanted him, that much he knew. The rest, if he had to fight to get them to the place they needed to be, he'd do it and anything else necessary to make certain they were *them* again. Now and for always.

"Before we head," she pointed to the bed, "over there, we need to talk."

"Okay, baby." He took a step back and leaned against the wall again, forcing himself not to cross his arms over his chest. "Talk."

"I adore you, *mi amado*." Fuck yeah. That's what he's talking about. "You've been the breath in my lungs since the day we met."

Yup. This was going exactly where he wanted it to go. "Which is why when you cut my heart out, I filed for divorce."

Reflexively, his arms crossed over his chest. "You gonna explain that shit, 'cause I have no idea what you're talking about."

Her whole body caved in on itself like she'd been punched in the gut. She backed up and sat on the edge of the bed. "Santa Monica." She put her hands on her thighs and squeezed.

Normally, he'd get over there and show her how it's done, but right now, he had to know what fucked-up shit she had twisted in her head so he could unravel it and get them heading in the right direction.

"Santa Monica," he ground out.

"I was attending a one-day Heart Association conference." She stopped and stared at him.

She didn't seem capable of saying more than a few words at a time. No problem, he'd help her along even if it took hours.

"I remember. You left early so you could stop and get yourself a latté at Caffe Luxxe before you headed down the PCH." What he didn't say was why he remembered it so well. Six days later she'd dropped divorce papers and left him.

"Right." She nodded. "So. At lunch. I wanted to get some fresh air." Again, she stopped like she couldn't go on.

"Nice hotel. It's on the water. Good place to take a walk." He was jumping out of his skin, but he wouldn't do anything to scare her. He had to know, finally, what the hell she had been thinking when she fractured them.

"You would know," she mumbled.

What the fuck? Everyone knew that hotel. They'd been to two weddings and a bat mitzvah at that hotel.

"You too, baby. We've been to a few things there over the years."

She sighed so huge her shoulders practically went up to her ears before they dropped. "True." She gripped her knees and he knew she was going to spill it. "When I was crossing the lobby, I saw you coming out of the elevator with a beautiful blonde woman."

He looked at the floor and thought *it couldn't be this simple*. "Yeah, you did. She's Arvid's woman. She was visiting from Denver. They were staying at the hotel for a long weekend. We were supposed to meet for lunch at True Food Kitchen. He had to go in 'cause one of his patients coded. I was turning off Wilshire when he called and wanted to know if I was in Santa Monica yet. When I told him I was, he asked me to swing by the hotel and collect her—her name is Holly—at their room. He gave her my description and phone number so she could call me when I was standing outside the door." Her eyes went wide. "Yeah, you can't be too careful with the woman you love."

He held her gaze to make sure she understood his meaning. "I agreed to bring her to the hospital so he could take her out to eat after he got done with his patient since he *knows* me and understands why I wouldn't have lunch alone with a woman *my wife* and I didn't know."

"Um…oh."

Oh? Fuck no. He was so furious he couldn't see straight. "Oh" was not going to cut it after he'd suffered—as a dying man walking across the desert looking for water suffered—without her for one hundred and twenty-three days. He forced himself to stay against the wall, but couldn't help swinging his arm out when he raised his voice and asked, "When you saw me, why didn't you call out so I'd turn around? Or, better yet, come up to me?"

Her hands were clasped together and tears were running down her face. He couldn't stand seeing her like that. He crossed the room and squatted in front of her.

"Baby." He brushed the tears off her face with his pinkie. "What were you thinking?"

"I…I…I thought I…I…I saw your hand on her waist, like…like you were holding her to you. And…and I was so shocked I felt like I was going to vomit. I didn't want to see the look on your face if you were really, you know, with her, so I ran."

"Angie. Do you really think I'd ever cheat on you?"

She shrugged and he hated her defeated expression. "You'd been…I don't know…different for a while."

"Ange, how many times did I tell you nothing was wrong?"

She sucked in a deep breath through her nose, clearly trying to pull it together. "All the time."

"Why didn't you believe me?"

"Because you were different. Distracted. Remote. Distant. I felt shut out. Cut off. Alone. I told you all this."

"Baby. And I told you, huge house payment, Victor's salary, two new cars, both of us with surgeries in the morning, patients all afternoon, and we have late office hours on Thursdays. I wanted us to start a family." He laid his hand on their babies' bump. "I thought we'd have to put it off until we had more bank." He moved his hand under her top and started rubbing her bump. "I was preoccupied and sometimes a little stressed, but never about us. You're my everything, Ange. How can you not believe that?"

"I don't know." She began sobbing and he'd had enough.

He stood, damn his knees protested, scooped her up, and walked to the side of the bed where he laid her down. Then he went to the other side of the bed, climbed in, and got up right behind her, draping his arm under her even more substantial breasts.

"Listen to me, baby, 'cause you need to get this, hold on to it, and believe it for the rest of your life." He squeezed her gently, and she knew what that meant. She sucked in air, stopped sobbing, and turned in his arms to look him in the eye. "I love you. You're my happy. You're my best friend, an unbelievably great fuck, my lover, and my biggest adventure. There is absolutely no one anywhere who could usurp what you mean to me. Believe it right down to the marrow, Ange. The only thing that's going to change," he glanced down at her bump, "is in a few months I'm going to have two more people to love, and each of them will be better than perfect because they're half you. Get it?"

She rested her forehead on his chin. "I get it. I'm such an idiot. I can't believe I did this to us."

He gathered her as close as he could. "I can't either, but I understand you got something in your head about us not being on the same page and when you saw me with Holly, it confirmed what you thought. You were wrong, but apparently I didn't do a good enough job letting you know you had nothing to worry about. I hope I have now."

"You have, *mi cielo*."

"Good." He tilted her head up with his forefinger and kissed her plump, delicious lips. "In the car, on the way to Gayle's office, you call your lawyer and tell him we are *not* getting divorced. I want whatever fuckin' papers he needs to file filed and sent over to my lawyer by close of business tomorrow. And right now, baby, you have to swear to me that if you ever see or hear anything that scares you or makes you doubt me or us, you will ask *me* what the fuck is going on. I'll tell you the truth every time."

She nodded.

"Swear it, Ange. I'm not playing here."

"I swear it." He kissed her again, this time a little longer and with more tongue. She pulled back and said, "Before we get busy, can I just say, you've gotten even bossier, and I didn't think that was possible."

"That's what happens when I haven't tasted you or been inside you for four fuckin' months."

"So what are you waiting for?"

He grinned before he licked the seam of her mouth, nibbled on her bottom lip, then, when she gasped, he speared his tongue against hers and proceeded to take everything while he poured all his love into that kiss. When her legs tangled with his, he put his hands under her scrub top and pulled it up over her head.

"Baby. Gotta say, those are some serious tits."

She smacked his arm. "So romantic."

He unhooked her bra, and damn, those girls weighed six pounds each. He lowered his head and inhaled her warm, spicy scent. "Tender?"

"A little. Go easy. I'll let you know if I can handle more."

He answered by circling her darkened nipple with his tongue and took great pleasure in sucking the hardened peak into his mouth. He didn't pull, but he nibbled lightly and teased her with the tip of his tongue. When she started to moan and squirm, he felt like he was king of the world.

"More," she whispered.

He sucked harder, and with his hand, he lightly squeezed the other nipple between his thumb and forefinger. Damn. She began panting in his ear. He trailed kisses down her torso until he got to her belly, then he worshipped the bump. Kissing top, sides, center, and finally licking his way down the barely-there *linea nigra*. When he put his hands in her panties, she lifted her tush and helped shimmy the soft cotton down her legs.

Holy shit, her scent was stronger than usual—sweeter and more pungent—entirely intoxicating. He nuzzled her dark soft curls and grabbed her thicker thighs and held on as he pushed them open.

Brett reached out with his tongue and tasted ambrosia. She was wet and dripping for him, and he lapped up every drop before alternately nibbling on her clit and tonguing her channel. He'd missed everything about her more than he could articulate, but having this sweet heaven on his lips started to soothe the holes in his soul.

He knew she was close when she grabbed his hair and pulled. Yeah, he was going to make her come hard. He'd heard pregnancy sex made the orgasm more intense, which made sense, more hormones, greater blood flow to the region—a recipe for a slamming climax.

Brett didn't have to work hard, although none of having her all over his face, lips, and down his throat was anything but fantastic, but it didn't take long and she was screaming his name, had her legs locked around his shoulders, and was practically pulling his hair out by the roots. He rested his mouth on her inner thigh, letting her come down before going at her again.

"That was a-mazing," she panted.

"Love I can give you that, baby, but have to be real here, too long without, and pregnancy sex… I can't take all the credit."

"Oh yeah you can. You've always been *really* good at that."

"Enjoy the taste of you, Ange. Always have, always will."

"I'd love to reciprocate. You know I adore your cock."

He chuckled. "I've noticed." He squeezed her thigh. "How about in a few days when I'm sure I won't blow my wad in about twenty seconds."

"Makes me feel all kinds of sexy to have this kind of power over you."

"*Ketzelah*, you've always had all kinds of power over me."

"Let's call it a draw since you announced I was your love slave after we spent our first night together."

He grinned. "You are." He got on his knees and took off his shirt, then unbuttoned his jeans and pulled down the zipper. "I'm gonna prove that to you right now."

He yanked her ankles and gently tugged her down the bed until her legs hung over the edge. Then he stood, took off his pants and toed off his socks, went to the head of the bed and grabbed a couple of pillows, then stuffed them under her tush.

"If anything I do hurts or is uncomfortable, you tell me immediately."

She nodded.

"Don't move, Ange. I don't want to come within a minute of being inside of you."

"'Kay."

He positioned his dick at her entrance, and swear to god, he felt stupid giddy for a moment. Slowly, he sank into her sweet, tight, hot pussy, and when he touched her cervix, he stopped. He was big, and he'd always been careful not to ram himself into her.

"Damn, baby, you feel so fuckin' good."

"Hmmm," she hummed. "You too, *cariño*."

He grabbed her hips, and she wrapped her legs around his thighs. Slowly, he began to slide out and push back into her. He kept the motion smooth and easy, willing himself to hold off until he got her to come again. As he felt her body tighten, he took her clit between his thumb and forefinger and in time with his motion he squeezed and released the swollen nub until she fisted the blanket and let out the longest moan he'd ever heard.

That did it. He moved his hips faster, and while she was still coming, he joined her, his balls pulling up so tight, he thought he'd pass out.

He leaned over her, holding all his weight in his arms. "Best sex of my life."

Then he kissed her until neither of them could breathe.

Seven

Angie was lying on the table, watching the picture forming on the monitor. Gayle stopped the live picture and moved the cursor to show Angie and Brett baby number one. "A boy." Gayle depressed a key and the live picture was back. After about a minute, she stopped it again, moved the cursor, and said, "Another boy." Then she let the live picture resume and waited, moving the transducer under Angie's belly. "Aha," Gayle muttered, then stopped the live picture and moved the cursor again. "As I thought. Boy number three."

"What the fuck?" Brett boomed.

"They're called triplets, Dr. Shapiro," Gayle poked. "It's a complicated medical term."

"Back up, smart-ass. Three weeks ago you told Ange they were twins."

"Three weeks ago I wasn't positive they were triplets. I'm pretty sure boy number three is a fraternal and he's being nudged aside by the dizygotics, who, as you know, share the same chorion and placenta, but they grow in a separate amniotic sac from the fraternal triplet. We're going to keep a close eye on boy number three, make sure he thrives."

"Three," Angie whispered because she couldn't suck enough air into her lungs.

"Do I get to do my Tarzan now?" Brett asked.

"Only if I get to do my Jane," Angie snapped, her voice coming back.

"Jane was sweet and accommodating," Brett stated.

"Uh, no. Jane whipped Tarzan's ass into shape."

Gayle started laughing as she printed out a series of pictures. "Here." She handed Brett a couple of towels. "Clean up your wife and meet me in my office when you're ready."

After she left, Brett went to the sink and ran hot water over one towel, then wrung it out and walked back to Angie. "Damn, Ange.

Three in one go. If you don't want to do this again, we're good for life."

"Let me get through this pregnancy and when they're all out of diapers, I'll let you know if I want to do this again."

"Fair enough." He cleaned off her bump, dried it, then helped her off the table. With gentle hands and sweet care, he helped her get dressed, and they left to go to Gayle's private office.

They were sitting at her desk for a couple of minutes when she walked in. "So," she began, "I know you weren't surprised about twins, but triplets changes the game."

"I'll say," Angie deadpanned. "This probably explains why I can't eat much at one sitting."

"Indeed," Gayle said. "Lots pressing on all your organs."

Brett leaned forward and put his elbows on his knees. "Let's talk about boy number three."

"From what I can hear and see, he seems healthy, but vying for room in there. It's possible he'll be smaller than the twins, but that might change as the pregnancy progresses. In cases like these, we have more frequent visits and do more sonograms. Initially, I'm putting Angie on a schedule of a visit every two weeks. If either of you think there's a need to come in, don't worry, I'll see you when you get here."

"How much longer can I work?" Angie asked.

"Realistically, another couple of months. You're right at the beginning of your fifth month and in the next couple of weeks you're going to experience major changes. In your case, your hard watermelon," she pointed to Angie's bump, "is going to grow bigger at a faster rate than you've experienced so far. You can look up all the ancillary symptoms, as I know you've been doing all along," Gayle smiled, "but you need to read about multiples. Exponentially, your pregnancy is going to be more difficult because you've got three guys in there feeding off you like limpets."

"Nice, Gayle. Way to make Ange feel all warm and fuzzy."

"Brett, Angie doesn't want warm and fuzzy from me, she wants, and will get, the facts and the truth. Though, I gotta say, I like the limpets analogy."

"Back to stop working at seven months," Angie interjected.

"You're going to find surgery difficult by the end of this month. You'll want to get busy offloading your patients to your colleagues.

Your feet will be too swollen after standing for hours at a time, your back will be killing you, and your legs aren't going to be too happy either. You can see patients in your office until somewhere near the end of the sixth month, but after that, you'll be too big to feel comfortable in real clothes and those boys will be too active for you to be able to concentrate. I'm guessing the twins will settle on the same sleep/awake cycle, but the fraternal will probably have an opposite cycle to capitalize on your time when his brothers are sleeping. Which means you're going to be bothered by them twenty-four seven. Most of all, by month six, you'll be here once a week because we have to keep a close eye on your blood pressure and signs of preeclampsia."

"What about sex?"

Gayle smiled. "That's the Brett I know and love." He made a circling hand motion and Gayle laughed. "For now, whatever works and feels comfortable. As the pregnancy progresses, we'll make adjustments based on how Angie's doing. I will say, orgasms near the end of the sixth month might jump-start labor, and we want those guys to stay in there as long as possible. Having said that, most triplet pregnancies last thirty-two weeks. Our goal is that number or longer."

***

"Get ready, baby, we're going to have more sex this month than sixteen-year-olds," Brett told her when they stepped into the elevator after leaving Gayle's office.

He was good to his word, and then some. More times than not, she passed out before he finished cleaning her up. The man was insatiable, and Angie loved every minute of it.

Gayle was right. By the end of Angie's fifth month she had to stop doing surgeries. She'd planned for it, and her colleagues in their practice took up the slack. She never thought she'd feel so exhausted, and by the end of the sixth month, she was thrilled to stop working. The boys were tearing it up inside her body. It felt like they were playing full-blown basketball games, running up and down the court about twenty-one hours a day.

She became enormously pregnant and had perfected the waddle by the second week of the sixth month. When she stopped working—and she never thought she'd love being home as much as she did—she went downstairs in the morning and didn't go back up until nighttime. The couches were her friends, and she never knew how much she loved Victor until she became a beached whale. While Brett was at work—he called at least three times a day— Victor catered to Angie, told her jokes, and watched movies with her. Victor couldn't wait for the babies to arrive, and took classes to prepare for becoming their manny when Brett and Angie went back to work.

Brett. For as long as Angie lived, she'd never understand why she doubted him. When she looked back on the series of events that led to her asinine decision to divorce him, the only thing she could come up with was she'd convinced herself that they were drifting apart, and once she'd gone down that rabbit hole, she couldn't drag herself out. When she saw him with Holly, that'd confirmed all Angie's fears, including those apparently left over from childhood.

To his credit, after Brett's lawyer got the necessary papers from Angie's lawyer that ended the divorce proceedings, Brett never said another word about it. They resumed their lives, but honestly, it was better. They were better. She treasured every moment with him, and he listened to her with an intensity she'd never known. She felt more than she thought possible.

Brett was her full partner in preparing for the boys' arrival. He was part interior decorator, part massage therapist, part sex god— okay, he was that full-time—and most of all, he was sweet, and patient, and funny, and he loved her hard. She felt it every day, and never doubted it.

She stayed healthy and made it to thirty-three weeks. The boys were delivered by C-section, and Brett was in the operating room, of course.

Twins David and Daniel were three pounds six ounces at birth, and their fraternal brother, Dagon, was three pound three ounces at birth. They were in the NICU for three weeks, and guess who gained weight the fastest? The "little" one, Dag, who, at his rate of growth, they expected to be a linebacker one day. Dag was four pounds eleven ounces to his brothers' four pounds three ounces when they came home.

Both Brett and Angie had dark hair, and by two months old, all the boys had dark fuzz on their heads. By the time their hair grew in, they all had thick, unruly hair like their dad. Body type: these kids were Brett's. Temperament: David and Dag were Brett to a T. Daniel was more like Angie. Facially, the boys favored Brett, but their eye shape was more like hers. Aside from that, it was like her genes hadn't mattered in making these kids.

Dag was the first to eat solid food, walk, talk, and say no. Daniel often slept wedged between the dogs. David never really walked, he ran everywhere and banged into everything. They had a mini surgical station in their house, mostly for David.

The boys loved Angie, hung on her legs, and were generous with their hugs and kisses, but they thought Brett was a superhero and followed him around every minute he was home.

Two years, three months after the boys were born…

Brett smacked Ange's marvelous ass as he pulled out of her delicious pussy. She rolled to her side and looked at him with such love he swore he felt his heart would burst from it. He got out of bed, went to the bathroom, cleaned up, and brought a warm washcloth to clean Angie. When he was done, he threw the cloth on the floor, pulled her across the bed, and tucked her against his chest.

"How you feeling, baby?"

"Like I have no bones in my body."

He grinned. He loved doing that to her. "Sounds about right."

"Do you ever get tired of being smug?"

"Ah, nope."

"So arrogant."

"But you love me."

"With all my heart, *mi amado*."

He squeezed her and kissed her eyelids, cheeks, and chin. "I'm going to take the monsters to Noah's to get bagels. Give you some lie-in time."

She gazed up at him and smiled. "Want a daughter?"

His head jerked. "Really?"

She nodded.

"You sure, baby? I'm totally happy with the way things are."

"We'd said four if we had twins. It's one more pregnancy."

"The truth? I'm scared shitless about anything happening to you. The boys were rough on you, and I'm a selfish man who wants to enjoy his wife's body, and loves it exactly how it is."

She tilted her head and smirked.

"You're fuckin' kidding me?"

"We have sex like it's going to be outlawed."

"We also use birth control."

"Yeah, and we did when I got pregnant with the boys."

He dropped his head on the pillow and pulled her up so she was lying across him.

"How far along are you?"

"Just. Maybe four weeks."

"I'm warning you, Ange, you go for a sonogram at seven weeks. I need to know right fuckin' away if we have to buy a bigger house."

She laughed. "So bossy."

"But you love me."

"'Til time ceases."

ABOUT THE AUTHORS

Diane Benefiel

National Readers' Choice Award winner for her novel, *Solitary Man*, Diane Benefiel has been an avid reader all her life. She enjoys a wide range of genres, from westerns to fantasy to mysteries, but romance has always been a favorite. She writes what she loves best to read – emotional, heart-gripping romantic suspense novels. She likes writing romantic suspense because she can put the hero and heroine in all sorts of predicaments that they have to work together to overcome.

A native Southern Californian, Diane enjoys nothing better than summer. For a high school history teacher, summer means a break from teenagers, and summer allows her to spend her early mornings immersed in her current writing project. With both kids living out of the house, in addition to writing, she enjoys camping and gardening with her husband.

Diane loves hearing from her readers.
Website: dianebenefiel.com
Twitter: twitter.com/dianebenefiel
Instagram: diane_benefiel
Pinterest: diane_benefiel
Facebook: facebook.com/DianeBenefielRomance
BookBub: bookbub.com/authors/diane-benefiel
Goodreads: goodreads.com/author/show/8075321.Diane_Benefiel
Newsletter: https://landing.mailerlite.com/webforms/landing/n1i2u8

Joan Bird

A fourth-generation Californian with roots in (among other places) Ireland and Wales, Joan Bird is a daughter, sister and the fourth of six children, a black sheep, a musician and songwriter, a poet, a gardener, a lawyer, a woman of great faith, and the mother to two stepdaughters and five grandchildren. Gifts of the loud-in-a-good-way, and a loving husband whose jokes she vowed always to laugh at grace her life. She's been writing since she was ten, not always successfully, married twice, not always successfully, but faith in something greater than herself keeps her looking forward, never back. Her philosophy? The past offers lessons. It may shape a person, but it's the future that holds all the promises.

Connect with Joan:
facebook: http://www.facebook.com/joan.m.bird
twitter: @AuthorJoanMBird

Emily Mims

The author of over forty romance novels, Emily Mims combined her writing career with a career in public education until leaving the classroom to write full time. The mother of two sons, she and her husband split their time between central Texas, eastern Tennessee, and Georgia visiting their kids and grandchildren. For relaxation Emily plays the piano, organ, dulcimer, and ukulele for two different performing groups, and even sings a little. She says, "I love to write romances because I believe in them. Romance happened to me and it can happen to any woman—if she'll just let it."

Connect with Emily:
facebook.com/emily.mims.756
twitter.com/emilymimsauthor
instagram.com/mims_emily
website: emilymims.com

J.K. Winn

J. K. Winn has many stories to share. After years of working in the real world, including practicing psychotherapy and teaching at the college level, she decided to reinvent herself midlife to pursue her love of story.

She has six previously published novels, a play produced by the Actor's Alliance of San Diego, and poetry anthalogized in *The Love of Writing* by the San Diego Writer's Workshop. Her play *Gotcha!* was selected for a reading at the Village Arts Theater in Carlsbad, California.

She lives by the beach in San Diego County, California.

CONNECT WITH J.K.
Website: jkwin.com
Instagram: @authorjkwinn
Facebook: authorjkwin
Twitter: @authorjkwinn
LinkedIn: j-k-winn

Elle Wright

Elle Wright has been writing stories since she was a child, which led her to a career in journalism. She enjoys reporting life as much as making up a world she can control. She lives on the east coast of the United States where most of her large, noisy family resides. When she isn't in front of her computer, she loves to travel, garden, hang out with her dogs, and take in the brisk sea air that she's told is supposed to help calm her. She's been testing that theory for a while now.

CONNECT WITH ELLE:
Twitter: @ElleWright18
Instagram: @Elle_Wright_Writes
FB: facebook.com/elle.wright.1460

www.BOROUGHSPUBLISHINGGROUP.com

If you enjoyed this book, please write a review. Our authors appreciate the feedback, and it helps future readers find books they love. We welcome your comments and invite you to send them to info@boroughspublishinggroup.com. Follow us on Facebook, Twitter and Instagram, and be sure to sign up for our newsletter for surprises and new releases from your favorite authors.

Are you an aspiring writer? Check out www.boroughspublishinggroup.com/submit and see if we can help you make your dreams come true.